"It's New Year's Eve, Maggie."

"I know."

"Fourteen . . . thirteen . . . twelve . . ."

"Everybody kisses everybody on New Year's."

She dragged in a deep draft of air. "Yes. I know."

He stepped closer, his body barely brushing hers.

"Eight . . ."

Her tongue moistened her lips, leaving them shiny.

A low moan escaped from Rush, and his other hand joined the first, circling her throat. His thumb tilted her head back to an angle more accommodating to his height.

"Four . . . three . . ."

His head began its descent . . .

Dear Reader:

Nora Roberts, Tracy Sinclair, Jeanne Stephens, Carole Halston, Linda Howard. Are these authors familiar to you? We hope so, because they are just a few of our most popular authors who publish with Silhouette Special Edition each and every month. And the Special Edition list is changing to include new writers with fresh stories. It has been said that discovering a new author is like making a new friend. So during these next few months, be sure to look for books by Sandi Shane, Dorothy Glenn and other authors who have just written their first and second Special Editions, stories we hope you enjoy.

Choosing which Special Editions to publish each month is a pleasurable task, but not an easy one. We look for stories that are sophisticated, sensuous, touching, and great love stories, as well. These are the elements that make Silhouette Special Editions more romantic...and unique.

So we hope you'll find this Silhouette Special Edition just that—*Special*—and that the story finds a special place in your heart.

The Editors at Silhouette

SERL-7/85

SANDI SHANE
Sweet Burning

Silhouette Special Edition

Published by Silhouette Books New York

America's Publisher of Contemporary Romance

To the group—Diane, Kathy, Marian and
Peggy—thanks for caring and sharing.

SILHOUETTE BOOKS
300 E. 42nd St., New York, N.Y. 10017

ISBN: 0-373-09257-1

First Silhouette Books printing August, 1985

10 9 8 7 6 5 4 3 2 1

America's Publisher of Contemporary Romance

Printed in the U.S.A.

Silhouette Books by Sandi Shane

No Perfect Season (IM #91)
Sweet Burning (SE #257)

SANDI SHANE

is a wife, mother and full-time writer of romance. She's also an animal lover, sharing her North Louisiana home with three smug cats, numerous dogs and keeping thoroughbred horses. She likes rain. And autumn. And loves stories that make you cry.

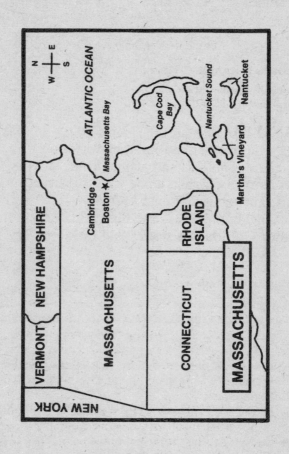

Chapter One

The strains of "Silent Night" incompatibly coupling with those of harsh punk rock from the apartment next door drew Maggie Spencer's mouth into a downward grimace and hastened her to the conclusion that it was a darned good thing she had planned to go out. Otherwise she was destined to spend the evening in the annoying overflow of youthful Rose What's-her-name's holiday party.

The Christmas holidays. They were downright unfriendly, Maggie thought with another frown, this one immediately softening, however, to the semblance of a smile as she truthfully admitted that they were less unamiable than they'd been this time last year. She congratulated herself that she'd hit upon such a successful means of coping with them and with parties in general. With one dialing of the telephone she could take her social life from complex to simple, from wracked with frustration to a satisfaction as smooth as placid water.

Water. Maggie realized the bathroom tap was still running and immediately shut it off and stood her toothbrush in its oriental-figured porcelain stand. Glancing at her watch, she panicked at the late hour and threw herself into putting the finishing touches to her makeup. She applied a final coat of mascara to lashes that framed bright, sapphire, almond-shaped eyes and brushed a cloud of rose onto inordinately high cheekbones; she next dusted an extra dollop of blush onto an almost-square chin and jawline framing a face too angular and too thin to expect to be pretty, but a face she had been told defied the odds with a regal loveliness.

Moving quickly from bathroom to bedroom, she slipped her perfect, but constantly fought-for, size-eight figure into a chic, long, straight-skirted black taffeta dress, then eased to the side of the bed, where she slid her foot into a strappy gold sandal and wrapped the thin leather about her ankle. She repeated the action for the other foot. That done, she raced to her dressing table, grabbed an ivory-handled brush and skimmed it once, twice, three times through her rich, darker-than-dark, coffee-brown hair that was fashionably coiffed into a multilayered style that grazed her shoulders. Suddenly, as her eyes tuned in to the image in the beveled, gold-framed mirror, she stopped in midstroke.

Forty. The big four-oh loomed on her horizon like an uninvited guest, taking insatiable, chunky bites out of the one month, three weeks and I'm-not-really-counting days she had left. Did she really look forty years old? The answer, she knew, depended on the generosity of her mood at the moment of contemplation. On those dark days when nothing on God's earth seemed to go right she told herself she looked, felt and acted like forty-plus, but at those times when she was honest, like right now, she had to admit that, though not beautiful—she'd never been a bona-fide beauty— she was attractive and well preserved. There were only faint character lines about her eyes, no slackness whatsoever to her neck and no charcoal smudges beneath her eyes. Well, none that a thin layer of makeup wouldn't hide. And her skin, although occasionally thirsty, did not yet slurp up moisturizer. No, she sometimes tended to forget that she had the glow of good health on her cheeks and a body trim and taut from conscientious dieting and structured exercise. She tended to forget that taking care of herself had paid off. She tended to forget . . .

A sudden frown tugged at her mouth and she squinted, sending her heavy but shapely winged brows upward.

"Oh, no, it couldn't be," she muttered, screwing up her eyes even more tightly as she studied the hairline revealed in the golden light of the lamp.

Cursing her farsightedness, she marched across the room, where she dumped the contents of her gold-filigree bag onto the bed and scooped up a pair of tortoiseshell-framed glasses. She thrust them on, at the same time impatiently striding back to the mirror. Tilting her head downward a bit, her fingers foraged in the hair slanting across her forehead. She grimaced. A gray hair. A bold gray hair. An audacious, bold gray hair. She yanked, cursed and, whipping the glasses from her face, wiped away a tear that had instantly sprung up in sympathy with her tender scalp. Irreverently tossing the glasses onto the dressing table, she sighed heavily. Now be reasonable, Maggie, she ordered herself, feeling her generous mood scattering like a smoky morning mist. One gray hair doesn't make you old. Not any more than the inability to see that gray hair without wearing glasses. You are not old. Forty is definitely not old.

Thankfully, the phone rang. Clearing her throat and her head, she crossed the room and stretched out a hand with red-lacquered nails. "Hello?" she answered as she sat down on the side of the bed. Her taffeta skirt belled slightly and made a crisp, crinkling sound.

"He's going to be late."

Maggie immediately recognized the voice, a very distinguishable drawl deliberately and zealously retained, as belonging to April Newbern, her friend, her only real confidante, her undeniable sanity for the last two and a half years.

"He just called, said the weather was worse than he'd thought. Gee, Mags, have you looked outside lately?" At the question, Maggie glanced up to see crystal-like shards of ice and snow pelting the windowpane. "I hate Boston in the damn winter. For five friggin' cents I'd haul myself back to Texas where they know how to have cold weather."

"You could probably catch a late flight," Maggie offered, a genuine smile stretching her full, lower lip and at the same time causing her upper lip, sharp-edged rather than smoothly curvaceous, to tilt in a way that had reduced the oxygen intake of more than one male. How many times had April threatened to return to her native state in the ten years Maggie had known her? More often than Maggie could count, that was for sure. So many times that it had become a running joke.

"You laugh," came the mockingly surly reply. "One of these days I'm going to do it. Daddy only sent me up here to go to the prestigious Radcliffe, to get some eastern charm and to learn how to crook my pinkie, not to become a damn Yankee . . . and certainly not to freeze to death in the winter."

Maggie's smile broadened. "You can't go home. If you did, you'd have to explain to your dad what you're doing with the fifty-thousand-dollar-plus degree in sociology he paid for. Somehow I don't think *Daddy*"—she gave it all the southern emphasis she could with her Bostonian accent—"is going to understand your male escort service."

The laugh suddenly skittering across the line qualified as delightfully raucous, and Maggie had a quick mental flash of jeans far too tight, hair far too frosted and curled to a wavy frizzle, cowboy boots far too pointy-toed and a feathered western hat that had never been beyond the Charles River. For the thousandth time she wondered how two such polar opposites as she and April ever could have been attracted to one another and struck up such a solid, lasting friendship.

"You're right," April agreed, "Daddy might want his money refunded." Then, slipping back into business without missing a, beat, she added, "Your date said to tell you he was just leaving and that he should be there by ten to eight. Said to tell you he was sorry about the delay."

"That's all right," Maggie answered. "It's only one of those obligatory and probably boring as sin Christmas parties and . . ."

"How many times do I have to tell you?" April interrupted. "If you do sin right, it isn't boring."

Maggie ignored the often heard comment. ". . . and all we have to do is arrive at a decent hour and stay a credible length of time. But it was nice of him to call." She shifted the phone to her other ear, nestling it beneath a curtain of hair, and in the brief interim the word *sensitive* crossed her mind. It had been a sensitive thing for—she stretched and looked at the name on the writing pad by the phone, squinting in the process— Michael Rusheon Barrington to do. The name conjured up the image of a stately, sophisticated gentleman. Maggie fleetingly wondered what led a man to this type of job, the job of escorting strange women for an evening's entertainment.

"He's not only nice," April agreed, "he's absolutely gor . . . geous." She trailed off until the last was totally inaudible, then made a big deal of coughing.

"He's what?"

"Gracious," the other woman rushed out. "He's gracious. Graciousness personified. What are you wearing?"

The question came out of left field, but then, most everything April said came out of a never expected, often outrageous field. "The black taffeta with the black and gold jacket."

"Good," she replied in a pleased tone. "That looks fantastic on you. You wearing the sexy gold sandals?"

Automatically, Maggie looked down at her feet. One leg was crossed over the other and, peeking out from beneath the fabric of her long skirt, was a three-inch heel and toes playing hide-and-seek in the thin webbing of gilded lamé. "I'm wearing the gold sandals. The sexy I'm not sure of."

"They are, believe me. And men love high heels."

Maggie frowned. "April Newbern, what are you . . ."

"Ah, damn, my other line is blipping. God, I hate being such a success. Look, I'll talk to you tomorrow." There was a scrambling of the phone, then the added, afterthought words, "Do yourself a favor, Mags. Reconsider your position on sin."

The woman hung up, leaving Maggie's perplexed frown still securely in place. And there it remained for a full thirty seconds before she finally convinced herself that her mind was only being overactive. April was always off the wall. No more so this evening than at any other time. But for all of her insane ways, she was dead serious about her escort agency, a fact proved by the black ink her bookkeeper repeatedly used. She wouldn't risk playing cupid. Would she? No, of course not. She'd had plenty of time to do just that during the three months Maggie had patronized her business, and she'd refrained. Of the seven escorts she had sent to Maggie—and never the same one twice—each had been a paragon of professionalism.

No, Maggie thought, rising from the bed and slipping the black and gold jacket from its hanger and onto both arms, where the sleeves puffed fashionably upward, she had never regretted her decision to use the Newbern Agency. In fact, she admitted as she tied the jacket's gigantic bow into asymmetrical perfection, it was the best move she'd made in two and a half years. She was sick to death of well-meaning friends who wanted, following her divorce, to "fix her up" with eligible gentlemen, most of whom turned out to be less eligible than believed, and the closest any of them had ever been to a gentleman was when they'd accidentally stood next to one. She'd had no idea there was so much groping going on in the world. Nor had she realized that as men grew older, they also selectively grew deaf to the word *no*.

It was April who finally pointed out her agency as a solution to the problem. For a reasonable sum of money a woman could get an intelligent, attractive, attentive companion, a companion who understood the no-hands rule from the very beginning. Though Maggie had been skeptical at first, she now admitted her friend was right. April's service had made the evenings when she had been forced to socialize for the art gallery's sake a lot more comfortable and enjoyable. It had uncomplicated a complicated problem. And only April knew she was buying the men in her life.

No, she could trust April, Maggie thought as she fitted diamond-and-gold studs into her pierced ears. Michael Rusheon Barrington would be standard issue. He would be intelligent, attractive, attentive. And nice. He would be . . . gracious.

The clean, five-year-old, silver-gray Monte Carlo pulled up to the curb—or as close to the curb as it could get, considering the evening's mucky build-up of slush and ice. Snow, in virgin flurries, peppered the windshield, while sleet, as hard and brazen as a seasoned streetwalker, pounded away at the same expanse of glass. The wipers groaned in a valiant effort to scrape away the winter elements, but when the masculine hand, strong-veined and fringed with heavy, dark hairs, snapped off the ignition, the wipers stopped midswipe, and the window was immediately smothered in white wetness.

Throwing open the door, the driver stepped out into the cold night, turned up the collar of his heavy black wool coat, adjusted the white wool scarf more closely about his already freezing ears and hurried toward the old Balsam mansion, which had been converted into plush condos, as had several other large, history-steeped structures in the Back Bay area.

He was late. Late wasn't his style, but then, he'd

underestimated Mother Nature. She could be harsh in Boston in the month of December. A slightly guilty smile crept to his well-shaped mouth. Of course, it hadn't helped that he'd had his head stuck in a law book long past the hour he'd promised himself to stop.

Agilely jumping a puddle that threatened to dampen his elegant and brand-new patent leather shoes, shoes he had been able to afford the month before only by making hamburger the mainstay of his diet, he yanked open the door. A young woman, smelling subtly of an expensive perfume and blowing her frosty breath into the air, arrived at the same moment and, after a near collision and profuse apologies, he allowed her first entry. She walked to the black, wrought-iron-enclosed elevator; he followed and, sliding back the door, again allowed her to precede him. She punched the button for the third floor, then looked to him for a comment.

"Three's fine," he answered her silent inquiry. He gave her a brief, friendly smile.

The doors whisked closed; the elevator began its ascent.

The female, young and strikingly beautiful, stared openly at the male figure. Brown hair, the color of polished pecan shells, had obviously seen an attempt to part on the right, but the frigid wind had blown it in a helter-skelter fashion until it fell into a short, mussed, tiered look. His eyebrows, much darker than his hair, were heavy and straight, slanting only near the outer ends, and his eyes, hypnotic, endless brown depths, were quite the loveliest she'd ever seen. And the cleft in his chin, looking almost as if someone had indented it with a powerful push of a thumb, did crazy things to a feminine heart. Crazy things, indeed.

"I don't suppose you're going to Rose Marie's party?" she asked. Hope shone on her face.

Dark brown eyes coasted to her. " 'Fraid not."

"That's a shame," she added frankly.

He negligently ran a hand into his coat pocket and smiled. "I'm working tonight."

A pretty eyebrow arched upward. "Working? Couldn't get you to call in sick, could I?"

He laughed, a pleasing sound in the small cubicle now flashing the number two on its upward climb. " 'Fraid not. But thanks, anyway."

She shrugged her fur-covered shoulders in acceptance and smiled beguilingly. The elevator door slid open. She slid out. With one backward glance, she added, "I'm in the phone book—Constance Cross."

His only reply was a nip of a smile she didn't see. He stepped from the elevator, hurriedly scanned the numbers above the apartments, and ultimately followed his elevator companion, who was quickly disappearing down the hall. He smiled, this time openly, at the woman's blatant come-on. Her interest hadn't offended him, but neither had it impressed him. It happened too often. He had learned at a very early age that he had been gifted with two things: a good brain and good looks. The first he cultivated; the second he exploited. In fact, he exploited the good looks in order to cultivate the good brains. That was why he was working this job. In his view, any—well, almost any—means justified the end. And the end was graduation from law school.

He stopped in front of number six and pressed the doorbell that doubled as a lion's mouth. He took one last look at Constance Cross's legs, which he had to admit were nice. Real nice. Maybe he would break his usual rule and call her . . .

The dark, wooden door of number six swung open. The man's attention shifted.

His legally trained eyes made a blitzkrieg survey of

the woman before him, taking in brown-black hair, sapphire-blue eyes, a sharp-featured but lovely face, a model-thin but undeniably feminine figure and stocking-nude toes peeking from beneath black fabric and out of gold sandals.

. . . then again, he amended his thought, maybe he'd forget about Constance Cross. There was definitely something to be said for an older woman.

"Hi," he said, his lips arcing upward as he raked a strand of wind-teased hair from his forehead. "I'm sorry I'm late."

Maggie's eyes made an equally quick scan. Pearlescent flakes of snow peeping from dark hair and nestling on the upturned collar of a black wool coat. Eyes, piercing, spellbinding, eyes that whispered, "Come here. Let me tell you a secret." A narrow, straight nose, a pronouncedly cleft chin, a face that screamed handsome. A face and body that, likewise, shouted youth, a youth in his prime.

Unable to keep her lips from returning his smile, she answered, "I'm afraid you're going to be even later." Then, with a slight tilt of her head that sent her hair into a gentle cascade, she added, "I think you want next door."

With no other word, she closed the door, turned around and took two and a half steps back into the room.

The doorbell buzzed again.

A deep crease furrowed Maggie's forehead as she retraced her steps and opened the door once more. The man before her wore a similar expression.

"Number six?"

"Yes," Maggie confirmed, her face still puzzled.

"Margaret Spencer?"

A ridiculous idea crossed her mind—but it was too

ridiculous to even entertain—and yet she heard herself answering in a fatalistic way. "Maggie. Maggie Spencer."

The downward tug of his mouth inched upward into a hint of a grin. "Rush."

The crease in Maggie's forehead deepened to a questioning groove. "Rush?"

"Rush Barrington." He extended his hand. She lowered her eyes to it and extended her own simply because she had been conditioned to do so. When her eyes found his once more, he added, "I'm your escort for the evening."

Life relaxed to the pace of a slow-framed movie and became a montage of sounds and sights, smells and touches. The hand holding hers huddled between degrees of warmth and cold. It was also large and slightly rough. He smelled of a fresh, woodsy scent that quickly dragged her attention to her own sweet, flowery fragrance, and as she stood there the two bouquets seemed to visibly mix and mingle. He looked tall and trim, and in some indefinable way, capable and comfortable, with himself, with life and with this situation. In the background, wafting from Rose What's-her-name's condo, came the sound of giggles and Michael Jackson vocalizing "Beat It." Which was exactly what she wanted to do, she thought, pulling her hand from his, because *she* didn't feel comfortable with this situation. No, actually, she thought, shock receding and ire awakening, what she'd really like to do was beat April—to a pulp not even her "daddy" would recognize.

"There's been some mistake," she said, knowing full well there hadn't been. Unless you counted trusting your best friend a mistake.

A frown once again slipped to his lips, lips that had

been on the verge of smiling in a most enchanting way. "What kind of mistake?"

Before Maggie could respond, a couple of partygoers passed by, heading for next door. Their faces were wreathed in gaiety, while laughter tripped easily into the corridor. The two glanced curiously at the open doorway, where a good-looking man stood talking to a pretty lady. All four smiled tentative, cordial smiles.

"You think I could come in until we settle this?" Rush asked after the couple stepped on by.

Silently, Maggie moved backward in an acquiescing gesture. Rush stepped over the threshold and closed the door behind him.

"Now," he said, looking directly at her, "what's the problem?"

What was the problem? she wanted to shout, but restrained her actions admirably. She searched her inner self, corralling all the tact, honesty and maturity she could find, then stumbled around an answer that best befitted a lamebrained adolescent. "You're . . . I'm . . . I mean . . . You're . . ." If there were an award for bumbling incoherency, she thought, stricken with mortification, she'd just won it. "I mean . . ."

From the confused look on his face, it was obvious he'd tried to follow the maze of her reply. It was equally obvious he hadn't succeeded. "Exactly what do you mean?"

She opened her mouth, hesitated, then closed it without a word being uttered.

"Aren't I dressed appropriately?" he asked, as if the idea had just struck him. "April told me a tux."

He pulled back his heavy overcoat to reveal the elegant black of his tuxedo. A crisp, pleated white shirt offset the midnight-dark color, and a precisely executed black bow tie was the perfect accent.

"No . . . no . . . you're dressed fine," Maggie hastened to answer, her eyes taking in the man before her. Involuntarily, she scanned the well-tailored fit of fabric over the length of his legs, a length that easily put him beyond six-foot-one or -two. Her own tall five-foot-seven seemed suddenly dwarfed, just as her own willow thinness seemed swallowed up by the solid breadth of his utterly masculine shoulders. "No," she heard herself repeating, "you're dressed fine."

Rush massaged his forehead in a pose of deep thought. Snapping his fingers as if just recognizing the problem, he teased, "Let me guess, you don't like brown-haired, brown-eyed escorts."

"No . . . I mean, yes, I do like brown hair and brown eyes. . . ." She trailed off and took a fortifying breath before adding, "Look, it's nothing personal. It's just that you're . . ."

"Younger than you were expecting?" he supplied, tossing his teasing tone aside. He seemed suddenly torn between wanting to ease her discomfiture and delighting at the way the delicate rose of her embarrassment tinted her prominent cheekbones.

"Ah, you finally noticed," she answered with a smug look and a slight nod of her head as she took refuge behind the veneer of sarcasm.

"I noticed, but I didn't know I was supposed to be so impressed." He paused, his right hand slipping past his coat to ease into a pants pocket. The action splayed fabric in a provocative way. "Look, Maggie, I'm big people. I sleep without a night-light, and I've been seeing PG movies for a long time without parental guidance. Besides, age is relative."

If it was one thing she didn't want at this point, it was logic. "All that may well be true, but . . . I'm sorry, you're just too young."

He watched as she took determined steps toward the phone and lifted it from its cradle. "Mind if I stay while you call the agency?" he asked.

"Suit yourself," she shot back, squinting her eyes and punching in April's number. As the phone rang, Maggie tapped out a nervous tattoo with her foot.

Rush, with contrasting calmness, walked toward the floral-printed sofa that blended with the Regency-red paper covering the walls with dramatic flair. A lemon-yellow and white rug overspread a floor of hardwood marquetry, and black, yellow and red pillows reclined in thoughtful abandon in every nook and cranny. One red and one white chair were arranged around a pale yellow oriental table, while a chair, upholstered in the same floral-print material as the sofa, had at its side a shiny brass trunk. With the gold and black she was wearing, and with her foot still tapping in agitation, Maggie looked like a bumblebee flitting about a garden of brightly colored flowers. Again, by contrast, Rush looked as though he had leisurely lit among the same brilliant blossoms.

For the briefest of moments, their eyes met—collided really. Maggie quickly diverted hers.

"Newbern Agency. I've got the man for you," the southern voice suddenly crooned in Maggie's ear.

"Not this time you don't," Maggie answered, her own voice sitting precariously on the edge of irritation.

"Mags? What's wrong? He didn't show up?"

"Oh, he showed up all right, but . . ."

"Isn't he gorgeous?" April cut in. "Lord, what a bod. . . ."

"What are you trying to do, April Newbern?" Maggie likewise interrupted in a low hiss.

"What do you mean?"

"You know what I mean."

Silence. Followed by a deep sigh. "C'mon, you're not hung up about the age difference, are you? So he's a little younger. So what?"

"A little?" Maggie's voice rose with her irritation. "He's young enough to be . . ."

"Uh-uh," Maggie heard from behind her. Rush had removed his coat and wool muffler and now sat on the sofa, both arms negligently hugging its back, one leg casually squared over the other. "I'm not young enough to be your son unless you hit puberty at an abnormally early age."

"Will you be quiet?" Maggie said, throwing him her most quelling look.

"Then why did you call?" April asked over the phone.

"Not you," Maggie quickly denied. "Look, *friend,*" —she coiled the phone cord around a finger that was doubling as April Newbern's neck—"I want another escort."

"Sor . . . ree," April singsonged. "I don't know whether you've noticed it or not, but it's the Christmas holidays. And a Saturday night to boot. Escorts are at a premium. Everyone is booked. The only other male I can offer you is the janitor."

Maggie sighed a full whoosh of air from her lungs. Her eyes once again darted across the room. The smile in Rush's eyes said he was definitely amused.

"How old?" Maggie asked.

"The janitor?" April drawled.

"Rush Barrington," Maggie said, her glance never backing down from his.

"Twenty-nine. I'm not a kid," he answered just as April said, "Twenty-nine. He's not a kid."

Long, long moments passed. Maggie studied him, he studied Maggie and April Newbern waited, a mischievous, I've-cornered-my-opponent smile plastered on her elfin face.

Finally April said, "C'mon, Mags, the worst that can happen is that everyone thinks you're having a fling with a younger man. And every woman at that party would trade places with you in the bat of an eye."

Maggie heaved a weary sigh, turned her back on Rush, draping the cord around her firm derriere as she did so, and whispered into the phone, "I won't forget this."

A bawdy laugh skipped over the lines. "That's what I'm counting on."

Maggie hung up the phone, relieved that one couldn't be tried for thinking of murder. She could easily throttle April's pretty Texan neck! If this party wasn't so important . . .

"Well, what's the verdict, judge?" Rush asked, drawing her attention back to him. "Do I get to go sip champagne with the adults, or am I going home to milk and cookies?"

Blue eyes battled with brown ones that seemed to be enjoying the whole situation.

"Let's go," she said, striding toward her fur coat and jamming her arms into it. "Your mommy probably wants you in early."

He laughed, a rich, full sound that only aggravated Maggie more.

"Are you coming?" she snapped frostily.

He unhurriedly pulled himself up from the sofa and reached for his coat and scarf. "Yes . . . *ma'am.*"

The look she gave him could have sizzled steel. The warm, crooked smile he returned could have thawed the outer reaches of the Antarctic. To her chagrin, Maggie felt its cooling effects.

Chapter Two

$\mathcal{T}$he car door on the passenger side opened, sending frigid air inside the Monte Carlo's warm interior. Lost in thought, Maggie glanced up in surprise at the speed with which they'd made the journey from Hereford Street to Beacon Hill. She peeked at Rush, who stood waiting politely for her to get out of the car. His features were schooled into faultlessly proper lines that made him look considerably older. Well . . . *older*, anyway. Nothing at all like the memory of him lounging indolently against her floral sofa, his dark eyes dancing in amusement while she voiced her complaint to April.

His eyes weren't dancing now, she thought. They were probing hers with an intensity that forced her to lower her dark lashes in protest and confusion. Resolutely, she swung her legs to the red-brick sidewalk.

Rush held out his hand to assist her, causing her lashes to fly upward once more. His gaze was correctly solicitous. Exactly what she expected, and undoubtedly what April demanded from her escorts. Maggie placed her gloved hand in his and felt his fingers curl around hers as she straightened her body to a standing position and started up the walk.

Rush's grip tightened, holding her at his side while he pushed down the lock button and slammed the car door. "You might slip," he cautioned. "Hang on."

She did. Although the distance from his car to the off-white brick house—one of a select few that comprised fashionable Louisburg Square—was a matter of only a few feet, Maggie was grateful for his support as she crunched gingerly through the rapidly freezing slush and rock salt someone had sprinkled in an attempt to make a more secure footing. Cold numbed her toes, and she mentally cursed her "sexy" gold sandals. She'd give a week's worth of commissions for a pair of fur-lined galoshes—or a pair of April's cowboy boots. The thought of lizard boots paired with her elegant gown caused her lips to curve upward.

Rush, who had gained the steps and was already reaching a long finger toward the bell, happened to catch the smile as he glanced over at her. A nearby gaslight threw her profile in relief, from the fall of hair over her forehead to the slight turn of her nose and down to the angular line of her chin. Snowflakes swirled, indiscriminately dusting her wind-tossed hair and the ebony blackness of the three-quarter, sealskin jacket she wore.

A snowflake settled on her lashes, and her smile faded. She blinked rapidly and raised a hand to wipe it away. From the corner of her eye, Maggie saw Rush's tanned fingers as they reached out and closed ever so gently around her wrist. Their eyes met, Maggie's mirroring her surprise, Rush's filled with humor. Without a word, he leaned near and, reaching out a slender finger, retrieved the melting snowflake.

Before Maggie could do more than register the uniqueness of his behavior, the door of the house, bedecked with a traditional wreath of holly and red ribbon, swung open, and the Farnsworth butler, clad impeccably in black, stood staring down his straight British nose at them.

The man's appearance caused all of Maggie's anger and frustration at April to come rushing back. How could she have done this? The Farnsworths could trace their ancestry back to King George IV for goodness' sake! How dare April send a . . . a callow boy to escort her to such a prestigious gathering? He'd probably be able to carry on a conversation only if it were about drinking, girls or sex. Sex! Maggie shifted uncomfortably. Now why in the world would she think of that?

As she pondered the situation, Rush grasped her elbow and ushered her into the waiting warmth. His voice was firm and confident as he announced their arrival. "Margaret Spencer and Michael Rusheon Barrington."

The butler permitted a hint of a smile to soften the severe line of his thin lips as he nodded. "Cramer, sir. Miserable evening, isn't it?"

"Very," Rush concurred with a smile, sliding the fur from Maggie's shoulders and relinquishing it to the man before removing his own coat.

Cramer settled the jacket onto a hanger and inclined his head toward the hallway. "Straight on to the right, sir," he said, indicating the whereabouts of the party, even as the sounds of laughter and music penetrated Maggie's misery.

Thank God! Cramer wasn't going to announce their

arrival. At least now she wouldn't have forty or fifty pairs of eyes condemning her at once. Granted, Rush Barrington had conducted himself commendably so far, but . . . She sighed. No one knew she used April's service. They would think Rush was a real date and that Margaret Spencer, divorcée of two years, sole owner of a growing-in-popularity art gallery—the woman who seldom dated and was the mother of a college sophomore—was following her ex-husband's lead and robbing the cradle. Maggie wavered between anger and embarrassment.

It seemed Rush could read her mind as he grinned engagingly, offering her his arm and the solemn question, "Ready, ma'am?"

Maggie saw the glint of humor lurking in the depths of his beautiful dark eyes. Like a mischievous boy he was pushing her, gambling that his charm would keep her from being too angry, just as Lacey used to do when she was little. Lacey! The thought of her nineteen-year-old daughter leaped into Maggie's mind. Nineteen? Lacey would be twenty come spring, Maggie reminded herself. Things suddenly fell into a very clear but unsettling perspective. Her daughter was a far more suitable date for Rush Barrington.

With a ragged sigh, Maggie's fingers closed around Rush's proffered arm, her scarlet nails unconsciously digging into the black fabric covering the firmness of his biceps. Without a word, he led her into the room filled with music, laughter, cigarette smoke and the buzz of a dozen different conversations.

"Maggie Spencer!" The voice, whiskey husky, halted Rush, who had taken no more than a dozen steps into the room. Maggie was instantly enveloped in an ample-bosomed hug exuding *Giorgio* perfume. Maggie invariably connected both the hug and the expensive Rodeo

Drive scent with her hostess, Sylvia Farnsworth. Sylvia released Maggie and held her at arm's length with plump hands flaunting diamonds on every finger. Then, Sylvialike, she launched into one of her typically one-sided conversations, making one of her typically erroneous deductions.

"You're looking positively marvelous, darling! The holidays definitely agree with you!" She slid a less than oblique glance in Rush's direction and cooed, "Or do we give the credit to this delightful thing?" Her tone seemed to suggest he looked ·good enough to pass around as a canapé. "Have pity, Maggie! Introduce us!"

Maggie's horrified eyes met Rush's. He smiled at her, almost understandingly, it seemed, then shifted his attention and his smile to Sylvia as he offered her his hand. "Rush Barrington, Mrs. Farnsworth."

When the older woman's eyebrows lifted in surprise at his knowledge of who she was, Rush explained. "I'm an avid newspaper reader, and you're a very visible person in Boston. And this is my first date with Maggie, so I'm afraid I can't take credit for the marvelous way she looks."

Sylvia, who prided herself on never flustering easily, bounced back with a coy smile that encompassed them both. "I see. My apologies, I'm sure. Still, Maggie, darling,"—here her dark eyelashes climbed daringly, dramatically upward—"one can always hope."

Maggie's breath caught in a silent gasp. Her eyes flew to Rush's, cornflower blue clashing with darkest chocolate. Warm, liquid chocolate. A smile twinkled in their dark depths. Damn April! Damn Michael Rusheon Barrington! And damn her traitorous heart, which was ignoring the difference in their ages by shifting to a faster speed.

Before Maggie could do more than frown back at him, Sylvia linked her arms with theirs. "You must meet my husband, Mr. Barrington. Oh, and Maggie, he wants to know what you think about that British artist, whatever his name is."

Maggie let the nonstop conversation flow on around her. Several years of dealing with Sylvia Farnsworth had taught her one thing: Normal conversation with her was an impossibility. Her husband, Daniel, was another matter. As staid as his wife was flighty, Daniel Farnsworth was steeped in the importance of his own family history and deeply interested in world affairs, besides keeping his finger on the pulse of the art world. Daniel was known for keeping everyone on their conversational toes.

She chanced a look up at Rush and felt a sinking feeling wash over her. There was no way he could hold his own with someone like their host. She sighed once more. It was a pity, but pretty—young—Rush Barrington was about to be chewed up and spit out.

Three hours later Maggie huddled in the furry depths of her sealskin jacket, hunching her shoulders and burying her face in its sleek smoothness while Rush maneuvered the Monte Carlo away from the curb and out onto the slippery street. The heater blew valiantly against the icy air, but so far hadn't done much toward overcoming the miserable coldness of the car's confines. She shivered.

Rush glanced over at her. "I'm sorry it's so cold. I should have come out earlier and warmed up the car."

"No. It's all right," she told him. "It'll warm up in a minute."

Silence, broken only by the sound of the heater fan, monopolized the next few moments. As the air

warmed, relief that the important party had gone so
well and that Rush had not been an embarrassment to
her began to ooze throughout Maggie's pleasantly tired
body.

She scoured her mind for some topic they could
discuss on the drive home. She owed him at least the
courtesy of polite conversation after the way he'd come
through for her. She was surprised at how easily he'd
mingled with her friends and contemporaries, discussing everything from the president's foreign policy to
classical music with apparently no difficulty.

Besides holding his own in any conversation, he had
been very solicitous of Maggie's needs, bringing her
more wine when she wanted it, helping her select food
from the lavish buffet and even rescuing her from the
drunken advances of a man she'd turned down more
than once after discovering that the old one-night stand
was the extent of involvement he desired. All in all,
she'd found Rush Barrington much, much more than a
beautiful face and a superb, masculine body.

Settling herself more comfortably, she relaxed
against the seat, completely free from the worry that
had plagued her from the first moment she'd realized
April had sent a younger man to escort her. Maggie's
lips tilted upward at the corners as she thought of his
meeting with Daniel Farnsworth.

Rush turned his head and saw the smile as they
passed beneath the glow of a streetlight. "Why are you
wearing that smirky smile?"

A soft expulsion of laughter escaped her lips. "I was
thinking about how well you handled our host."

Her laughter turned into a definitely girlish giggle.
"For the first time since I've known him Daniel actually
looked uncomfortable when you asked him about that
fifteenth-century painting." She turned in the seat to

look at him. His profile was as perfect as the rest of him, she thought randomly, her mind more fully occupied with the reality that he'd handled himself with poise and intelligence. "I'm curious. How did you know about that particular painting? It isn't something a person with a passing knowledge of art would be familiar with."

Rush took his eyes from the icy streets for a moment, the whiteness of his smile slicing through the darkness. "Piece of cake! I'm a first-class spermologer."

The fourth—and totally unnecessary—glass of wine she'd polished off in an attempt to soften the blow should Rush prove disastrous as her escort, combined with the cozy warmth of the car, suffused Maggie with light-headedness, causing her thoughts and her smile to teeter at the edge of the risqué. "Does that have anything to do with what it sounds like?"

Rush laughed, his voice low and intimate sounding to Maggie, whose head rested contentedly against the seat. "Hardly. A spermologer is a person who gathers trivia. Trust me. My mind is a veritable quagmire of obscure tidbits. A couple of other guys and I spend a lot of time playing Trivial Pursuit when we aren't studying."

"Studying?" Maggie's interest was piqued. He seemed a little old for a college student, but then, a lot of people picked up classes now and then. "What are you studying?"

"Law. I have one more semester at Harvard Law School before I can take the bar exam." He heaved a ragged sigh. "God, I'll be glad to finish!"

"Why aren't you in school now?"

He flashed her another quick grin. "Money. It costs a bundle to go to Harvard. Unfortunately, I don't have it." His voice held no self-pity as he added, "I've had to drop out a couple of times to gather up enough money to go on."

Maggie was surprised, but some part of her mind told her his interest in law was logical. She had sensed a brilliance in his attitude and conversation from the directness of the questions he had leveled at some of the other guests during the course of the evening. Looking back, she could see that he'd very cleverly picked everyone's brain while disclosing very little about himself.

"So what do you do to make money?"

He shrugged. "Whatever it takes."

Genuinely intrigued, Maggie prodded, "Like working for April?"

"Yes."

"Does it pay well?"

"Not too badly."

Maggie silently considered his statement. It did take a bundle to go to Harvard. He must have really worked hard and sacrificed to get as far as he had. He rose a notch in her esteem. "Do you have a daytime job, too?"

"Yes. I work as a clerk for a law firm here in Boston. And occasionally I . . . model."

The words were spoken with more than a little hesitation.

She pictured him again, lounging against her sofa, the white, pleated shirt stretching tautly over his broad chest, the fabric of his close-fitting tuxedo pants hugging the muscles of his thighs as he stretched his legs out before him. He was beautifully put together, she thought. It was easy to picture him as a model. "But you don't like it."

"You could say that," he replied. Then he sighed.

"It's terrific pay, but it drives me crazy to stand there for hours with either a smile or a look of arrogant boredom plastered on my face. I'm just not geared for that sort of thing."

"You certainly have the looks for it," Maggie said truthfully.

Rush shrugged. "Anybody can look good if they have a makeup artist who knows what he's doing."

Maggie was silent, impressed with his casual attitude toward his looks, which were, in all honesty, superb.

"Well?" he prompted, cocking his head sideways to look at her. Their eyes met briefly before he turned his attention back to his driving.

"Well what?"

"Aren't you going to give me your opinion of the kind of man who'd make money exploiting his looks?"

Maggie shook her head, the action causing soft strands of dark hair to brush gently against her cheeks. "No. There's nothing wrong with modeling. It's an honest way to make a living, and that's all that matters in the long run."

Rush was silent for a moment. Then, very quietly, he said, "Thanks."

"What do you plan to do when you finish law school? Do you have anything lined up?"

"I'm leaning toward criminal law. I've heard from a firm in New Jersey that handles a lot of big criminal cases. There's a firm here in Boston, too. I don't know. The main thing is to get through. That's why I'm working for the Newbern Agency at night on top of my other jobs. Escorting isn't usually very demanding. After a day with my head in law books, I'm ready for something pretty low-key."

"I imagine so."

Silence pulsated throughout the car's interior in sync with the hum of the engine. Finally Rush broke the stillness. "What about you, Maggie? We've spent the evening together, I've even fought off one of your admirers, but I don't know anything about you except that you own your own art gallery. Tell me about Maggie Spencer."

His voice was low and held an unmistakable note of interest. April was right. Rush Barrington was gracious. Maggie laughed, the sound stilted with embarrassment. "What do you want to know?"

He smiled briefly at her. "For starters, I'd like to know why a woman who is as obviously charming and lovely as you feels it necessary to use an escort service. Surely you don't have any trouble finding dates?"

Maggie's laughter was genuine this time. "You mentioned my admirer. If you'll recall, he was getting a little free with his hands. He's even worse in a car or on a dance floor. And so far all my experiences tell me that his actions are representative of ninety-five percent of the male population of the world. In short, I got tired of doing battle every time I went out. Unfortunately, my business requires a certain amount of socializing—especially during the holiday season—and usually an escort. So when April saw my predicament, she suggested I give her agency a try."

"And has it worked?"

"Definitely. I get all the pluses of a date without the hassle at the door. The men April sends have always been everything they should be. Well mannered, courteous, attractive . . ."

"And older," he cut in.

Her eyes met his. "Yes. Older."

"Other than the age, was I satisfactory?"

She smiled. "Of course. Look, I'm sorry I caused such a fuss earlier, but you have to admit that if our roles had been reversed and you'd opened the door to find an older woman waiting to escort you, you'd have felt the same way."

Rush sat in silent consideration for a moment. "I think maturity, more than age, should be the factor in any relationship. If I'd found you at my door, I would have been pleased to think April believed I'd have anything in common with someone who's as successful and knowledgeable as you. And I doubt that I'd have worried about age differences." His eyes found hers again. "I'd have been too impressed by your looks."

Good Lord! What should she say? Was he flirting, or just being flattering so she'd give April a good report? She wasn't beautiful, and she knew it. If she *had* been beautiful, or more clever, then Jarrell . . . No, she was definitely too . . . too angular. All over. From the curve of her lips and the line of her jaw right down to the slender bones in her feet. Rush Barrington might be young, but it seemed he had eye problems, too.

"Have you been single long?" he asked suddenly.

"About two years," Maggie said shortly, unhappy with the subtle turn of the conversation.

"Divorced?"

"Yes."

Maggie willed him to stop the questioning. Mercifully, he did. Perhaps he sensed he was getting too personal, or perhaps he heard the anger seeping into her voice.

Divorced.

After more than two years she still couldn't think about her breakup with Jarrell without a feeling of utter failure sweeping over her. Funny. She'd thought she was doing everything right. She'd helped him get through college, sacrificed through those first rough years while he was establishing his advertising firm, worked and kept his home, had his daughter and fulfilled, to the best of her ability, the role of mother.

Everything had seemed all right until the night of June thirteenth, two and a half years earlier . . . just three weeks after Lacey graduated from high school, three days before their anniversary and right in the middle of her strawberry shortcake. Somewhere between the tart taste of strawberries and the smooth, sweet flavor of whipped cream, Maggie's world had fallen apart. To this day she couldn't abide strawberries, nor tolerate whipped cream.

"I've found someone else, Maggie. I want a divorce."

No prelude, no preamble, no warning. No softly executed announcement that might have helped lessen the blow. Just the severest economy of words, delivered with the severest economy of emotion. Just that her husband of nineteen years had found someone else—my God, she hadn't even known he was looking! —and that he wanted release from the matrimonial chains chafing his independence. Never once had she suspected Jarrell was unhappy. To say his announcement had taken her by surprise was the classic understatement.

That night Jarrell Spencer, self-made advertising executive and the only man to ever be her lover, had packed and left—going, Maggie was sure, to the side, to the bed, to the life of the other woman. He had left Maggie, stunned and near shock, with a sink full of dirty dishes, with eyes stinging from soon to fall tears, and with a heart brimming over with despair.

Planning what she and Jarrell would do after Lacey graduated from high school had been one of her favorite pastimes. She wouldn't be so tied to the house anymore. She would be free to take business trips with her husband, combining work with the pleasure of his company, since her main purpose at the gallery was the discovery of new, exciting talent.

Adjusting to life again without a child in the house would be difficult, but it would free them to do so many things that had been curtailed when Lacey came along and altered the tenor of their lives. Not that they hadn't loved her. They had. But having a child around was inhibiting in many ways.

Maggie had found herself looking forward to sleeping in the nude and wearing sexy negligees as she had during the early days of their marriage. By the time she no longer had to worry about a child crawling into bed with her and Jarrell, she'd gotten used to wearing a gown. And so she'd anticipated Lacey's departure for college, totally ignorant of anything amiss in her marriage and looking forward to surprising Jarrell with nights of utterly decadent marital bliss.

They would rediscover one another and the feelings of youthful passion that had once blazed so brightly between them, the passion that work and obligations had dimmed. She didn't know Jarrell had already rediscovered those feelings of youthful passion with a younger woman and had no interest in reacquainting himself with the love he and Maggie had once shared. He wanted a new love and a new life with Rita, the vivacious young woman who worked beside him. Rita, who was only nine years older than their daughter and eleven years younger than Maggie. Rita, who was a tender twenty-six to Maggie's ancient thirty-seven.

When he walked out the door with his golf clubs and his briefcase, the sun glinting off the Piaget watch she'd given him, he took with him most of what was good in Maggie's life. He took her laughter, her usual joie de vivre, her natural confidence. He stole her self-esteem. Suddenly she felt used, inferior, discarded. She had felt instantaneously old.

"Maggie?" Rush's voice interrupted the morbid train of her thoughts. "Are you all right?"

Maggie's head jerked toward the sound of his voice, the memories causing a resurgence of the feeling of aging she usually managed to keep at bay until faced with some situation that triggered it—like sitting in a dark car with a man a decade younger than she was. "I'm fine," she murmured softly.

He glanced over at her, concern carved into his features. Then, somehow, as if he knew the turn of her thoughts, he said gently, "Don't be so hard on yourself."

Impossible, Maggie thought. There was no way he could know what she was thinking. Or was there? He was terribly sharp. Wasn't it necessary for a legal mind to be able to think like the people it would try? To have some idea what thoughts were held silent and secret? He might have guessed his question about divorce would bring to mind memories best left in the past.

He braked the car to a halt.

"One Newbern Agency date delivered safe and sound in spite of hazardous driving conditions," he quipped lightly, once more saving her from searching for a suitable comeback to his observations. His hand reached out and touched her arm. "Stay put while I come around. That sidewalk looks slick."

Obediently, Maggie waited while he opened the door

and moved slowly around the hood of the car. In seconds he had opened her door, allowing the entrance of a deep breath of chilly air. He helped her out, keeping her elbow in a firm grip as they eased up onto the sidewalk.

Maggie could feel the strength in the hand and arm that steadied her as they walked slowly toward the door. That goal was but feet away when without warning she stepped onto the now frozen patch that hours before had been the puddle Rush had sidestepped when he'd arrived to pick her up. She gave a startled cry as her feet flew out from under her. Twisting her body around and flailing for the support she knew Rush's solid body could provide, Maggie crashed into the wall of his chest. Hard arms closed around her as her face scraped against the scratchy wool of his coat. Her arms grabbed the first thing they came into contact with—his wide shoulders. Her fingers tightened convulsively.

"Easy," his voice, which was very near her ear, soothed. "I've got you."

Maggie raised her head and looked up at him.

He smiled, his beautifully angular upper lip pulling cheekward, stretching the fullness of his lower lip in a way that snatched her breath from her already heaving chest. His eyes sparkled with warmth and life, inviting Maggie to reach out and take hold of that warmth and life with both hands.

She fought the urge and said unsteadily, "I'm okay. Just a little shaky."

Rush loosened his hold and allowed her to resume her place beside him as they made their way gingerly across the walk and up the steps to the door. Once inside, and without waiting for Rush, Maggie's gold sandals tapped a rapid rhythm across the marble entrance to the elevator. A slender, scarlet-tipped finger jabbed impatiently at the up button.

The doors slid open almost immediately, and Maggie scurried inside. Her eyes were wide and bright as she watched Rush enter behind her and press the button for her floor. Turning, he leaned negligently against the pale green walls and, as the elevator began its smooth flight, granted Maggie another of those captivating smiles. Her stomach gave a gentle lurch that she thought best to attribute to the elevator's upward motion.

Funny, she'd never before realized just how small the inside of this elevator was. Or was it Rush's broad body that made it seem so? She tried to keep her eyes from meeting his, but, like the heroines in the torrid romance novels she'd taken to reading this past year, her eyes kept straying to his.

Rush's penetrating gaze seemed to miss nothing. Maggie felt her cheeks growing warm beneath his thorough perusal and allowed her lashes to veil the confusion she knew must be mirrored in her eyes. Why, why wouldn't the elevator hurry?

She hazarded another glance at him and found his mouth quirked in a gentle smile. Oh, God! He was gorgeous. Rush Barrington was beautifully, wonderfully, blatantly male. From the top of his glossy dark head to the tips of his patent leather–shod feet. Her insides began to quiver and her knees felt weak from his nearness. No! she thought. Not with Rush. I don't want to feel this awareness—sexual awareness, she qualified —for him.

But she did.

What would April think of her circumstances? She could almost hear her friend's voice saying, "He's got a nice body. He's handsome. Admitting it doesn't make you a dirty old woman. It makes you normal, for heaven's sake. Remember, Mags, you're divorced—not dead."

The silent, inner conversation with April made her feel much better and it burned away the edges of her guilt. She chanced another look at Rush.

Electric blue melded with cocoa brown. He was so close . . . so close she could easily touch him.

And she wanted to, she realized suddenly.

Is this how it happened to Jarrell? she wondered in a moment of sympathetic understanding for what he might have felt. Had his hand touched Rita's at lunch one day? Had he leaned over to check one of her advertising layouts and, when she'd looked up, had the awareness just been there? Had the unbidden attraction sprung to life as it was now springing to life for her—unwanted, unasked for, but undeniably *there?*

Neither spoke. Neither moved.

He was so young. Too young. A man, to be sure, to make her feel what she hadn't felt in more than two years. But a young man. Reality smothered the burgeoning feelings inside her. Reality was the ten-year difference in their ages. Reality was a daughter in college. Reality was the indisputable fact that men wanted younger women, not older ones. Reality was that even though Rush Barrington made her heart go pitter-pat, he'd die laughing if he knew it.

Fool!

The elevator jerked to a stop. Maggie moved toward the doors before they were fully open, hurrying ahead of him, her fingers rummaging frantically through her gold evening bag for her key.

She had it in her hand and almost to the keyhole, when Rush's fingers closed around hers. Maggie froze.

"Let me," he commanded softly.

Maggie's fingers relaxed their grip on the key. Turning slowly, she discovered that she was imprisoned between the door and Rush, who stood only inches away.

She lifted her gaze to his as the key clicked in the lock. Their bodies were so close Maggie could see the faint lines fanning out around his eyes and she marveled at the extraordinary length of his dark lashes. The faint woodsy scent of his cologne wafted to her nostrils. His breath, smelling faintly of brandy, caressed her face.

Maggie was suddenly assailed with the age-old fear that attacked women of all ages when faced with a man at the door at the end of an evening—afraid that he would try to kiss her, afraid that he wouldn't. Her eyes mirrored her quandary.

One corner of Rush's mouth lifted in a half smile. He dangled the key in front of her. "Thank you for the evening, Maggie Spencer."

"Yes. Thank you for being so . . . helpful." Her words and tone of voice sounded stiff even to her own ears. Where had the easy conversation they'd shared in the car gone? She took the key from him, her cold fingers brushing his before she plunged both hands into her jacket pockets.

"Dammit, Maggie," Rush growled suddenly, urgently, "I . . ."

"I thought you were working!" came a softly accusing feminine voice from Maggie's left. She swiveled her head and saw a beautiful woman approach them, her long, slim legs carrying her toward them with the sinuous grace and easy confidence of the young and beautiful.

Without turning, Rush recognized Constance Cross's

voice. His breath escaped in a long hiss as he saw the guilt quickly crowd out the anticipatory look in Maggie's eyes.

He forced his eyes and a smile toward the younger woman, idly noting that she wasn't as pretty as he'd thought earlier. Her face had an almost babyish roundness that spoke of a recent acquaintance with her teen years.

"Just finishing," he said as pleasantly as he could.

Constance looked pointedly at Maggie and smiled knowingly. "Sure."

Without another word she moved past them and toward the elevator.

Rush turned back toward Maggie, an apology already taking shape on his lips.

"Good night," she said with a wide smile as brittle as old paper. One hand moved from her pocket and pushed open the door.

"Maggie . . ."

The shrill ringing of the phone interrupted him and sent Maggie's gaze flying thankfully toward it. She glanced back at him, relief written clearly on her striking features. "Thanks again, Rush. Good night."

Before Rush could do more than open his mouth to answer, the door shut very quietly in his face.

Chapter Three

"Where do you want to hang this?"

Maggie looked up from the pile of sales receipts, her eyes, framed by glasses, moving first to the vibrant splashes of color of the abstract painting, then upward to the pleasant, expectant face of Jerri Fitzgerald.

"What about upstairs?" Maggie suggested, pushing back her chair, standing and rounding the corner of the gracefully lined, Georgian-style desk. "What else did we get in the shipment?"

"Lots of goodies," the other woman replied as she, with undeniable enthusiasm, began to show off the numerous large and small prints and reprints of contemporary art.

"This is unusual," Maggie commented of a serigraph by an Israeli artist named Agam. Its bold, geometric pattern was a visual delight.

"Yes, that is nice, isn't it?" Jerri responded, studying the work with a critical eye. "We ought to put it in a frame with crisp, clean lines, something cool, like silver. What do you think?"

"Sounds terrific," Maggie answered, as usual bowing to her assistant's instinctive knowledge of framing. To put it succinctly, Jerri Fitzgerald was the best Maggie had ever seen at delicately balancing picture and frame. It was a talent as necessary to selling art as the ability to recognize which pieces would and wouldn't sell. Maggie had been lucky to find her. Smiling to herself, Maggie rephrased the statement. She'd been lucky that Jerri had found her.

Eight months earlier Jerri Fitzgerald had literally walked in off the street, announced that she was looking for a job in an art gallery, likewise announced —and bluntly so—that she hadn't worked in years, had no formal training in art, and that there was absolutely no reason such a prestigious gallery should hire her . . . except that she'd once been good at framing and was willing to work hard at learning whatever else she needed to know. She'd also admitted to being a widow, a mother whose fledglings had newly flown the nest, and a woman who was going certifiably crazy from the sound of her quiet house. Maggie had liked her directness and her candor. So much so, she had hired her on the spot.

In truth, Maggie thought as she now watched Jerri awkwardly negotiate the spiral, corkscrewlike, black iron stairway with the bundle of prints tucked under her arm, the woman reminded her of herself. Oh, not physically. Jerri was short, as in petite, and a few pounds overweight compared to her own tall and thin physique; the woman had cropped, full-fluffed blond hair to her longer, sleeker black-brown; and Maggie would guess her age to be somewhere near fifty. But there was one basic similarity. Maggie had gotten her job in very much the same way Jerri had gotten hers and, in all honesty, with less reason. She hadn't even known about framing.

What, or rather whom, she had known was a friend of Jacob Simon. The Simon Gallery, located on Newbury Street, a street well known for housing more than two dozen of the best contemporary galleries in America, was one of Boston's finest. And Jacob Simon, an art legend. A successful painter in his own right, a specialist in seascapes, he had turned to selling art in his later years and had reaped even more success at that. He had an eye for knowing what the buyer wanted and the ability to discover greatness just crucial seconds before everyone else did. All this he had taught to the inexperienced Maggie, who had been brazen enough to beg a friend to introduce her to him at a party.

That had been six years ago and at a time in Maggie's life when she'd wanted something to fill the long hours that Jarrell spent at work and Lacey at high school. She'd also wanted something just to get her out of the house and add a little challenge to her life. So proficient did she become at her job that as Jacob Simon's health deteriorated, she shouldered more and more of the responsibility of running the prestigious Simon Gallery. When he'd died two years earlier, Maggie, with a lump in her throat and with a lump sum in her bank account—Jarrell's guilt-generous divorce settlement—had bought out the business.

She had changed little; only superficial things, like having a fireplace built in, like smothering the hardwood floors in Persian rugs boasting bright colors, like keeping coffee hot in a silver urn and ready to pour in delicate, white, gilt-edged demitasse cups. A sturdy masculine desk had given way to a more feminine Georgian one, and green plants in pounded brass pots—bushy palms and marbled dieffenbachia and treelike schefflera—filled up many previously empty spots. The loft, used for storage and framing, had been enlarged, the second story repainted a straw-colored neutral and the first floor made to more closely resemble the cozy home it had once been to high society a generation ago.

The quality of the gallery's business had remained unchanged, however, just as had the old, three-story brownstone's outer appearance. And still tacked to the heavy wooden door, which rumor had it had been imported from France during the Revolutionary War, was a brass plate stating in small and finely chiseled letters: THE SIMON GALLERY. Maggie had adamantly refused to change the name to her own, though she did take a special pride in the fact that verbally, and in all the right art circles, it was now referred to as the Simon-Spencer Gallery.

Thank God she'd had the gallery, Maggie thought as she slipped the glasses from her eyes and abandoned them on the paper-strewn desk. If April had been her sanity, the gallery had been her salvation. Stepping to the coffee urn, she poured out a cup of the aromatic brew and walked toward the blazing fireplace. Beyond the window, soft, fleecy snowflakes laced the air in a peaceful, lazy design. Maggie sipped, sighed an end-of-a-Friday-afternoon sigh and luxuriated in the welcome warmth seeping through her royal-blue-and-black-plaid woolen skirt. Easing one stockinged foot from a black leather high-heeled pump, she angled it to the fire, held it a moment, rubbed the front of it up the calf of her other leg, then slid her toasty toes back into the shoe. For a reason she couldn't explain, the warm feeling reminded her of Rush Barrington.

But then, almost everything this week had reminded

her of Rush Barrington. From the moment she had gently—unhappily?—closed the door in his face the Saturday before, he had become a haunting memory in her mind. He had also been one other thing. He had been the first, the only man since Jarrell, to awaken her sleeping sexuality.

Though alone, she blushed at the admission. My God, she thought on a wave of disbelief, how could she be attracted to him? Oh, what April had said was true; he was gorgeous, with a face so handsome it could stop a woman's heart and a body so firm and muscular that that same feminine heart, stopped only moments before, could easily lurch into rapid double time, but . . .

She set the cup on the mantel, nestling it beside the glass-domed clock, and sighed. She had to put him out of her mind. Good heavens, what would people think? What would Rush think? Nothing, she quickly supplied, because no one, and certainly not Rush, would ever know of her foray into insanity. And not only that, if she were to see him again—which she wouldn't, because she'd made it plain to April she wanted no escort on a repeat basis—she was certain her response would be more sane. It had been nothing more than the madness of a wild moment.

The cluster of bells tinkling as the front door opened scattered Maggie's thoughts like dandelions in a whispered puff of wind. A frosty wave of air skipped into the room and with it the hint of a Christmas carol from a nearby boutique. In also came a man. Maggie's eyes sought out the male figure, a smile of greeting forming on her full, glossed lips. The smile froze, almost comically, in midstretch, while her breath caught in her throat. Her heart stopped, started again, then pranced into double time. Oh, damn! she thought, snatching at the remnants of her sanity. It was more than the madness of a wild moment. It was just . . . madness.

Rush's lips curved into a slow, languorous smile at the exact moment that his eyes gently, but totally, connected with hers. He looked at her. She looked at him. For how long, neither could have said.

"I wasn't sure I had the right place," he said at last. One gloved hand was stuffed into the pocket of his heavy, buttoned-up overcoat. A woolen scarf was coiled about his neck, hiding part of his chin in its folds, and comfortable, casual boots encased his feet. Dying snowflakes glistened on upturned collar and wind-ravaged hair. His nose shone a chafed rose-red from the blistering, stinging cold, and Maggie had the urge to warm it with the soft touch of her hand.

But she didn't. She concentrated instead on a reply and heard herself say, "You have the right place." She was aware that she hadn't asked "The right place for what?" She also felt a sudden, crazy, empty feeling in the pit of her stomach, the kind a woman feels for a man, and had a pang of guilt for feeling it. She killed the unwanted feeling with an on-target shot of determination.

"Your name's not on the outside," he pointed out.

She shook her head. "No, it isn't."

"I canvassed the whole area and finally had to stop and ask which gallery was yours."

"I'm sorry."

"There's no need for you to be," he said, smiling and brushing a lock of hair from eyes presently taking in the fireplace. "Look, if you're selling heat, you've got yourself a customer at any price."

Maggie moved back in open invitation to the roaring hearth, and Rush, removing first the gloves, then unwinding the scarf, stepped forward as he unbuttoned his coat and slipped from it.

"Here, let me have your things," she offered, taking the woolen garment and hanging it on a brass rack. When she turned back, she was forced again to battle that empty feeling in her stomach.

Saturday night Rush had been wearing a tux and he had looked—Maggie searched her mind and settled on the only appropriate word—fantastic, but now, standing before the fire, his back to the orange-red flame, his hands warming behind him, he looked even more fantastic. Beige corduroy pants, not old, but worn just enough to mold to his body in an intimately familiar way, covered the long length of his legs, while a pullover sweater, in shades of tan, chocolate and lime green, nestled over a white shirt. And from the vee of the shirt and sweater peeked hair, hair a much darker brown than that on his head . . . and thick, sinfully thick, wonderfully thick. Maggie couldn't keep herself from wondering if it matted his whole chest in the same rich density. The thought that it might initiated another string of feelings she thought best to squelch.

She dragged her eyes from his chest and wiped her moist palm down the side of her skirt. "How have you been?" she heard herself ask.

He shrugged, seconds later spreading his legs to equally distribute his weight. "Fine. April's keeping me busy." His eyes melded with hers and held for the duration of a question. "How have you been?"

Maggie had the curious feeling he was asking not so much about her health as whether she, too, had been doing the party scene that week and if so, had she used the agency. Was he wondering why she hadn't asked for him if she had? He probably worked on commission; the more he went out, the more he made.

"No," she said. Suddenly realizing that she had in no way answered his verbalized question, she added, "I mean, I'm fine. I've stayed in pretty close this week."

Some emotion passed across his brown irises; Maggie thought it looked like relief, but since that emotion made no sense, she told herself she must be wrong.

"You were wise," he said. "It's been miserable weather."

"Miserable," she agreed. "Boston at its winter finest."

Again, they exchanged long, quiet looks.

"Well, what can I do for you?" Maggie was finally moved to ask when she suddenly realized they were both just staring. Her words seemed to jar him back to the moment as well.

He smiled, somewhat sheepishly, and slid one hand into a pants pocket. "I came in to buy something, but I think I may have gotten in over my head. Financially speaking." This last he said with an encompassing gesture that took in the gallery. "Why don't you just send me on my way before I make a total fool of myself?"

"I will not," she said, immediately coming to his defense. "How much do you want to spend?"

"I'd like to spend a lot—it's for my parents for Christmas—but I can't go over seventy-five dollars, tops a hundred." He grimaced. "Don't laugh too loud."

"I'm not laughing," she said, instantly empathizing with him and mentally going over her stock. Finding something in his price range was going to be a challenge, but she didn't tell him that. Instead, she implied the reverse. "We have pieces in the gallery at all prices." Which wasn't a lie, she placated herself. "Let's see if we can find something you like." She started off toward the back of the gallery; Rush easily caught up with her and tempered his long stride to match hers.

For the next few minutes Maggie led him from picture to picture, tactfully guiding him only to those within his budget. They laughed over some, discussed in pseudo-intellectual terms the deep, hidden meaning of others, which usually led to more laughter, and even outright grimaced at a few. All Rush vetoed at his disliking or what he imagined would be the disliking of his parents.

"How about flowers?" she suggested, answering her own question and moving forward at the same time. "No, Dad probably wouldn't like flowers. Not masculine enough."

They stopped in front of the next painting, both pairs of eyes automatically glancing upward. A sudden twinkle appeared in Rush's. "Ah, now I think we've found something Dad would really like. Although I'm not sure Mom would be crazy about a nude."

"What makes you think women don't like nudes?" Maggie countered.

His mouth pursed thoughtfully. "Point well taken. Do women like nudes? Or does it depend on the woman and the nude?"

The gallery suddenly grew quiet, and Maggie would have even believed that it shrank in size, shrank from a three-story brownstone down to a world only the size of the man before her. In that moment she admitted that the past week had dulled her memory. Why hadn't she remembered the dark brown warmth of Rush's eyes? Why hadn't she remembered the simple beauty of his smile, the smile now teasing her for an answer to his question? In the distant reaches of her mind she heard the phone ring. Heard it ring again. And again. Abruptly, she tore her eyes from his.

"If you'll excuse me," she said, backing away several paces, then turning and almost racing for the phone. Racing *for* the phone? Or was it racing *from* Rush?

When she returned minutes later Rush stood with feet apart and hands clasped loosely behind his back, contemplating a picture. "I like it," he announced over his shoulder at the sound of her footsteps. The *it* was a colorful, oriental-flavored etching called *Songbird.* "How much?"

Maggie gave an inward grimace. She wanted to lie. It wouldn't have been the first time she'd sacrificed the profit from a sale. But this time she couldn't do it. Not to a man who so intimately knew the value of a dollar. Not to a man who had struggled so hard to get where he was. Not to a man who had such obvious pride.

"I'd have to look it up to be sure," she answered, an apology in the blue depths of her eyes, "but I think it's one hundred seventy-five dollars, maybe even two hundred."

Rush gave a low whistle. "I think I'll pass."

"Maybe not," Maggie returned as a sudden thought took form. "Why don't we just reframe it in something less expensive? Sometimes you pay as much for a frame as for the artwork." As she explained this, she reached upward to disengage the etching from the wall.

"Sounds good. Here, let me do that," Rush offered, reaching out to take over the task.

His fingers brushed against Maggie's, and at each point of contact a tingling erupted. His eyes moved quickly to hers just seconds before she jerked her hand away and called out in a scratchy voice for her assistant. When Jerri descended the stairway Maggie introduced the two and explained their problem. Jerri was, as always, quick to find a solution.

"We have a dark brown bamboo flecked with gilt that

would look real nice," the woman suggested. "It's a simpler frame, but certainly it would be as attractive, and to be honest it's probably more appropriate than this." She indicated the already framed picture with the thump of a finger.

"How does that sound?" Maggie asked, looking over at Rush.

He shrugged and smiled. "Sounds great."

"Do you still want it triple-matted?" Jerri asked. "That costs a little . . ."

"Yes, leave it triple-matted," Maggie cut in. Like it or not, Rush would accept a measure of her generosity.

Moments later Jerri was once again ascending the stairs to the loft, the etching in her hand, while Rush and Maggie were finalizing the sale. Maggie was writing out a ticket, or rather, trying to do so without the aid of her glasses. She told herself it was pure vanity that kept her from reaching the few inches and scooping them up from the desk. But vanity or not, she didn't reach.

"Would these help?" Rush offered, handing the dark-framed glasses to her. There was the hint of a smile playing around his lips, almost as if he understood her dilemma and was amused by it.

She smiled halfheartedly and with even less amusement. "Thank you," she said, hoping the words seemed imbued with sincerity, and slid the glasses on. Forcing herself to look him fully in the face, she shoved the charge papers at Rush, who scrawled his name boldly, then, with a rustle of paper, she pulled his copy from the others.

"We could deliver it tomorrow," she offered.

"Great," he confirmed, slipping back into his overcoat and twining the scarf about his neck. "Thanks," he said as he pulled on one glove, then the other.

"You're welcome," she said, watching his hair-covered wrist disappear inside the leather. "I'm glad we had something."

She smiled. He smiled. Time glided by. The atmosphere suddenly seemed charged with an indefinable tension.

"What time do you close?" Rush asked.

"The gallery?"

"Uh-huh."

"Six." She knew what was coming. As a woman, she intuitively knew what was coming. The very thought both frightened and electrified her.

Rush pulled back the edge of his fur-lined glove and checked his watch. "If I did some shopping for an hour and came back at six, could I buy you a drink?"

"I don't . . ." She hesitated. Actually hesitated. Oh, God, she wasn't seriously considering going out with a man ten years her junior. Was she? "I . . . I can't . . ." She heard herself making a decision. Her answer didn't feel good, but it did feel right. "I mean, I've got other plans . . ."

She would have bet money he knew she was lying, but he smiled, a soft, sincere flexing of his lips. "I understand." He stepped back. "Well, thanks again." He took another step, another, then turned around and walked toward the door. When he opened it, bells jingled and the sound of "Joy to the World" flitted into the shop, along with the tinny chords of coins clanging in a Salvation Army kettle. His hand on the door, he turned and smiled once more. "Merry Christmas, Maggie," he said softly, in a rich, masculine voice. Before she could reply he was out the door.

Slipping from the desk to the window, she watched as he raised the collar of his coat against the bitter wind and snow, watched as he wove in and out of the crowd of holiday shoppers, watched as he dug in his pocket for a coin and tossed it into the contribution kettle, watched as he turned and disappeared at the end of the street. Disappeared. She suddenly felt a sensation of emptiness, this time not the stomach-emptiness of desire but the soul-emptiness of being alone. All alone. In fact, she felt so alone that had he been standing before her with the offer of a drink, she would have been helpless to answer anything but yes.

Lacey wasn't coming home for Christmas! The thought stabbed at Maggie's heart, leaving a vicious pain in its wake.

"Mom? Are you there?"

Maggie wrapped the old bathrobe around herself, as if she could somehow keep the emotional cold at bay with the thin fabric, and squeezed the telephone to her ear with achingly clenched fingers.

"Sure, honey," she said in a voice that fought hard for normalcy, but fell a little short of victory.

"It just sort of happened, Mom," Lacey explained. "I mean, all us girls were gab-festing in the dorm, and someone said 'Hey, let's go skiing for Christmas.' And before anyone knew what was happening, we had reservations at this fabulous resort in the Poconos. But it won't cost that much," the nineteen-year-old hastened to add. "There's twelve of us going, and we'll stay four to a room."

Maggie had a quick vision of twelve college girls descending on an unsuspecting resort in the Poconos and leaving the entire state of Pennsylvania in a condition just short of shell shock.

"Who's going?" Maggie asked.

Lacey spouted off a quick list of names, most of whom Maggie recognized as young women her daughter had known since high school or had met the year before when she'd first entered Skidmore College in Saratoga Springs, New York.

"And what about New Year's?" Maggie added, knowing the answer even before she asked.

There was a long, uncomfortable pause at the other end of the line. "I'm still going to spend it with Dad and . . ." Lacey trailed off.

"Rita," Maggie supplied. "Her name is Rita and we both know it."

"I know," Lacey Spencer said, still sounding to her perceptive mother's ears like the little girl she had known and loved so well, the little girl with blond braids, braces and blue eyes, the little girl who had grown into a beautiful, sensitive woman. "It's just . . . I don't know, Mom. . . ."—Maggie could almost see her daughter shrug—"It's just that things are so different now."

"I know, Lacey. They are for all of us." Maggie shifted the phone to her other ear. "Your dad loves you, though, honey, and you try and have a good time on New Year's with them. Okay?" Jarrell may be guilty of a lot of things, Maggie admitted in fairness, but he wasn't guilty of not loving his daughter.

"Sure," Lacey answered in a tone that could have been either sincere or insincere. Maggie thought it probably fell somewhere in between. "Look, Mom," Lacey added, "if you don't want me to go Christmas . . ."

"Of course you can go skiing," Maggie broke in with great expense to her composure. "I haven't done a thing toward Christmas dinner." This last was a lie, but she told herself the frozen turkey would keep and the mincemeat pie she had planned, Lacey's favorite, was too fattening anyway. "Do you need any money?"

Another pause. "No, ma'am." The "ma'am," used

now only when Lacey thought she was veering toward a head-on collision with disfavor, alerted Maggie that she wasn't going to like what she next heard. And she didn't. "Dad's going to send me some for the trip."

"You've already talked to your dad about this?"

"Yes, ma'am. He said it was okay with him if it was with you."

Well, why the hell shouldn't it be okay with him? Maggie thought in a sudden lightning bolt of anger. It wasn't interfering with his precious plans in any way. He was still spending New Year's with their daughter. And Maggie wouldn't get to see her until heaven knew when. It wasn't fair! It just wasn't fair! It . . .

"Mom?"

Maggie sighed, at the same time raking back an errant wisp of dark hair from eyes cloudy with tears. It wasn't Lacey's fault that she was growing up . . . that she'd already grown up. And it wasn't Lacey's place to entertain her or save her from the hungry jaws of loneliness. "Promise me that you'll be careful."

The younger woman's voice held the jubilant notes of relief. "I will, Mom. I promise. And I'll call you."

"Okay, honey. Have a good time."

There was a slight hesitation before Lacey added, "I love you, Mom. More than chocolate-ripple ice cream."

The tears that had threatened moments before now pooled in Maggie's blue eyes, making them appear as shiny as polished glass. "I love you. More than chocolate-ripple ice cream." It was an expression begun when Lacey was little and now lovingly worn by time. It was an expression no amount of money could buy.

"Good-bye, Mom."

"Good-bye."

The phone went dead in Maggie's hand. Slowly, she stretched and levered it back into its cradle. She straightened and wiped at a lone tear. Lacey wasn't coming home for Christmas. Her only family wasn't coming home for Christmas or New Year's. Suddenly the holidays looked dark and dismal and not at all worth going through.

Just as suddenly Maggie realized she could use the drink Rush had offered her earlier that afternoon. And she realized one other thing as well. More than the drink, she could use the smiling, teasing company of Rush Barrington.

The seven days preceding Christmas were miserable. Maggie deliberately worked long hours at the gallery and deliberately accepted only two party invitations, both of which she deemed absolutely essential to business. On both occasions she relied on the Newbern Agency for escorts. Both of the men April sent were professionally charming, acceptably courteous and outrageously dull when compared to Rush, a comparison Maggie seemed intent on making despite her wish not to. At the end of the second and last social obligation, Maggie breathed a sigh of relief and sat back to await Christmas Day.

It arrived with a lonely vengeance.

Maggie woke late and with a dull headache that refused to go away. She had been up only a short time when her parents called from New Jersey to wish her a merry Christmas, and in some indefinable way the call upset her. Her parents had sounded old and as lonely as she. With a start, Maggie realized *their* daughter hadn't come home for the holiday either. She vowed to somehow make it up to them.

Midmorning, her ex-in-laws called, two people she

cared a lot about, people she'd remained close to despite the tragedy of her failed marriage. Then, at about noon, April called, insisting for the thousandth time that Maggie join her and Sam for dinner. For the thousandth time Maggie refused. Sam was April's current love interest, an interest that had lasted beyond the usual three months, and it was the first time in Maggie's memory that April had cooked a meal for anyone, maybe even the first time April had cooked a meal, period. Maggie knew the dinner was special to her friend and she had no intention of being an awkward third wheel.

So Maggie ate her dinner alone—a turkey sandwich, the makings of which she had bought at a deli the day before. It was nutritious, she told herself as she choked it down, and it was the traditional holiday turkey, even if in a slightly different form. Later that afternoon she sat around the small tree, hung with red-and-white-striped candy canes and dotted with red bows, and opened her presents. Lacey had sent her a soft pink angora sweater that promised to do exciting things for Maggie's complexion and figure. Maggie would have traded it for fifteen minutes with her daughter.

The fifteen minutes came via telephone at nine-thirty that night. Lacey's voice was so full of the fun she was having that Maggie felt an instant guilt for even daring to wish her daughter were there with her. The Poconos were beautiful; the resort was "rad," which Maggie interpreted as greater than great; the skiing was wonderful; the males fantastic.

"Oh, Mom, there's a whole group of Harvard guys here," Lacey cooed. "They're seniors . . . well, most of them are . . . and they're . . ."

"I know," Maggie supplied with the first smile of the day, "they're rad." The smile slipped a little,

though, when she realized that Rush was at Harvard.
She hastened to tell herself he was older than the
men Lacey was talking about and almost finished with
law school, but some traitorous voice deep inside
insisted he wasn't that much older. The voice was depressing.

Maggie hung up with the sensation that the call had
made her feel both better and worse. She was also left
with Rush Barrington on her mind. Showering and
slipping into a warm flannel nightgown, she eased
between cool, clean, blue-flowered sheets and tried to
go to sleep. A vision of Rush—brown hair mussed and
brown eyes flirting—drifted before her. Had he gone
away for Christmas? Had he spent the day in town with
friends? Had he spent the day alone?

Turning over with a groan, she jabbed at the pillow
and settled her head in its soft depths. Moments later
she was asleep. Her last conscious thought was of Rush.
She wondered what he was doing.

Three days later Maggie reached for the phone and
dialed the Newbern Agency. She'd just received an
invitation to a New Year's party that she couldn't pass
up for professional and personal reasons. The professional reason was that the artist who was giving it,
rumored to be ultratalented, was looking for a gallery
home; the personal reason was that one more holiday
spent alone in the apartment and they'd carry her out
screaming and in a straitjacket.

"The Newbern Agency. I've got the man for you,"
came April's drawled response.

"Hi."

"Oh, hi, Mags." The voice instantly changed from a
business tone to one of friend-to-friend. "How's it
going?"

"Fine."

"How was your holiday?"

"Long," Maggie responded without hesitation. "*Real* long."

Maggie could almost see the frown on April's pixie-ish face. "I knew it. I knew you should have come to dinner. Why didn't . . ."

"No," Maggie broke in, "I shouldn't have. And speaking of the holiday, how was it your way?"

A full-blown sigh escaped April's lips. "Wonderful. Simply wonderful."

Maggie's mouth curved into a smile. "How was your dinner?"

"The turkey was overcooked, the dressing too dry, the cranberry sauce too tart, the yams too sweet and Sam loved it."

Maggie's smile turned into a laugh. "That wonderful, huh?"

"That wonderful. Of course, it was all Sam's fault that the turkey was overcooked."

"I don't think I'll pursue that," Maggie said.

"Don't want you to," April responded, "although I will say that the bird wasn't the only thing cooking."

Maggie laughed again, a sound of genuine happiness. "April, you're wild."

"Funny, that's what Sam said." Now both women laughed. "Is this a social call or something else?" April asked finally.

"It's something else. I need an escort. For a New Year's Eve party."

"Okay. What time do you need him?"

"Have him pick me up at about seven-thirty."

"Seven-thirty it is," April repeated, obviously recording the information on paper. "How do you want him to dress?"

Maggie pursed her lips thoughtfully, then decided. "I guess a tux."

"One man in tux at seven-thirty on New Year's Eve. Anything else?"

There was a pause, slight but full of feeling, and Maggie's heart accelerated to a pace just short of a scamper. "Is . . ." She cleared her throat, adding as casually as she could, "Is Rush Barrington already booked?"

Chapter Four

$\mathcal{M}$ aggie leaned nearer the lighted mirror, painstakingly outlined her lips, then filled in their fullness with a rich, vibrant carmine. She straightened and examined her appearance carefully. Her thick, coffee-colored hair was swept upward into a jumble of curls whose very casualness spoke of her recent trip to one of Boston's most notable stylists. Soft tendrils fell onto her forehead, caressed the line of her jaw and invited attention to the delicate nape of her neck.

She wore a crimson silk-jersey skirt slit high in front to reveal glimpses of long, silken-clad legs when she walked. Her blouse was a matching long-sleeve, shadow-striped silk chiffon that fell full and loose from shirred shoulders. Its softly draped V-neck exposed bare flesh almost to her waist. The look was fashionable and elegant . . . and too darn revealing, she thought, even though she did have on one of those bras especially designed for plunging necklines.

Maggie made a small sound of irritation. She'd been trying for days—without luck—to reach her host to check on appropriate apparel for his New Year's Eve party. She hated not knowing what to wear! A quick glance at the clock further provoked her annoyance. There was no time to change, so she'd just have to try to fill up the bare space!

Her host for the evening, who called himself by the unlikely name of Rafael Brown, and who some were calling Boston's Van Gogh, was an unknown element to Maggie. She'd heard about him through the grapevine and understood he was trying to affiliate himself with a gallery. She wondered why some of her competition hadn't snapped him up if he was half as good as rumor had him.

So she'd taken the bull by the horns and called him about looking at his work. In return, he'd invited her and an escort to his New Year's Eve party, where he promised all his paintings would be displayed for her perusal. Excited by the fact that the man seemed receptive to a small gallery, Maggie had accepted. And since Lacey had plans, it would be better than being alone.

It was only later that she remembered the need for an escort. And much later that she'd screwed up her courage and called April to see if Rush could go with her. She still blushed when she remembered April's teasing comments.

Even now, as she hooked several fine gold chains around her neck, she wondered if her friend's statement was true and Rush had really asked to be assigned to her, or if April was just playing another of her matchmaking games. Who could tell? All Maggie did know was that April's statement, and the fact that she herself *had* asked for him for the party tonight, made her terribly nervous.

Maggie had admitted during the long, lonely week since Christmas that she was physically attracted to Rush. He was charming, handsome, intelligent. And he made her laugh. She admitted that his nearness and the strange, indecipherable message she sometimes thought she saw in his eyes set her heart clamoring in her breast. She admitted it, but she hadn't accepted it.

What did he want with her? Why had he come to her shop when there were dozens of others he could have chosen? And there must be hundreds of women his age who would give their eyeteeth to have a drink with him. Why ask *her*?

Unable to find an answer, and darting another glance at the clock to find it was almost time for Rush to arrive, Maggie heaved a troubled sigh and put on a chain with a diamond teardrop that fell to rest between her breasts. There! The bare expanse of skin wasn't quite so noticeable. She began rummaging around in her jewelry box for the matching earrings only to find that they weren't in their proper place. She tapped at her lips with one finger. *Think, Maggie, think! You wore them two weeks ago to the Carruthers' party.*

It had been late when she'd come in. She'd cleaned her face somewhat haphazardly and fallen into bed. The earrings had made sleeping uncomfortable, and somewhere in that nebulous realm between being awake and asleep, she'd taken them off and . . . A wide smile lit her face as she remembered where she'd put the earrings. The drawer of her nightstand.

Maggie hurried to the bed, seated herself on its edge and pulled open the drawer of the bedside table. The first things she saw were the ivory combs she used to hold back the sides of her hair. The combs she couldn't find last week, she remembered with mild irritation as she scavenged through the drawer's contents. Eyebrow tweezers. A magnifying mirror. A jar of night cream. The usual assortment of items she dumped inside whenever she was trying to clean up in a hurry.

Aha! There was one. As Maggie shifted some items to get the earring, her fingers brushed a small, black velvet case. Her movements stilled suddenly before her fingers closed almost convulsively around the jeweler's box.

She swallowed low in her throat and, against her will and her better judgment, found herself taking out the black case and flicking open the lid. It gave a mocking clank. The gold and jade cuff links looked the same as they had when she'd bought them for Jarrell and the celebration of their nineteen years of marriage—and the same as they'd looked the hundred or so times she'd flipped open the lid in just this same punitive and pondering manner.

She smiled, the crooked, sad smile she almost always wore when viewing the cuff links, a smile that expressed eloquently the irony they represented. Her husband hadn't remembered their special day. Maggie's lips curved into an arc of sarcasm. But then, a man could be forgiven for not remembering his anniversary when it fell just three days after the day he'd asked for a divorce so he could be with another woman.

The sharp, intrusive peal of the doorbell jarred Maggie from her black reverie.

Rush! She jumped, snapped the case shut with a click that symbolically locked out the past one more time and replaced the velvet box in the bedside table. Her gaze lighted almost simultaneously on the errant earring.

The doorbell rang again, impatiently, it seemed. A nervous, almost sick feeling knotted her stomach. Oh, God! Had April told Rush she'd asked for him? Surely her friend wouldn't do that to her!

Rising from the bed, Maggie went into the living room, putting the diamond drops in her ears as she went. She had just put the back on the last earring and was turning the doorknob when the bell pealed for the third time.

She swung open the door and found Rush standing in the opening, his hands thrust into the pockets of his wool coat, his hair, as usual, attractively disarrayed.

Her eyes clung to his features, charting the bold sweep of his heavy brows, the perfect outline of his lips. As always, she fought the urge to press her fingertip to the deep cleft in his chin. She also did battle with the breathtaking plunge her heart always took when she first saw him. Her mind hadn't played tricks on her. He was as beautifully masculine as she remembered.

"Hi." Maggie offered him a nervous smile, fingering the chains against her breast and stepping aside so he could enter. "Sorry I kept you waiting. I couldn't find my earrings. Let me get my coat and I'll be ready." She knew she was rattling on, but couldn't seem to stop the flow of words.

"I thought you'd stood me up," Rush said, closing the door behind him.

Maggie turned to smile at him, the teasing tone in his words alleviating much of her discomfort. "Not on your life! I'm going to a stranger's party and I'd like at least one familiar face around." She disappeared through the bedroom door.

"Where are we going?" Rush asked, combing his fingers through his hair.

Maggie stuck her head back around the door. "An

artist who's looking for a gallery is having a party. Are you ready for this? His name is Rafael . . ."—she paused for emphasis—"Brown." When she saw Rush's brows draw together and his mouth silently forming the name, she laughed. "Precisely," she said, her head disappearing from the doorway. She returned to the living room in a matter of minutes, a mink jacket flung over her arm. She handed the coat to Rush, their eyes meeting again before she turned to offer him her back so he could help her into the coat's warmth.

It would be all right, she assured herself. She would have a good time with him—laugh, talk and tease. But that didn't mean there was anything more to her feelings than just that. Rush was someone she could count on as pleasant, undemanding company. *And that, Maggie Spencer, is all there is to it.*

"Are you *sure* this is the right place?" Maggie asked, her breathing labored and the calves of her legs aching as she gripped Rush's hand tightly and looked toward the top of the flight of stairs they still had to climb—the fourth and hopefully the last.

Rush grinned down at her and cocked one eyebrow. "That depends on whether or not you gave me the right address."

When Maggie frowned he laughed softly and looped his arm around her waist. "Come on. We'll help each other."

Together, they trudged slowly up the stairs, but somehow Rush's arm around her didn't help. Instead, the brush of his thigh against hers and the feel of her shoulder against the solidity of his body only added to her breathlessness and the heavy beating of her heart.

She forced her mind to the meeting with Rafael Brown. Good Lord! Who would ever believe someone could actually make their home in something like this? The building was five stories of what? Old offices that had been vacated years ago? Hundreds of years ago, she thought grimly.

"What kind of person would want to live here, anyway?" she muttered, reaching the top and clutching the banister while she tried to control her breathing.

Rush, who, much to Maggie's perverse delight, was breathing more heavily than normal himself, shrugged. "Who knows? Although the wharf area is becoming popular. A lot of people are renovating places like this and turning them into homes."

"Well, it may be tacky to point this out, counselor," she grumbled, "but this place has never heard the word *renovation*—let alone seen any." She lifted her hand from the rail and looked disgustedly at the grime on her glove. "Would you look at the dust?"

"Come on, Maggie! Think of the commissions you'll make if you can snag Brown for the gallery." He gripped her elbow and propelled her toward their destination, a bright, cerulean-blue door that obviously led to the Brown apartment. Surprisingly, there was a doorbell. When Rush pressed it, it sounded like temple bells tinkling in the wind. They looked at each other questioningly.

The door swung open. A man wearing chains of varying thicknesses around his neck and a skintight, black leather body suit decorated with nuts and bolts stood before them, his short, bleached-blond hair standing straight up as if he'd stuck his finger into an electrical outlet. "Hey," he said with a wide smile, "what's happ'nin'?"

Maggie's eyes widened, then swung upward to Rush. His features were schooled into impassivity as he said, "I'm Rush Barrington. And this is Ms. Spencer from

the Simon Gallery. We're looking for the Rafael Brown
party."

"You found it. I'm Sylvester, but call me Sly. Come
on in. I'll tell Rafe you're here."

Rush took Maggie's hand in his, and they followed
Sly inside. Maggie absorbed her surroundings in
shocked disbelief. The apartment was nothing more
than a huge, open room with bare wooden floors in dire
need of refinishing. There wasn't one stick of furniture
that she could see, and the only decorating that had
been done was the strategic placement of Rafael's
paintings against brick walls that had recently received
a fresh coat of stark white paint. The other guests,
dozens of them, looked as if they were going trick-
or-treating instead of attending a New Year's Eve
party.

Sly led them through the maze of people, then
spotting their host across the room, waved his arm in
the air—setting his chains rattling—and headed toward
Rafael yelling loudly, "Rafe! Come here, man! Rush
Barrington and his old lady are here!"

Maggie cringed, both at the style of his announcement and at his phraseology. Old lady, was she? She
stopped mutinously where she was. Let Rafael come to
them.

As if reading her mind, Rush tightened his hold on
her fingers. "It's only a figure of speech!" he whispered.

She glared up at him, tried without success to jerk
her hand free of his and hissed back, "Is that right,
kid?"

Then, when she saw his lips twitching with the urge
to smile, she pressed her own tightly together to control
the same need. In a concerted effort to keep from
disgracing them both with the laughter that bubbled up

inside her—once she let loose with it there would be no going back—Maggie glanced around her, quickly realizing that if she hoped to keep from laughing, she had chosen the wrong tack.

She couldn't recall ever seeing such a motley group. Nor could she remember ever feeling so overdressed and out of place as both she and Rush were at that moment.

"Ms. Spencer." The attractive masculine voice drew Maggie's attention from the scene before her to a man of perhaps fifty whose arm was draped around the shoulders of a petite young woman of no more than twenty.

They were an odd couple, she thought. The girl, for she was little more than that, was dainty and feminine in an antique dress of black velvet with ecru lace at the collar and cuffs. Her eyes were large and a luminous blue, set in a face reminiscent of a Victorian china doll.

The man, though a good thirty years older than his companion, was fit and trim, a fact emphasized by the close fit of his paint-splattered jeans and dark purple T-shirt whose bold yellow caption read: ARTISTS DO IT ON CANVAS.

Oh, no, Maggie thought. It couldn't be . . .

"I'm Rafael Brown, and this is my wife, Deanna."

"This is Rush Barrington, Mr. Brown. Thank you so much for inviting us," Maggie said as the quartet shook hands.

"It's our pleasure. And please call me Rafe."

Maggie inclined her head in acquiescence.

"You don't mind if I call you Maggie and Rush, do you?" Rafael asked with an unusual familiarity.

"Of course not." *Okay, Maggie, he's strange. So what? Who cares how weird he is if he can paint?*

"Would you like to look at the paintings now, or can I offer you a drink?" Rafael asked.

Maggie looked up at Rush, who indicated that she should make the decision. "I'm fine for the moment. Let's look at the paintings."

"Fine," Rafael smiled, leading the way to a far wall, where a group of three paintings had been hung.

One was of an old man in a Salvation Army soup line at Christmas. His face was lined, his emaciated body covered with tattered overalls and topped by an ill-fitting sports coat that hung on his spare frame. The second depicted a ballet scene that somehow portrayed, instead of the dance's grace and beauty, the agony of hours of practice and the torture of torn muscles. The final canvas was of a child of the barrio, ragged and forlorn, clutching the railing of the stairs outside the building that housed him, his eyes staring unseeingly at the rubble surrounding him.

They all had several things in common. All were painted with the pure, vibrant color and the thick, swirled brush strokes associated with Van Gogh during his expressionist period. But more importantly, each captured the pain of life, as well as an agony of the spirit. Each was excellent.

The man was a kook. The man was weird. But the man could paint. Maggie knew the paintings would sell. "They're fantastic, Rafe," she said quietly, turning to look at him.

"Thank you."

Deanna, who stood patiently at Rafael's side, looked up at him adoringly and said, "Wait until you see the silk screens. Rafe is committed to capturing adolescent androgyny on silk screen."

Maggie glanced up at Rush and saw the telltale

tightening of his lips. She felt the same overwhelming urge to laugh tickling her insides. What on earth was adolescent androgyny? She smiled at her host and murmured, "How interesting."

Rafael laughed and dropped a quick kiss on Deanna's soft, pink lips. "Don't get her started. She's my staunchest supporter. We'll leave you to look things over at your leisure." He smiled at both Rush and Maggie. "Just relax and have a good time tonight. We can talk business later."

"Thank you," Maggie said, smiling as Rafe and Deanna walked away. She looked up at Rush, whose gaze was focused on some point across the room. "What do you think?"

Rush turned his head slowly toward her, laughter dancing in the depths of his dark brown eyes. "I think Rafael is definitely on the strange side, but he's sensitive and smart."

"Smart? Why?"

"Because he was sharp enough to marry money."

"Marry money? Deanna? That poor, undernourished thing?"

He laughed softly, the sound falling like a springtime breeze on Maggie's ears. "That poor, undernourished thing is Deanna Danvers."

Maggie's mouth dropped open. "Danvers? The newspaper Danvers? The ones who also own the Milwaukee brewery?"

Rush nodded. "One and the same."

"How do you know?"

Trailing a finger down the bridge of her nose, Rush shook his head in wonderment. "Maggie, Maggie, don't you ever read the paper?"

"Not if I can help it," she retorted saucily to negate the rapid tripping of her pulse caused by his touch.

He laughed again, and Maggie fleetingly thought that she could become addicted to the sound. "There's someone with a tray of drinks. Want one?" he asked, his eyes still twinkling.

Maggie nodded. "I think I'm ready now."

Rush waved at the woman bearing a silver tray of drinks, who promptly made her way toward them. Maggie looked at the woman and glanced up at Rush in what was quickly becoming standard procedure every time her attention was snagged by another of Rafael Brown's strange guests. Rush met her laughing-eyed look with one that crinkled the corners of his dark eyes before they rolled ceiling-ward in disbelief.

The woman was probably older than Maggie, but had on black plastic pumps and white bobby socks. Her jeans were faded and tight, and she wore a hot-pink mesh shirt over a man's sweat shirt. Her hair had been shaved at the sides and what was left on top had been sprayed with pink, green and orange. Three inches of various sized safety pins hung from one ear. A star-shaped stud pierced the other. She smiled. "Hi. I'm Nancy. Would you like something to drink?"

"Do you have any white wine?" Maggie asked, eyeing dubiously the tray of drinks the woman carried.

Despite her attire, Nancy's smile looked quite normal and was contagious. "Sorry. This is a group of artists, remember? Very creative."

Rush looked at the tray, which held several concoctions—all in expensive glassware. A wineglass held a raw egg covered with something clear and topped with salt and pepper.

"A Prairie Chicken," Nancy said, seeing the look of question in his eyes. "It's Sly's favorite."

Maggie turned her head aside and moaned, her stomach rebelling at the very thought of the drink.

"This one looks okay," Rush said, indicating another.

"That's a Yellow Parrot. It has yellow Chartreuse, apricot brandy and Pernod," Nancy explained.

Maggie shook her head.

"What's this?" Rush asked, pointing to another drink.

"Oh, that's called a Pussyfoot. Grenadine, ginger ale, ice . . ."

"We'll take it," Rush said, picking up the glass.

Nancy laughed. "It'll have you purring in no time."

"Really?" Rush leered at Maggie, who glared back at him. He pointed to the last drink on the tray, an old-fashioned glass garnished with a twist of lime. "What about that one?"

Nancy grinned wickedly at Rush and said, "It's Pimm's, tequila and lime juice . . . a Dowager's Downfall."

Rush turned to Maggie, an innocent smile curving his beautifully shaped mouth. Their eyes met and held. "A Dowager's Downfall. It sounds . . . interesting. We'll take it," he said softly, teasingly.

Maggie blushed at the implication of his words. Her color deepened even more when Rush winked at Nancy and said, "If the Pussyfoot doesn't work, maybe the Downfall will."

Nancy's laughter floated through the room as she left them there and went to serve the other guests.

Maggie looked at the man standing beside her and was assailed with a sudden, sobering feeling. The strangely and suggestively named drinks Rush Barrington held were no threat to her, regardless of their content. But Rush himself was another matter. Another matter altogether.

Thirty minutes later Maggie leaned against the wall with a ragged sigh. "My feet are killing me!"

"I'm surprised they aren't frozen solid in those flimsy sandals. This isn't the warmest place I was ever in."

Maggie held out a slender foot, shod in the gold sandals April thought were so sexy. Her mood mellowed by the Pussyfoot she'd chosen over the Dowager's Downfall, she observed in a thoughtful tone, "'Flimsy,' the man says. He obviously has no consideration for what we women go through to make ourselves attractive."

Rush leaned against the wall beside Maggie and smiled down at her, an action that caused her to feel warm even in the drafty room. "Granted. The sandals are sexy. Very. But then, so are the feet, which I'd hate to have to treat for fallen arches or frostbite just because you wanted to be sexy."

A blush stole over Maggie's face, and she quickly sought to change the subject. "More like cramps in my calves if I don't get to sit down soon. Do you see a chair anywhere?"

Rush's eyes made a slow survey of the room. "Yeah. There's one." He grabbed her hand and led her through the crowd to a corner where a Papasan chair stood, its floral, chintz pad making the large, rattan seat resemble a bowl of exotic flowers.

Maggie looked at it, blinked, looked at Rush, lifted a brow in question and said softly, "Watch my lips, counselor. I said a chair. That thing looks like a giant coolie hat turned upside down."

"Come on. We'll share the space."

"Rush, do you see this skirt? It's tight. And it has a

slit up the front. If I sit down on that thing—in this outfit—with you—I'll be arrested for contributing to the delinquency of a minor."

Rush grinned and began shrugging out of his tux jacket. "Don't worry about a thing, ma'am. I'll be your defense counsel."

Maggie watched as he took off the coat. "What do you think you're doing?"

"We're going to sit down." Rush lowered himself onto the chair and held out his hand. "Come on." Reluctantly, Maggie placed her hand in his and seated herself on the chair's edge.

The next thing she knew, Rush had looped an arm around her waist and had pulled her back into the middle of the bowl-shaped seat. Maggie gasped in surprise, her eyes flying to his. He smiled, removed his arm from around her, pushed her back into the chair's depths and covered her legs with his jacket.

"There'll be no arguing, Maggie. When I make up my mind about something I do it."

She looked up at him with wide sapphire-blue eyes. Somehow, his statement seemed a portent of things to come.

"Lean up a little," he commanded.

Unhesitatingly, she did as he requested and felt his arm slide beneath her shoulders before he relaxed beside her with a soft "Ahhh" of contentment. She stiffened when she felt his body roll against hers, the hard warmth of him touching her all the way from her shoulder, which was tucked just beneath his raised arm, to her hips, which fit snugly beside his in the deepest curve of the bowl, on down to her thighs. Her head rested against his shoulder.

"Relax. I'd never attack a woman old enough to be my mother," he said laughingly into her ear.

Maggie's head whipped around, an action that brought her face close to his. His eyes were closed in complete relaxation. "I'm *not* old enough to be your mother!" she snapped.

His eyes opened, some disturbing emotion drowsing in their enticing depths. "I'm glad you finally realized it." The words were spoken lightly, but Maggie knew he was referring to her hang-up about their ages.

"Geez! Look at that one!" he said suddenly—more, Maggie thought, to change the subject than anything.

She turned in the direction of his rolled eyes and saw a tall, buxom woman of perhaps twenty-five with frizzled hair caught up in a ponytail atop her head, wearing a semitransparent red-vinyl raincoat belted with some sort of frayed-at-the-ends rope. She wore nothing beneath but a pair of bikini panties decorated with the famous Playboy emblem.

Maggie groaned at the explicit sight, burying her face against Rush's chest in embarrassment. She felt his arms go around her. His touch was impersonal. She told herself his reaction to her suddenly close body was mechanical, nothing more than a programmed male response, yet the feel of the warmth of his hands through the thin chiffon of her blouse and the sound and feel of his heart beating against her cheek intensified her awareness and started a curious ache in her middle.

Rush chuckled against her ear, the sound low and incredibly sexy. "What a group this is!"

She denied the warm feelings coursing through her, replacing them instead with normal conversation. "I know. I didn't know there were so many strange people in Boston."

"Me either," he admitted. His eyes swept the room,

then met hers with probing intensity. "So what do you think about the paintings?"

Maggie braced her right hand against the cushion near Rush's head. "I think Mr. Brown is an incredible talent." She was silent a moment, her eyes fixed on, but not seeing, something across the room. When she spoke, her voice sounded perplexed, wondering. "Why do you suppose she married him?"

"Deanna?" Rush asked.

Maggie nodded. "He's got to be twenty-five or thirty years older than she is. Do you think she was looking for a father figure?"

Rush moved his arm from behind Maggie and began to loosen his tie. "She has a perfectly legitimate father. Who, by all accounts, is a pretty good one."

"Oh." Maggie lowered herself back against the cushion, half turning toward Rush. She chewed thoughtfully on her bottom lip, her fingers working unconsciously with his tie and loosening the top button of his shirt with the unconcerned ease born to women. It was a task she'd performed innumerable times for Jarrell during the course of their marriage. "I just don't get it."

Rush reached out and placed the knuckles of one hand beneath her chin, raising it until their eyes met. "Did you ever entertain the possibility that she loves him?"

"Loves him? But the age difference!"

Rush's thumb brushed back and forth against her chin. "Love isn't bound by rules and regulations, Maggie, because it comes from the heart, not the mind."

Maggie was suddenly conscious of the fact that she and Rush had turned and now faced each other in the chair's depression. She was acutely aware that she lay flush against him, her body pressed to his in a most intimate and disturbing way and—heaven help her—it felt so good! His right hand rested against her hip, while his left held her chin.

Her own hands were flat against the vertically pleated front of his shirt, one resting against his racing heart, the other higher, so that her thumb rested in the hollow of his throat and the heel of her palm brushed the crisp, dark hair that grew high on his chest. She thought idly that she must have undone two buttons.

Her eyes lifted to his and found that they were making a thorough survey of her blouse's deep vee neckline and the diamond teardrop that rested on the slight rise of one breast. His fingers began rubbing slow, concentric circles against the swell of her hip, fanning the embers of Maggie's sexuality, which had been banked down for two long years. She wanted to finish unbuttoning his shirt, wanted to run her palms over the hair that grew so abundantly over his broad chest. Wanted to rest her fingertip against the cleft in his chin and trace the sensuous curve of his mouth.

She felt the sharp, staccato beat of his heart, heard the quickened tenor of his breathing, felt his fingers tighten on her hip.

"Rush!" Her voice sounded breathless and, even to her own ears, seemed to hold a note of urgency.

"It's eleven-thirty!" The announcement was yelled by someone across the room, ending the mesmerizing spell with the suddenness of a magician snapping his fingers to bring someone out of a trance. It left Maggie feeling lost and somehow spent. What was happening to her? What was Rush Barrington doing to her safe, predictable world?

Rush muttered something under his breath, then turned a scowling countenance toward her. "Let's get out of here. I don't think either of us is ready for the way this bunch will usher in the new year!"

In a matter of minutes Maggie found herself inside Rush's car. He had practically dragged her down the stairs after finding their coats and making the excuse of another party to their host.

"Where are we going?" she asked at last.

"Home."

He didn't sound as if their destination was negotiable, so Maggie curled into her corner and tried to dissect the evening. No. Not the evening. Just what had happened between her and Rush . . . what had been happening between them since the first time April had sent him over.

She was attracted to him. She'd ceased denying it days ago. Now she not only faced the realization, but accepted it. She was falling for Rush Barrington like the proverbial ton of bricks. The knowledge filled her with a vague pleasure that was almost completely overshadowed by her feelings of guilt and fear.

She was falling for Rush Barrington. Perhaps if she repeated the statement often enough it would take on an air of reality. She was attracted to Rush Barrington. Sexually attracted.

But it was more than just sexual attraction. She *liked* Rush Barrington. She admired him for his single-minded determination to get his law degree, especially in view of the length of time it was taking him. She liked his no-nonsense attitude, his strength of purpose, his supreme confidence in himself and his capabilities.

Stop it, Maggie Spencer! This is ridiculous! You have nothing in common with the man.

Her thoughts returned to the party they'd just left. There were people her age, and older, attending; and people Rush's age, and younger, but out of all of them, she and Rush could communicate comfortably only with each other. Maggie faced an irrefutable fact: successful relationships weren't formed on the basis of age, but on intellectual and emotional compatibility. As Rafael and Deanna proved.

"We're here," Rush announced, forcing her thoughts back to the moment at hand with the realization that she had been completely unaware of the drive back to her apartment. She turned to face him, certain that what she felt for him must show, even in the dark. He sat facing her, his left arm hooked over the steering wheel.

Maggie said the first thing that came to mind. "What time is it?"

"Pretty close to the witching hour, I imagine. Come on. Let's go in."

The walk to the front door seemed longer than usual, and the elevator ride interminable, especially because Maggie concentrated so hard on not letting her eyes stray to Rush. When the elevator doors slid open she felt his hand grip her elbow as he escorted her from the small cubicle. Neither spoke as they made their way toward her condo. The sound of people making merry filled the hallway. Rose was having another party.

When they reached her door Maggie saw Rush extend his hand, palm upward. She opened her small gilt evening purse, made a hasty search for her key and placed it in his hand. His fingers, surprisingly warm, since he hadn't been wearing gloves, closed around hers. Maggie's baffled blue eyes met the deep, warm brown of his.

"I enjoyed the evening," he told her, his hand tightening over hers for a moment before he slipped the key into the lock and opened the door.

"So did I."

"I don't suppose you'd ask me in for a cup of coffee?" he asked, holding the key out for her.

Was there a hint of longing in his voice? she asked herself as she dropped the key into her purse. Maggie shook her head once in negation and offered him a wan smile. "I don't think so. I'm a little tired."

Rush's head nodded in acquiescence. "Sure. Another time. Is the gallery open tomorrow?"

Again, Maggie shook her head. Why did she have the ridiculous feeling he was trying to prolong their time together? Her stomach churned in nervous reaction. How long until midnight? Would he try to kiss her? Would she let him if he did?

"What time is it?" she asked again.

Rush held out his arm and pushed back his coat sleeve. The plain gold-tone watch that encircled his wrist sparkled in the light of the hall. "Thirty seconds and counting."

As if in response to his announcement, the guests in Rose's apartment chorused, "Twenty-nine . . . twenty-eight . . ."

Their eyes locked as Rush lowered his arm and, reaching out a hand, caught Maggie gently behind the neck. His fingers were slightly rough against the tender flesh of her nape. He exerted the tiniest bit of pressure, encouraging her to move just a little closer. She did.

"Twenty-one . . . twenty . . ."

"Rush . . ."

He smiled, a crooked, half smile that seemed tinged with—uncertainty? Almost as if he expected her to protest, he argued, "It's New Year's Eve, Maggie."

"I know."

"Fourteen . . . thirteen . . . twelve . . ."

"Everybody kisses everybody on New Year's."

She dragged in a deep draft of air. "Yes. I know."

He stepped closer, his body barely brushing hers.

"Eight . . ."

Her tongue darted out and moistened her lips, leaving them shiny and wet.

A low moan escaped Rush and his other hand joined the first, encircling her throat while his thumbs tilted her head back to an angle more accommodating to his height.

"Four . . . three . . ."

His head began its descent.

Maggie's lashes fell.

"Two . . . *One!*" There was a loud roar of *"Happy New Year!"* from the apartment down the way, and an even louder roar inside Maggie's head as Rush held her immobile with hands that cupped her head while his mouth took hers in a kiss as soft as the brush of a butterfly wing.

This time it was Maggie who groaned as her heart stopped, then took up a ragged beat that pulsed throughout her body. His hold on her tightened fractionally, and his mouth worked slowly against hers as he seemed to savor the very taste and texture of her lips.

His lips were firm, warm and extremely practiced, she thought as she felt herself responding to the pressure of his kiss. Just when she would have raised her hands to his face, she felt him begin to move away, felt his lips lift from hers.

Their eyes opened almost simultaneously. Bare inches from each other, breaths melding and mingling, their eyes collided—Maggie's slightly dazed with the wonder of the moment, Rush's holding a smoldering warmth that caused a reciprocal heat to sweep through her already throbbing body.

"Happy New Year." His voice was low, husky.

"Happy New Year." Maggie's voice was hardly more than a whisper.

Rush's hands slid from the sides of her face down to her shoulders as he moved a step away from her.

Maggie thrust her hands into the pockets of her coat so he wouldn't see their trembling. They stared at each other for long moments, the air around them encumbered with unspoken thoughts and turbulent feelings.

Rush spoke first. "I'll call you."

Maggie nodded. His hands fell from her shoulders, leaving her with the overwhelming urge to cry. His eyes moved to her mouth, and he raised one finger, gently touching the fullness of her bottom lip, before he turned and walked down the corridor.

Her eyes followed him until he turned the corner to the elevator. Then, slowly, she went into the apartment and closed the door. *I'll call you.* The words were a promise she knew he would keep. He would call, and when he did she knew he would ask her out for a real date, not just as an escort. And, by doing so, he would take their relationship from the professional to the personal.

Maggie took off her coat and dropped it onto a nearby chair.

What would her answer be?

Her eyes met the troubled blue ones of the woman in the gold-framed mirror, seeking an answer from her that she couldn't find within herself.

Rush leaned against the back wall of the elevator and rammed his hands into the pockets of his overcoat. His blood raced through his veins singing the name Maggie . . . Maggie . . .

He'd kissed her! He'd kissed her! And, without question, it had been all he'd hoped for. All he'd known it would be. The touch of her lips against his had triggered a depth of emotion he hadn't known existed, shaking him to the very core of his masculinity.

Maggie Spencer was a mass of contradictions, a cool, collected lady. Yet the fact that her apartment was decorated in bold, vibrant red and that the bright color was repeated in her wardrobe of sexy clothes suggested a personality outgoing and passionate. Will the real Maggie Spencer please stand up?

The elevator rocked to a gentle stop and the doors slipped open. Rush sighed and pushed himself away from the wall. Whoever the real Maggie Spencer was, one thing was certain. He was falling in love with her.

Chapter Five

$\mathcal{M}$aggie's big toe had just dipped into the warm, bubble-bath water when the phone rang. Yanking the manicured foot out with an appropriate word of protest, she grabbed her robe, threw it on and raced for the bedside table.

"Hello?" she answered, her voice on the outer edge of breathlessness.

"Maggie?"

The single word, simply delivered in basso profundo, brought her into the full fold of oxygen deprivation. Fighting for a decent breath—where had all the air suddenly gone?—she eased to the side of the bed and brushed back a tendril of hair springing loose from the knot piled capriciously atop her head.

"Hello," she repeated, sounding as ridiculously pleased as a teenage girl waiting for that all-important male call.

"Hello yourself," he responded, sounding as absurdly young and pleased as she. "Were you busy? Did I catch you at a bad time?"

Yes and yes, she thought, drawing the filmy robe tighter to her naked body and digging bare toes, one still sporting a sudsy bubble, into the royal blue, navy and beige rug. "No," she answered, "I wasn't busy and no, you didn't catch me at a bad time."

"Good. It was later than I thought when I looked at the clock."

Maggie automatically darted a glance at her own clock. Nine forty-three. What had he been doing to so absorb his mind that he had lost track of the hour?

"I've been reading a law book," he said as if he'd just picked up on her thought. "Know anything about *Barrington versus Spencer*?"

A gentle, playful smile sprang to Maggie's lips. "Absolutely nothing," she replied. "What's *Barrington versus Spencer*?"

"A very famous court case. Barrington claims Spencer robbed him of his ability to think straight."

The mouth smiling in enjoyment of his game suddenly went desert dry, and her breath, which was slowly returning to normal, took another nose dive.

"So Barrington just closed the textbook," Rush continued, "and called Spencer."

"How did it all turn out? This famous court case, I mean?"

"Don't know. The outcome's still pending. I think Barrington is hoping for poetic justice rather than legal."

"And what would that poetic justice be?" Maggie asked, her heart thumping in a faster rhythm.

"Barrington feels it would be fair retribution if ultimately he robbed Spencer of her ability to think straight."

They were both smiling crazy, silly smiles, and each knew the other was doing the same. They were both also aware of a heightened tension, aware that their relationship was taking a cautious step forward.

"So how's the new year treating you so far?" he asked, prudently changing the subject.

"So far, so good," Maggie replied, knowing, and being grateful for the fact, that he was deliberately easing back from the feelings stirred moments before. As she spoke, she propped herself against the mahogany headboard of the bed and straightened the robe to cover small, firmly shaped breasts. "How's it treating you?"

"So far, so good," he answered, slumping against the wall in lieu of a headboard and raking his fingers through the thick forest of hair covering his bare chest. "At least, I think so. I'll know more in a minute."

"Oh?"

"If you'll go out to dinner with me, the year will be off to a great start. Now before you say no," he threw in quickly, "just listen to my arguments. Okay?"

A smile, this one slightly mischievous, once again stole to her lips. "Yes, counselor."

"You have to eat, right?"

"Yes."

"And it would be just as easy to eat with someone, right?"

"Yes."

"And eating can be construed as only a culinary commitment, right?"

"Yes."

"No emotional commitment of any kind, right?"

She wasn't sure she agreed entirely with that, at least not under these circumstances, but she responded, "Yes."

"So what do you say?"

"Yes," she replied without hesitation.

"Look, Maggie, I'm only asking you out to din—" He stopped. Maggie's smile was broaching wide; it also seemed to tangibly flow through the phone line.

"You will?" he asked.

"I will. I've been saying I will for several minutes now." That her answer surprised him was evident, but then, it surprised her, too.

"Well, why the hell didn't you tell me the jury was already in?" he asked, trying to sound aggravated, but not quite doing so because of the curving of his own lips.

"You seemed so intent on pleading the case," she quipped.

"I oughta . . ." he threatened.

"You oughta what?" she taunted.

"I oughta take you to dinner. How does Thursday night sound?"

"Thursday is fine."

"I wish it could be the weekend, but I'm tied up with the agency. I'm only working weekends there now."

The thought of him escorting other women left her with an uncomfortable feeling, a feeling she didn't quite understand, but one she quickly ignored. "Thursday's fine," she assured him.

"Good. What if I pick you up about seven?"

"I'll be ready."

There was a slight pause, as if he was hesitant to hang up. "Well, I'll see you then."

There was a slight pause, as if she was hesitant to have him hang up. "See you then."

"Good night."

"Good night," she answered.

The phones clicked into muteness, and Maggie eased

the receiver back into place. Slow and silent seconds
passed as she stared at the recradled instrument. Suddenly she bounced off the bed and with light steps
headed back for the bathroom. A twinkle glinted in her
eyes, a smile curved her lips, a faint rosy blush glowed
on her face. Abandoning her robe, she stepped into the
bathtub. The water had cooled to an uncomfortable
temperature, a fact Maggie didn't notice for the
warmth flooding her body.

It was crazy. This fluttering feeling in her stomach,
like butterflies taking to air, was downright crazy. And
yet she wouldn't have traded it for all the sanity in the
world, for with the craziness came this wonderful sense
of anticipation, a sense of looking forward to something
—and this she hadn't done, not *really* done—since the
divorce.

Snuggling the pink angora sweater at the waist of her
gray wool skirt, Maggie thought back to Jerri's surprised expression when she'd announced she was leaving the gallery early, five o'clock instead of the usual
six. Giving Jerri instructions to lock up, Maggie had
made a mad dash for home, cursing the trolley's
slowness at regular intervals, and had bathed, done her
nails, styled her hair and dressed in record time. She
now stood in front of the mirror studding her ears with
coral earrings and at the same time slipping her feet
into snakeskin heels that blended gray and iridescent
shades of lavender and pink. As her hand fell away
from the rounded lobe of her ear, she forced herself to
assess her image . . . truthfully.

She looked slim and trim—she slid her hand to her
flat stomach—and her face, though as always too
angular, glowed with a radiance that was attractive
enough. Her hair shone—here she shook her head

slightly, swaying dusky brown hair about her shoulders —and her eyes, fringed with soot-black mascara, sparkled like blue ice. The only things she didn't particularly like were the faint lines—wrinkles if you were a pessimist, character lines if you were an optimist— radiating around her eyes.

The doorbell rang, thankfully ending her purgatory of doubt.

Rush's first comment on entering the apartment was a low, slow whistle, preceding the command for her to turn around.

She did, feeling a little bit foolish.

"You look . . ." He sought for a word and homed in on one. "You look like candy. Like raspberry cream candy."

"Is that good?" she asked, knowing that it was and knowing that she was flirting. Actually flirting!

But then, so was he. The smile, playing in only one corner of his mouth, was evidence of his flirting, an evidence that would have stood the test in any court of law. "It's better than good," he said. "And it tastes . . . divine." His eyes, a lazy, coffee-rich brown, lowered from hers to her mouth. And stayed there for a span of time that told her he remembered their kiss vividly.

"Let's go," he said suddenly, softly and with the tiniest rasp. As he ushered her out the door, his hand at her elbow, he added, "I hope you're hungry."

"Famished," she said, glancing upward until her eyes met his. And she was. She felt famished, flirty and full of life. She felt . . . young.

The car was cozy and warm, the night dark and cold. For the first time in days, the snow had temporarily abated, leaving the city blanketed in niveous white, but canopied by a still threatening ebony sky. The contrast between white and black, diametric opposites on the color spectrum, was exceptionally beautiful. And, like the work of a bold artist, Maggie thought, possessed of a stark visual power. But then, all of Boston, in every season of the year, had power. The power of history. A living history.

A thoroughly modern city, yet a city where the old is cherished and preserved, Boston had been born as an important shipbuilding center and fishing port and had gone on to become America's colonial hotbed of patriotism. Today, at practically every urban corner were reminders of America's hard-won independence, reminders like the Freedom Trail, with its stops at Faneuil Hall, the Old South Meetinghouse, the site of the Boston Massacre, and the Paul Revere House; reminders like the Boston Common, the oldest public park in the country, where cows once grazed, soldiers drilled and wicked witches were hanged; reminders like the site of the Boston Tea Party, the Old North Church, the Bunker Hill Monument.

She loved Boston, just as she loved being exactly where she was this very moment. In Rush's car. In Rush's company. Within the sound of Rush's voice.

That voice, warm, rich, enough to send shivers scampering through a woman's body, was presently making casual conversation, a conversation punctuated with teasing and laughter. Maggie listened and commented, teased and laughed, but all the while she did so, she was acutely aware of an exciting, almost scary, sense of newness. The newness of a relationship just beginning to delicately bud. Would it flower? Would it wither? Would she have the courage for either?

The car traveled down Boylston Street, past all the shops and galleries that were dozing away the night in preparation for the next day's commerce, and turned onto Arlington Street. Before Maggie knew quite what had happened, the car had pulled up beneath the portico of the Ritz-Carlton, the city's grande dame of hotels, and a man in livery was approaching her side of the car. She had time only to throw a sharp glance at Rush, a glance that asked eloquently, "What are we doing eating in one of the finest, most expensive restaurants in Boston?" before she was being escorted out of the car and joined by Rush. Taking her elbow, he guided her toward the hotel's entrance.

"Rush . . ." she chastised gently, knowing how hard he worked for his money, how little he had to fritter away carelessly and how guilty she suddenly felt.

"Hush," he returned softly as he looked down into her upturned face. "You're my Christmas present."

Minutes later, they were seated in the elegant second-floor restaurant by a blue-and-white draped window. Pale yellow light spewed from crystal chandeliers and soft piano music wafted wanderingly on the air. As Rush ordered their drinks, Maggie glanced out toward the Public Garden, presently peppered by snow, but with the promise of thousands of tulips and pansies in bloom come spring, then back to the man across from her. It was the first time she'd seen him in a suit and tie, a conservative blue-and-gray pinstripe, and she had to admit he did look the part of a lawyer. She also had to admit he looked unbelievably handsome.

"What do you mean I'm your Christmas present?" she asked when his gaze settled once again on her.

"Ever since I've been in law school, Mom and Dad have sent me money at Christmas," he explained, looking away briefly as the waiter returned with their drinks. "This year I'm dining out with their gift."

"I'm flattered," Maggie said, simply and seriously.

"By the way," Rush said as he picked up the chunky glass of bourbon and water, "they loved the picture."

Maggie smiled, again genuinely. "I'm glad. It's a pretty etching."

Rush nodded, took a sip of his drink and settled his wide shoulders comfortably back in his chair. His eyes sought hers, merged, and stayed. Seconds meandered by, along with the strains of a love song. A fine tension began to materialize between them.

"Well, what do we talk about?" he asked finally in a voice that sounded strangely forced. Before she could answer, he offered his own suggestions. "How about how much I've missed you this week? Or how I thought Thursday would never get here?" His voice lowered to the pitch of a sigh wrapped in satin. "Or how about how beautiful you are at this moment?"

Maggie swallowed, trying to drag her eyes from his, but discovering she couldn't. She moistened her lips self-consciously and attempted to tease. "It sounds as if you're majoring in more than law, Mr. Barrington. Which," she added, "gives us a perfect topic of conversation."

"Law?"

"Uh-huh," she nodded, cascading hair about her shoulders in a motion that caught and held the gilded chandelier light.

"Going from your beauty to law, Ms. Spencer," he teased in turn, "is like going from the sublime to the mundane."

"You are majoring in flattery, aren't you?" she tossed back playfully.

His laugh did gentle competition with the low conversation surrounding them. "I swear to God, I don't have a single class in it."

"You're already registered, then?"

Bringing the glass to his lips, he sipped and swallowed. "Yesterday. Classes start Monday. If I can just make this semester, there'll be nothing left before my bar exam, and then I'll be a full-fledged lawyer." He gave a short laugh. "And good ol' Harvard will probably be as glad to see me go as I will be to leave."

"Why?"

"I've been something of a problem student." At her obvious interest, he explained, "By the time you move into the last of your studies, the university likes to see you stay with it until you finish. Not drop out a semester as I did. In fact, I had to get a special dispensation to delay graduation. A couple of my professors went to bat for me."

Maggie's lips pursed pleasingly. "I'm impressed. That tells me you're good."

He shrugged, almost as if uncomfortable with her compliment. "Maybe just stubborn."

She studied him, studied the square, unrelenting jut of his cleft chin, studied the dark, piercing light that lived in his eyes. Yes, he was stubborn. She would concede that hands down. But he was also something else. He was a man dedicated to what he was doing. He was a man who wanted, totally and uncompromisingly, a degree in law. And she'd bet all she owned that he got that degree.

"Why law?" she asked pointedly.

Smiling wistfully, Rush traced an index finger down the side of his glass. "All because of a man I knew for about an hour," he said, his eyes moving from the glass to Maggie. "Give or take a few minutes."

"I'm intrigued," she said, her sapphire-blue eyes urging him to continue. He didn't right away, almost as if he was trying to decide how best to begin.

"I've always been something of a quiet rebel. Much to my parents' dismay," he added with a crooked grin. His hand went unconsciously—perhaps nervously, Maggie thought—to straighten his gray, knit tie. "After high school they wanted me to go to college, like all my buddies, but I insisted on the marines. After I did my stint there, I did sign up for college, went one year, then dropped out."

"Why?"

He shrugged. His nervousness suddenly seemed amplified. "I don't know that I can make you understand what I don't fully understand myself. Nothing was coming together in my life. I didn't know what I wanted to do. I just knew I wasn't doing it." Suddenly he shook his head, a smile curling the corner of his lip. "Do I sound crazy?"

"No," she said, shaking her head and smiling back. "Go on."

"I broke my parents' hearts again, bought a second-hand motorcycle and saw the U.S.A."

"How long did that last?"

"Almost nine months," he said, adding dramatically, "Then I met destiny head-on four miles outside of Taos, New Mexico."

So caught up in the story was Maggie that she resented having to take time out to order dinner, and the minute it was done she prodded, "So what happened four miles outside of Taos, New Mexico?" Her elbow was propped on the table, her chin resting in her hand, her eyes on Rush.

"About nine o'clock one Saturday night I stopped at this place, ordered a beer and before I knew what had happened I was in a fight with a motorcycle gang."

"The whole gang?"

"It damned sure seemed like it. Anyway, I got

arrested right along with the bad boys and tossed squarely in jail. I was assigned a lawyer who didn't even have to show up that night, but thank God he did." For a moment Rush was lost in the past. "To this day, I can feel those walls closing in on me, robbing me of the freedom I had always taken for granted." Suddenly his eyes focused again on Maggie and he smiled. "Suffice it to say, I was a big, bad, tough marine close to tears when Andrew Morris Williams walked in."

"The lawyer?"

"The lawyer," Rush confirmed. "He believed in my innocence, that I hadn't started the fight and had only defended myself, got me a special session in night court and gave me money to spend the rest of the night at a motel. He then gave me the best advice I've ever had. He told me to get the hell home and do something with my life besides get sleepy lawyers out of bed."

"And by the time you got home you knew what that something was," she stated softly.

"Yes, crazy isn't it? And one of these nights, I'm going to pay back old Andrew Morris Williams. I'm going to believe in a dumb, stupid, scared kid's innocence."

The meal had arrived long ago, and it gave Maggie something to do while she concentrated on the story she'd just heard. Over the green turtle soup, with a pastry turtle floating on top, she admitted to herself that the story had moved her and had definitely prejudiced her in Rush Barrington's favor. Over the Maine lobster "au whiskey," she conceded another vital point. Rush Barrington was a man, not a boy. A man with a man's goals, a man's dedication, a man's determination, a man's needs.

"Why did you go out with me tonight?" he asked softly.

Maggie glanced up sharply. They were waiting for the waiter to bring the check.

Before she could answer, he added, "April told me you asked for me on New Year's."

Again, the implication was *why*.

Maggie swallowed, lowered her head, then felt his finger gently raising her chin.

"Does it embarrass you that I know that?"

She shrugged. "A little."

"It shouldn't." He repeated his original question. "Why, Maggie? Why New Year's? Why tonight?"

Her eyes meshed with his and she offered the only truthful answer she could. "Would you believe that I don't really know?"

For long, quiet seconds he studied her. "Yes," he finally said, "I'd believe that."

Moments later, the bill paid and Rush and Maggie on their way to the elevator that would take them downstairs, he looked down at her and smiled.

"I have a confession," he said. "I asked April to assign me to you if you called and wanted an escort." His smile faded slightly, replaced with a look of dead earnestness. "And I know why *I* did."

"I don't want to take you home yet."

Maggie's eyes sliced through the car's darkness, alleviated periodically, in flashy neon fashion, by the streetlights. Rush's gaze met hers for a brief interchange before he turned his head once more to stare straight ahead.

"And I know just the place to take you," he added.

Thoughts of a loud, strobe-lit nightclub, disco or wherever the younger set hung out, jumped into Maggie's mind and uneasily resided there until Rush pulled into an underground parking lot and whisked her into the elevator of the Prudential Center.

"You're crazy," she said as the Tower elevator started its fifty-floor ascent to the popular outdoor Skywalk, from which the observer could get a 360-degree panoramic view of Boston.

"Yep," he agreed.

"I don't know whether you've noticed it or not, but it's cold outside. As in winter. As in January."

"I noticed."

"It's going to start snowing any minute," she taunted.

"Probably."

"We'll freeze."

"I doubt it."

"We'll . . ."

"If it's really too cold, we won't go," he said seriously as he held the door of the elevator that had just arrived on the observatory level.

"Are you kidding?" she answered, her face wreathed in a wide smile. "I wouldn't miss it."

He laughed, grabbed her hand—his and hers were bundled in gloves, but in some magical way she still felt a warmth reaching out to her—and moved to pay the two-dollar admission fee. Both fought over the task, Rush ultimately winning because Maggie refused to become embroiled in a scene. Finally, she adjusting her coat collar and he his neck scarf, they stepped forward.

As unlikely as it seemed at ten o'clock on a winter weeknight, two other couples were on the Skywalk, one snuggling to look through the coin-fed telescope, the other just snuggling. Maggie instantly wondered if the couples would believe that she and Rush had come there for the same reason, to share a private moment away from prying eyes, to touch, to hold, to kiss. The thought that these strangers might believe that left her feeling a little embarrassed. The thought that they might be right left her excited.

"Come here," Rush said, pulling her beside him to the railing and anchoring her there with an arm at her waist. "Look at beautiful Boston."

For long, quiet, peaceful moments, they stared downward at the glittering city. Thousands of golden pinpricks of light gleamed and winked and flirted outrageously with the viewer. By clear day the same sightseer could see for miles, as far as the distant mountaintops of southern New Hampshire, as far south as Cape Cod, as far east and north as the Boston Harbor.

"Look at all those dreams," Rush said pensively. "A dream for each light."

She angled her head to his, and her breath was a frosty vapor when she spoke. "Is your dream down there, Rush?"

His eyes coasted to her, and his breath was the same fine powder of cold crystals. "Sure." Pointing with his gloved hand, he added, "Right over there. See? There's my law office."

Maggie giggled. Giggled? Were soon to be forty-year-old women allowed to giggle? "Rush, I think your office is in the harbor!"

"Oh," he said, crestfallen. "Oh, hell, I'm making so much money I practice law from a yacht."

Maggie giggled again, a sound he answered with a beautiful smile. But the smile ebbed slowly away. "Do you have a dream down there, Maggie?"

A dream? Did she have a dream? Having a dream necessitated having a future. And she hadn't had a future since Jarrell. She couldn't afford a future. She'd had to spend all her time and emotional energy just getting through each day.

"I haven't dealt in dreams in a long while," she answered with a truthfulness that was somehow easy to share with this man.

"Start dealing in them." His eyes were black in the night, black and piercing, but piercing with a gentleness. The softly spoken command held a subtle promise, a faraway possibility that caused a delicate shiver to tremble through her body. "You're freezing," he said suddenly as he unwrapped the white woolen scarf from his own neck and wound it about hers. The scarf curled contentedly, draping across her chin. He pulled it up to nestle over her mouth . . . but his hands stopped in their mission.

Time crawled. Their eyes merged. Snowflakes began a downward fairy dance.

Slowly, Rush's thumbs pushed aside the scarf, revealing Maggie's mouth once more, now unprotected, now parted, now waiting. In that moment she silently confessed that nothing had ever felt quite so sensual, quite so intimate as her mouth being exposed to his consuming look. Oh, God, was he going to kiss her? Oh, God, please let him kiss her!

"Maggie," he whispered as his head slowly angled and his lips claimed hers.

His lips were cold, like the winter night around them; his lips were warm, like the forgotten feelings flowing through her; his lips were soft, like the gossamer threads of dreams. She moaned, a reticent, raw sound, and settled her palms against the front of his thick coat. When his tongue probed, not passionately, but tenderly, she gave him the right he sought, and for long moments he tasted her and in turn was sampled by her own mouth.

When he pulled back he was breathless, a breathlessness matched by her own.

"I feel . . . I feel a little drunk," she managed to say, her hands gripping his coat for support.

He smiled, a lopsided smile that sent a whole bevy of new feelings rampaging through her body. His hands cupped her shoulders, pulling her slightly into him. "Maybe it's the 'au whiskey' in the lobster."

"No," she whispered, slowly shaking her head, splaying hair in sweet disarray. "I don't think so."

Tiny snowflakes, each falling faster and with more daring than its predecessor, drifted around them and rained softly down on Maggie's upturned face; they fell on slightly shuttered lashes, fell on dusky rose cheeks, fell on kiss-damp lips.

"Let's go home," he said quietly, but with a huskiness possessed of promise.

"I'll make us some coffee," Maggie said, a nervous quiver invading her voice the moment the door of her condo closed behind them. She had just removed her coat and tossed it carelessly in a chair; it was immediately covered by Rush's.

"I don't want coffee," he said throatily, grabbing her by the wrist, turning her, pulling her against him. "And neither do you."

His mouth unerringly found hers. And she let it. In fact, she was helpless to stop it. Unlike the New Year's kiss, unlike the observatory kiss of twenty minutes before, this kiss instantly strained the bonds of sweetness and warmth and overflowed into the passionate and fiery. His mouth, open and intimate and wanting, moved over hers in a rhythm just short of delirious savagery; she encouraged it with an action just short of wantonness.

She was all feeling. All exploding firework feeling. Feeling that for so long had been a stranger to her passion-denied body. She told herself she shouldn't be giving in to it; she told herself she should be stronger. She told herself there were those who would criticize, chastise, condemn. She then told herself that those who would had no idea how good his lips felt against hers . . . they had no idea how good it was to feel again.

As if paying homage to that thought, Rush's tongue met hers, warmly, wetly, wondrously. She moaned, a sound echoed deep in his throat, and her hands crawled the front of his suit and slipped to clasp his neck. His hair was crisp and clean and cool to her fingertips. His hands moved to her shoulders, roamed her back, meandered leisurely down her spine and ended by palming her hips and drawing her close into his body. His aroused body. Maggie's heart flip-flopped. For almost twenty years the only aroused male she had been near was her husband. And she wasn't quite sure how she felt at this moment, so flush against the evidence of Rush's need. Embarrassed? No, this felt too natural. Did it seem lewd? No, never lewd. Never! Arousing? Oh, God, yes! And the instantaneousness of his arousal was only that much more arousing. Along with the fact that he made no effort to hide his male reaction to her.

Their mouths broke contact, merged once more, quickly, greedily, then broke away again. His eyes, opaque with desire, found hers.

"You can feel what's happening between us, can't you?" he demanded in a barely controlled rasp.

"Yes," she admitted, her own voice waveringly thin. "But it frightens me."

"Don't be frightened," he pleaded, a knuckle grazing the zenith of a cheekbone. "I'm a man; you're a woman. It's that simple, Maggie."

That simple? It didn't sound simple, at least not until his head nuzzled beneath the sable fall of her hair and his lips kissed her ear, his tongue tracing its shell-like outline, his teeth playfully nibbling at its lobe.

She moaned again, because she couldn't help it. And then again as he scattered a sensuous blaze of kisses down the slanting column of her neck.

"Oh, Maggie, you taste so good," he breathed against her nerve-tingling skin. As he spoke, his hands followed the delicate curve of her shoulders, then trailed lower, skimming her sides rib by rib by rib. One hand then brushed lightly, feather lightly, against the gentle slope of a breast. Then brushed by it again. Tentatively. As if giving her time to adjust to this deeper intimacy. "You feel so good," he whispered, his breath a warm whirlwind in her ear. "I love this sweater. It clings so beautifully to you."

Sweater. Pink sweater. Lacey's pink sweater. Maggie's heart increased its tempo and for a reason entirely separate from passion.

"My daughter gave it to me," she said, unaware of how much of a challenge there was in her voice. "My nineteen-year-old daughter gave it to me."

Rush's lips stopped midkiss and hovered at just that spot where neck slides into shoulder.

Maggie waited.

Rush hesitated.

Pulling back, his eyes joined with hers. He read there so many emotions. A kind of quiet defiance. A dare. An if-this-is-going-to-make-a-difference-I-want-to-know-it-now. Maybe even a little fear that it would make a difference.

"Your nineteen-year-old daughter has great taste in

sweaters," he said finally, adding, as his mouth once more lowered to hers, "and even greater taste in mothers."

Maggie felt a warm rush of relief, and this time when their lips met, she thanked him, silently, but completely, just as his kiss told her that he knew she was older and that he didn't give one single damn that she was. Maggie happily lost herself in the knowledge. So lost was she that she made no attempt to stop his hands as they edged beneath the sweater and slid upward to find both camisole-covered breasts. Sighing softly, she encouraged him to touch, to caress, to fondle. As thumbs slicked across satin to stroke against suddenly hard peaks, she moaned raggedly and swayed into him.

"Maggie, sweet Maggie, let me spend the night," he said hoarsely against her lips. "Let me make love to you."

His plea was tempting. It was also sobering. Dragging her lips from his, she pulled back. There was pleading in her eyes. "Please, Rush . . . don't ask me that. Please . . . oh damn!" she said, trying to pull from him. "I'm sorry. I didn't mean it to go this far. I didn't mean to tease. I . . ."

Rush's hands, still beneath the sweater, tightened over her rib cage, forcing her to remain before him. "It's okay. I understand."

Her eyes found his once more. "Do you?"

"Yes. I do."

"It's just . . ." Maggie sought for an explanation, one that would offer him a truthful insight into her mind and heart and soul. "I've only been with one man, Rush. And he was my husband."

"Is that what this is about?" he asked, his tone suddenly filled with new concern. "Are you still in love with him?"

"No," she answered quickly, so quickly she was a little surprised. She had loved Jarrell deeply, single-mindedly, but he had killed that love, smothered it in the pain of rejection. One could love only so long without its being returned. "I'm just not ready for us . . . you and me . . . not like this."

Soberly, Rush eased his hands out from under her sweater, straightening it at her waist. He then determinedly set her from him. The action made her feel young and vulnerable and made him seem so much older. He smiled slowly, sweetly, then said, "We'll play the game by your rules."

Turning away, he grabbed his coat and slid his arms into it. When he stood before her again he dipped his head for a quick, almost passionless kiss.

"Will you do me one favor?" he asked, his words still husky despite his efforts. "Tell me that some part of Maggie Spencer wants to make love to me."

Her eyes never flinched from the steady gaze of his. "I want to make love to you."

His eyes darkened to a sultry shade, and he swallowed low. "That's all the satisfaction I need right now."

Chapter Six

The persistent ringing of the telephone penetrated Rush's sleep-numbed brain with an ever increasing loudness. He blinked, searched out the clock at the side of the bed and concentrated his blurry gaze on the Roman numerals. Six-thirty! God, no wonder he felt so wrung out. He'd been asleep for only an hour. Being up most of the night before, then working until five at the office researching a big case was enough to make anyone tired.

The phone shrilled in his ear once more, and Rush's dull mind told him that if he wanted to make it stop, he had to answer it. He pushed himself up on one elbow, ran a hand over his haggard features and reached for the black plastic receiver.

"Yeah?" he snarled.

A husky giggle grated on his ears, and April Newbern, in her best Texas drawl, purred softly, "My, my, we're just a little ray of sunshine this evening, aren't we?"

In no mood to be teased, Rush said nicely, but pointedly, "What do you want, April?"

"I have a weekend job for you, sugar."

Even though it was Saturday evening and there wasn't a lot of weekend left, Rush moaned.

"Look," April said soothingly, "she wants you tonight, all day tomorrow and tomorrow night."

"All day tomorrow! April, in case you haven't noticed, I'm human."

"Oh, I noticed, all right," she cooed in a tone that would have made honey seem bitter.

"C'mon, cut it out. Give this woman to someone else, will you? I'm bushed and I still have tons of reading to do before Monday."

April sighed. "Okay, Mr. Barrington, whatever you say. But Maggie sure is going to be disappointed."

Rush sat straight up in bed. "Maggie? Why didn't you say it was Maggie who wanted me?"

"Does it make a difference?" April asked innocently. "Are you screening your escorts now?"

"Maggie makes a difference," Rush said softly, "and you know it."

There was a long pause, then April said only one word. "Good."

"So what am I supposed to wear? Where are we going?"

"Casual tonight. She'll tell you about it tomorrow when you get there."

"How casual?"

"Jeans or cords, I imagine. Oh, and Barrington, she was very emphatic about you bringing your books."

"My books! But . . ."

Rush's sentence was cut off by the sudden buzzing in

his ear. April had hung up. He sat staring at the phone for a long moment. What was up? Why would Maggie want him to dress casually and bring his books, for goodness' sake?

Maggie paced the living room, her black granny boots whispering restlessly across the floor as she waited for the doorbell to ring. Surely he would be here soon. What had April told him? Would he be mad when he found out what she was doing?

She didn't care if he was. She was worried about him. He was burning the candle at both ends, trying to study and work. In the two and a half weeks since they'd gone to the observatory, she'd seen him very few times—each time for about fifteen or twenty minutes, when he'd driven out of his way to stop by the shop and just say hello. Each time he had looked so exhausted that her heart ached for him. They hadn't been able to really talk at the gallery. And she hadn't gotten to touch him. She told herself it was for the best, but she still couldn't stop herself from calling April to set up the weekend, as much for herself as for Rush.

The chimes she'd been longing to hear suddenly tinkled throughout the room. He was here! Maggie struggled to subdue the wide grin threatening to split her features. She flung open the door and found Rush standing there in new, freshly laundered jeans and a brown-and-gray plaid shirt covered by a gray pullover and topped with a black-and-gray tweed sports coat. He had a stack of books under one arm and a frown on his handsome face.

"What's going on?" he barked, obviously bewildered by her strange request.

Ignoring his comment, Maggie smiled. "Why I'm just great, thank you! How about you?"

The teasing tone of her words brought forcibly home the fact that he'd given no word of greeting before jumping down her throat. A look of contrition replaced his scowl. "I'm sorry."

Maggie laughed. "Come in. Put your books down. Dinner is almost ready."

"Dinner? I thought we were going somewhere. What's going on?"

She turned to look at him, her hands clasped against her breast in a gesture that betrayed her nervousness. "Look, this is the last week of January. You've been back in school only a couple of weeks. You have classes all week, you've kept your clerk's job on Saturdays, you study every weeknight until God knows when and still hold down your job with April on the weekends. If you keep this pace up, you'll never live to get that law degree."

"So?" he prompted, a vague idea of what was going on taking shape in his mind.

"So I hired you for the weekend so you could rest. Or study. Whatever you want to do. But you don't have to worry about going somewhere else." She looked at him, trying unsuccessfully to gauge what he was thinking.

Rush put his books on the red floral sofa and approached her with a slow, measured gait. "You're paying April so she can pay me so I can rest?"

Maggie chewed on her upper lip and nodded. "Something like that."

"Exactly like that. So now on top of the indignity of being an escort and a model, I'm a kept man." He reached out and took her by the shoulder, his touch gentle through the white cowl-neck sweater she wore. "Why I oughta . . ."

"Rush!" Maggie's eyes flew to his.

"What I oughta do is kiss you."

Before Maggie could respond, he pulled her into the circle of his arms, his mouth swooping down and claiming hers with a hungry kiss. Her arms went around his middle and, without conscious thought, she melted against him, soft, womanly curves arching to a perfect fit against the steel hardness of his masculine body. It was crazy to feel what he made her feel, but she was helpless to fight her increasing attraction to him, and she was afraid to look any further into the future than today.

Rush's kiss deepened at her response, his mouth parting and slanting over hers. Then, in a journey of exquisite torture, his lips touched the corner of her mouth, his tongue tracing the angular curve of her upper lip, then dipping into the other corner before moving to her lower lip, which he kissed, then nibbled lightly with his teeth before drawing it into his mouth with a slow, sucking motion.

Maggie whimpered and pressed closer. Dear heaven, he felt so good. And what he did to her body was so . . . Her breath caught as Rush unfastened the wide, alligator belt that topped her sweater, tossed it to the floor and slid his hands up and under to the satin skin of her midriff.

She tore her mouth from his and leaned back to look at him. His eyes were half closed, his mouth glistened wetly from their kisses and his breath oozed from his body in an uneven sigh. Her voice was husky with suppressed emotion, and her eyes begged for understanding as she said the one word, "Please . . ."

Obediently, Rush removed his hands from beneath her sweater and placed them instead on the rounded curve of her bottom, drawing her closer to him and making her fully aware of his arousal.

"Please . . . please . . . I'd like to, Maggie-Mine," he gritted from between clenched teeth, rotating his hips slowly and firmly against her already throbbing femininity. "It would please me very much to please you."

"A part of me wants that closeness, too, Rush, but I didn't call you over for this," she said softly, "and I don't want to make you mad."

Rush cleared his throat and hauled her closer, tangling his fingers in the gleaming sable-colored strands of her hair and forcing her cheek against his sweater-clad chest while his other arm wrapped across her shoulders. He pressed a kiss to the top of her head and rested his chin on top of the kiss. "I'm not mad."

"Sure?" she asked, breathing in the peppery scent of his cologne.

"I'm not mad. I've become very calm, placid, docile. Probably all those cold showers you've forced me to take."

"Rush!"

He chuckled and released his hold on her only to take her by the shoulders once more.

"Do you know what really gets to me, Maggie?" he asked, studying each feature that made up her face with a thorough intensity.

She shook her head, causing his thumb to graze the edge of her bottom teeth and the tender inner flesh of her mouth.

"When I kiss you, you go absolutely boneless."

"I do?"

"Uh-huh. You just sort of melt into me." His eyes smiled into hers and he shook his head. "It's phenomenal. And when you go boneless . . . I go mindless."

Turning her head and pressing her mouth to his

fingers, she was suddenly filled with wonder at the feelings he insisted she created in him. Maggie, as Rush had urged her to do, began to deal in dreams for the first time in two years. If only she could have an affair with him and adapt to his absence when it was over. But she couldn't do that. She was too old-fashioned to participate in casual lovemaking. She was the kind of woman who would be destroyed at the end of an affair. Because she was the kind of woman whose heart had to be involved first. So much for dreams!

Hoping to alter the mood from the sensual to the friendly—a monumental task, but necessary if the weekend was going to work—Maggie looked up at him and smiled. "How about some dinner?"

Rush considered the question with mock-seriousness. "Well, it's second choice, but I'll take it." He looped his arm around her shoulders and they walked side by side to the kitchen. Maggie breathed a sigh of relief, thankful that he never pushed.

After a dinner of thick, chunky, beef stew and hard, crusty bread slathered with butter and washed down with three glasses of iced tea, Rush leaned back in repletion. "Thanks for the dinner. I was beginning to think the whole world existed on tuna fish and hamburger. I'd forgotten how good home-cooked food is."

"I'm glad you enjoyed it. How about some peach cobbler?"

Rush rubbed his flat stomach and groaned. "Maybe later. I couldn't eat another bite right now if my law degree depended on it."

Maggie propped her elbows on the table and rested her chin on top of her laced fingers. "So what will it be now? Rest or study?"

He grinned sheepishly. "It isn't the company or

anything, but I think I'll go for the rest. I'd been sleeping for an hour when April called, and I didn't get to sleep until about three-thirty this morning."

Maggie rose. "Fine. Go on into my bedroom and close the door."

"I'll just stretch out on the sofa."

"No, you won't," she said firmly, picking up her bowl and reaching across the table to get his. "I'm going to be doing the dishes and I hate trying to be quiet. Now get yourself in there!"

Rush laughed softly and grasped her wrist. "Bribe me."

"Rush . . ."

He exerted the slightest pressure on her wrist and she leaned nearer. "Say 'pretty please with sugar on top.'"

She smiled and repeated obediently, "Pretty please with sugar on top." When he didn't move, but sat waiting, she said, "Well, go on!"

"I'm waiting for the sugar."

"Rush Barrington," she said around a giggle, "you're impossible!"

"I know." His hand slid from her wrist up her arm. "Ornery . . ."

"Uh-huh. And irresistible," he added teasingly.

A sort of pain filled her eyes as they caressed his bold features. Her answer was a single breathless, "Yes."

She gave in to him, leaning down until their mouths brushed lightly. Then he pushed her purposefully away and stood up. "Show me where the bedroom is."

Three hours later Maggie rose to turn the television off. Rush had asked her to wake him when the news was over so he could go on home and get in a couple of hours of study. She crossed the living room and opened the bedroom door a crack. He'd kicked off his shoes and lay sprawled diagonally across the bed, flat on his back, one arm thrown up over his face, the other resting across his middle.

Maggie tiptoed nearer and sat down next to him. He was sleeping so peacefully. "Rush . . ." she whispered softly.

He didn't move. She covered the hand across his waist with hers and shook him gently. "Rush, wake up!"

He flung her hand away and murmured something unintelligible in his sleep. He was dead to the world, she realized, a curious ache filling her heart. Rising from the bed, Maggie took two comforters from the shelf of her walk-in closet. She covered Rush with one and slipped quietly from the room.

Back in the living room, she sat down on the sofa and pulled off her granny boots. Stretching, she turned off the yellow ginger-jar lamp, unfolded the other comforter, and with a feeling of utter contentment filling her because Rush was so near, she settled down beneath it and went instantly to sleep.

Wakefulness came slowly to Rush. He turned over on his stomach and drew in a deep breath, fighting against the reality of daylight and the fact that he had to get up. He could smell Maggie's perfume. It was almost as if she were there beside him. A smile lifted the corners of his mouth. Maggie . . . The thought of her filled him with a quiet happiness. She was everything he'd sought for in a woman. He wanted her. He loved her. And he'd better get himself in gear, since he was supposed to spend the day at her house.

He rolled over and, with eyes still closed, reached for the wind-up clock, the one he had bought when he realized he couldn't depend on fickle electricity with his tight schedule. Trying to juggle two jobs and law school demanded that he budget his time, and being late was something he just couldn't afford. He groped the top of the bedside table, but his hand encountered nothing but empty space. Muttering a mild curse, he forced his eyes open to see where in the heck the clock was. Instead of the battered nightstand that sat beside his double bed, his gaze lighted on a gracefully styled table with a dainty china lamp and a black-and-white photograph of a young girl.

Shocked awake, he sat up and ran his hand through his tousled hair, making a thorough perusal of the room and encountering not functional masculine furnishings, but an expensive Turkish rug topping parquet flooring and exquisite paintings hanging against grass-cloth walls. Good Lord! Maggie's bedroom! He'd fallen asleep in her bed, and for some reason she hadn't wakened him. His eyes sought and found her clock on the other side of the bed. Six thirty-five. He wondered if she was still asleep.

Smothering a yawn, Rush eased his feet to the floor and peeked into the living room. Maggie lay on the red-flowered sofa, her dark hair fanned out against the throw pillow beneath her head, her hands tucked beneath her cheek. A wave of tenderness washed over him, and a half smile quirked the corners of his finely chiseled mouth. He turned and headed toward the bathroom.

Fifteen minutes later, his teeth brushed with a new toothbrush he'd found in her medicine cabinet, his hair towel-dried and damp from the shower and smelling faintly of some feminine deodorant, Rush pulled on his jeans and shirt from the day before and padded in his socks to the living room.

He squatted down beside the sofa and looked his fill at the woman who was rapidly becoming the center of his life. At the sight of her, pleasure gleamed in his umber eyes. Her slim body spoke of elegance and class from the top of her dark hair to the plum tint that glossed the toenails peeking out from beneath the comforter. Her mouth was without lipstick, and her lashes, long and curled at the ends, made fanlike shadows on her cheeks. Why was it that women seemed to peak in beauty and sex appeal as they got older? He leaned nearer and pressed his lips to the sweeping arch of one eyebrow, then dropped a feather kiss on a delicate, blue-veined eyelid. She stirred and sighed.

He nuzzled the sensitive spot beneath her ear with his mouth and whispered, "Wake up, Maggie-Mine."

She snuggled deeper into the pillow.

"Maggie, if you don't open those beautiful blue eyes, I'm going to join you on that sofa and make mad, passionate love to you."

Her eyes, still dazed with sleep, flew open. "Rush!"

"You recognized me with the beard," he teased, running his hand over his unshaven face and scooting her hip aside with his so he could sit beside her.

Maggie attempted to smile around the fingertips covering a yawn. "Did you sleep well?"

"Like a log. But I'll bet you didn't." He stroked one finger lightly along the curve of her jaw.

"Yes, I did," she argued.

"Why didn't you wake me?"

"I tried, but you were really out of it, so I thought I'd just let you sleep since you seemed to need it so badly."

"You're some lady, Maggie Spencer," he said softly.

Soft color climbed the gentle rise of her cheekbones. Rush could see the uncertainty in her eyes and wondered why she was so distrustful of his praise. He gave an exaggerated sigh.

"Okay," he said, once again putting aside his feelings

in deference to hers, "if I can't seduce you with pretty words, then let's have breakfast."

At four o'clock that Sunday afternoon, Maggie, who'd been reading a swashbuckling historical romance, pulled off her glasses and glanced toward the window. It was snowing again. She untucked her feet from beneath her, tossed the glasses onto the table, stuck the book beneath a pillow out of Rush's sight and went to look out at the whirling, swirling whiteness blanketing the nearby buildings. She shivered. She was tired of the cold. But then, she always became impatient with winter once the holiday season was behind her.

Of course, she would have the opportunity to get away from Dame Boston's wrath in the middle of February. Nassau. A trip people dreamed about, unless they happened to be meeting with Giles Sutherland, world-famous landscape artist. Giles was in his midforties, handsome, charming, wealthy, and had more hands than a clock shop. Her last trip, that one to London, since he divided his time between England and the Bahamas, had been spent fighting off his advances while trying to talk business. If only there was some way she could dissuade him.

Maggie's mouth quirked in a wry smile. Maybe if she had a husband to take along, it might at least slow him down. *Sorry, Mags, no husband.* Well, a boyfriend, then.

"What's so interesting out there?"

Maggie turned and saw Rush standing in the doorway, his hair rumpled as if he'd repeatedly run his fingers through it, his shirt hanging free of his jeans and a pair of wire-framed, aviator-style glasses perched jauntily on the bridge of his strong, straight nose.

Maggie's tone mirrored her bemusement as she answered automatically, "Snow." Then she added, "You wear glasses?"

"Only when I want to see," he said with a smile. "I have an astigmatism and a problem with eye strain, so I wear them when I'm doing close work."

"Oh."

"What's the matter? You don't like men who wear glasses?"

"No! It's just that you seem so young . . ."

Rush laughed, crossed the room and pulled her into his arms. "I've been wearing them since I was a freshman in high school."

Maggie felt extremely foolish. Of course wearing glasses had nothing to do with age! She plucked at a button on his shirt and glanced up at him from beneath her lashes, broaching the idea that had been forming before he'd come into the room. "How would you like to go to Nassau?"

Rush gave a short, humorless laugh. "I'd love it, but unfortunately impoverished law students only get to see Nassau at the travel displays in the malls."

"I have to go the twelfth, thirteenth, and fourteenth of February for a long weekend . . . a British artist I'm trying to get for the gallery." She didn't tell him that her birthday fell on the thirteenth, and that she'd made her appointment with Giles purposely on that date so she would have something on her mind besides the fact that she would be forty years old. If she was wrapped up with business, maybe she'd get lucky and the day would seem just like any other. Ha!

"Three whole days," he mused. "I'll miss you."

"I said, I want you to go with me."

"And I'd love to, Maggie, but I just can't afford it."

"I'll pay for it because . . ."

"No way!" he interrupted, releasing her and striding to the fireplace, where he rested his forearm on the mantel and stared down into the flames. "You paid for this weekend, and I appreciate the break and the chance to be with you, but there's no way I'll let you pay my way to Nassau."

"Your pride is showing," Maggie teased, going to him and sliding her arms around him from behind.

"Damn right!"

Maggie rested her cheek against the warmth of his back, a slight, starchy scent tickling her nostrils. "Will you just let me explain? Giles Sutherland is a man who thinks every woman alive is just dying to fall into bed with him."

Rush was silent.

"I thought if I took someone with me—if he thought there was someone else in my life—it might discourage him. I think it'll work." When he didn't answer she continued, "Look, you'd get a marvelous weekend paid for, there would be a lot of time you could spend with your books if you needed, not to mention that Nassau in February has got to be close to heaven."

"I can't let you do it," he told her, loosening her grip on his waist and turning to face her.

She tugged abstractedly at a belt loop of his jeans. "I have the money, Rush. It's no big deal."

His laugh was laced with the barest trace of bitterness. "It never is when you have it."

Maggie lifted her troubled blue eyes to his and smiled a bit self-consciously. "I think we have a communication problem here. What I'm proposing, Mr. Barrington, is a business trip that would be mutually beneficial. I intend, through the Newbern Agency, to hire some man to go with me for the weekend—as an escort and as a deterrent to Giles Sutherland." She gave an embarrassed laugh. "You're an escort for the Newbern Agency. You're handsome, charming—exactly what I need. Look, the man's a lech. He's always got his hands where they shouldn't be. You'd be doing me a service by going along, believe me."

"Maybe. But I can't switch back and forth with our relationship like you seem to be able to do. We have a professional connection and a personal relationship. Sometimes I'm being paid by the agency to take you somewhere. The next time I'm taking you to dinner on my own. We seem to have something good going for us, but now you're wanting to hire me again—to pay my way to the Bahamas, so that I can be a buffer between you and some guy. Hell, I don't know when I'm supposed to stop acting like your escort and start acting like your real date." His brown eyes were bleak as they stared intently into hers. His tone of voice dropped a decibel. "I just don't know what you want from me, Maggie."

Maggie looked at him, understanding his irritation, yet recognizing his underlying patience with her and her reluctance to further their personal relationship. He'd said he'd play by her rules, and he had . . . even though he'd tried to bend them a time or two. She was thankful for his forbearance and, at the same time, a bit angry with herself for lacking the courage to go on with her life.

When she spoke, her voice quivered with emotion. "I want you to go with me to Nassau because if you don't go, I'll have to get someone else, and I'd really rather have you. And beyond that, I need time. Is that too much to ask?"

"Time," Rush repeated, nodding his head in acceptance. "You need more time. Okay. I can understand that, just like you've got to understand why I can't let you pay my way to Nassau. Call it pride if you like. I just can't do it."

The very quietness of his speech underscored his feelings much more strongly than anger could have. Maggie, misery welling up inside her, watched as he put on his jacket, gathered his books and crossed the room. There was something so final about his actions. When he reached the door he turned with a bittersweet smile playing at the corners of his mouth. "You've got all the time you need, Maggie-Mine, but remember that relationships can't stand still. They either move forward or they die."

She watched as the door shut behind him and knew that he took a large part of her with him. Then, for the first time since the day her divorce was declared final, Maggie Spencer cried over a man.

Later that night, after a hot bath, a cup of cocoa and several hours of deliberation, Maggie called Rush. She had no idea what she would say. She knew only that she couldn't stand leaving things as they were. Dialing his number proved no help, however, because all she heard was the irritating wail of a busy signal. With a disappointed sigh, she fluffed her pillows, reached for her romance novel and hoped she could read until she fell asleep.

She had just reread the same paragraph for the third time when her phone rang. She grabbed it so fast that Lacey, who believed in letting it ring at least three times so the caller wouldn't think you were too anxious, would have been utterly mortified.

"Hello?" Her voice sounded breathless, eager, and . . . anxious.

"So what do I take to Nassau?"

A broad smile sliced Maggie's features. "Rush?"

"Who else? Unless you've asked a whole slew of guys to go on this trip with you," he teased.

"No. Just you." She sat up straighter and pleated the floral sheet with nervous fingers. "I just didn't expect you to call."

"Neither did I," he admitted, "but I got to thinking about what you said, and believe me, men aren't the only ones groping out there. I've landed a couple of women through the agency who came on to me pretty strong." He heaved a deep sigh. "Anyway, I can relate to your problem. And you said you were going to take someone . . . so I thought, why the hell not me? Sometimes pride takes a tumble when money is involved." Then, before she could answer, he said, "No, that isn't true."

"What isn't?"

"The part about the money. Oh, sure, I can use it, but that isn't the reason I decided to go." His voice sounded tired. "The bottom line, Maggie Spencer, is that I can't bear the thought of another man spending the weekend with you when I can be with you myself."

Seventeen days later Maggie and Rush sat beside the hotel pool in Nassau. They had flown out of Logan Airport late that afternoon, after Rush had finished his classes for the week. They now sat at poolside, her thigh resting only millimeters from his, their feet playing in the warm chlorine-scented water. Evening toyed with the dangling end of day, pulling a curtain of pink gauze across the sun, which slid majestically behind the far horizon.

Rush trailed a fingertip from her knee up her thigh to the edge of her swimsuit. "You don't have much to say."

Maggie kept her gaze focused on the bottom of the

pool and shook her head. How could she tell him that the sight of him in brief black swimming trunks with narrow yellow, red and blue stripes on the side had robbed her of coherent thought, let alone speech. Good Lord! The man was so positively, so utterly masculine, he ought to be banned.

Catching movement from the corner of her eye, she turned and saw him lie back on the rough, cool deck, pillowing his head on his folded arms. The sight of him stretched out beside her sent her libido into high gear. He was dark skinned, and his shoulders and arms were muscular without making him look like a man too devoted to athletics. His abdomen was firm and, since he rested on his back, concave.

"Do you want to swim?" he asked, looking at her through partially closed eyes.

"I'd love to," she answered.

They stood and Rush immediately made a shallow dive off the side. He emerged seconds later, treading water, his hair slicked wetly back from the bold, masculine structure of his face. "Hurry up, slowpoke. It's great!"

Maggie untied the sash of her coverup and shrugged one shoulder free. She suddenly wished she had bought a swimsuit that wasn't quite so revealing.

"I'm gonna sink if you don't hurry up," he taunted. "I can't tread water indefinitely."

The teasing words struck home and, with quick movements, Maggie peeled out of the wrap, flung it down onto the deck and started for the ladder. The intake of Rush's breath was audible even to her.

"What's the matter?" she asked anxiously, searching his upturned face.

Rush eyed the gentle slope of her creamy shoulders, lingered on the roundness of her small breasts, encased in the teal-blue suit that fit like a second skin, skimmed the sweep of waist and hip and measured the firm length of her legs from her trim ankles to the high-cut sides of her suit, which showed a maximum of thigh, plus some hip.

"Wrong?" he echoed as his eyes traveled back up to tangle with hers. His voice was husky as he asked, "What ever gave you the idea something was wrong? On the contrary, Ms. Spencer, everything is fantastic."

Lowering herself into the water, she glided straight into Rush's arms, sliding her fingers through his wet hair and drawing his mouth down to hers. Their legs, moving back and forth in the water, brushed against each other, firm muscle against silky softness. Her breasts were flattened against his chest, and his hands rode the swell of her hips, his fingers insinuating themselves beneath the elasticized edge of her suit and pulling her into the heat of his arousal. "You're beautiful, Maggie," he whispered as he rained kisses over her face and shoulders.

She felt beautiful. And very much alive. Maybe it was time for her to get on with her life instead of burying herself in her work. She'd given Jarrell nineteen years as a wife, had given Lacey everything she could as a mother. Maybe now was the time to start giving to herself . . . as a friend.

Chapter Seven

*B*lack.

The nightgown was sinfully black, wickedly sheer and plunged so deeply in the front that it was guaranteed to drive any male instantly crazy.

Maggie looked furtively around her, as if everyone shopping in the small boutique on downtown Nassau's Bay Street knew what she was contemplating. With casual, nonchalant movements that would have been right at home with a slow, laid-back whistle, she eased the ebony confection from its hanger and walked to the nearest three-angled mirror. One arm about her waist, the other holding the bodice to her shoulders, she stared at her reflection.

"Oh . . . my . . . God," she whispered, dragging every ounce of meaning and sound from the three words. Even with her clothes beneath it, the gown was revealing. It was naughty. It was only threads away from scandalous. It was perfect.

Her mind quickly, and quite naturally, jumped to Rush. What would he think of the gown? If he were here this moment, instead of back at the hotel lost in a law book, what would he say? More importantly, what would he say of her decision to go to bed with him? *If* he asked her again.

She had lain awake long into the warm, balmy, tropical night, a night filled with the sounds of roaring ocean and rhyming cicadas, going over every reason she should and shouldn't have an affair with Rush Barrington. In the end, the shoulds had finally outweighed the shouldn'ts. She had decided, however, that she, Margaret Spencer, product of a twenty-year one-man relationship, could not initiate the affair. And not only that, she thought, it was necessary to her ego, an ego that had turned forty with the dawn, along with her physical body, that Rush do the initiating. She had to know that he truly wanted her, truly desired her as a lover.

But, she mused, still appraising the gown with a critical eye, it behooved one to be prepared.

"May I help you?" asked a smiling, deeply tanned young woman with a British accent and a boldly flowered skirt.

Maggie jumped, an action that combined being startled with being guilty. "Yes," she answered, clearing her throat and pushing forward the gown at the same time. "Yes, I'd like this."

The clerk's smile broadened to reveal white teeth that seemed even whiter in the sun-darkened face. "Isn't this lovely?" she asked, reaching for the filmy garment and moving off toward a counter at one end of the small room.

"Yes, lovely," Maggie responded absently, suddenly drowning in a wave of doubt and uncertainty. What in the world was she doing? What she was doing, she told herself, wrestling her runaway anxiety to the ground with a firm grip, was getting on with her life.

I'm entitled to the same happiness that Jarrell has, aren't I?

"Will this be a charge?" the woman asked.

"Yes!" Maggie answered quickly and with a defiance that the question didn't deserve. The saleswoman glanced up sharply.

Rush and I aren't kids, are we?

"Would you like this gift-wrapped?"

"No," Maggie answered out loud, but mentally added, *We aren't kids. Despite the fact that he's younger than I am, he isn't a kid. He's a man, a grown man; I'm a woman, a grown woman. It's that simple. Isn't that what he said?*

"Pardon?"

Maggie focused on the woman's one word and frowned slightly.

The clerk was also frowning. Just as slightly. But still with a lot of customer-relations courtesy. "You said something was simple."

The pink of intense embarrassment tinged Maggie's cheeks. "Simple? Ah . . . ah . . . the gown," she said, seizing eagerly on an obvious out. "The gown is simple, but lovely."

"Yes, ma'am," the woman agreed, though the small scowl slipped only a minuscule fraction and what did slip was replaced by an even more curious look that peeped stealthily from beneath mascaraed lashes.

And Rush was so right, Maggie added to herself, her attention once again diverted, *a relationship does not stand still. It either goes backward or forward. And it's time this one went forward. It's time . . .*

"One forty-seven," the lady from Nassau replied, looking at the thin watch on her wrist.

"Pardon me?" Maggie asked.

The clerk smiled, as if at a child. "The time, ma'am."

Maggie angled her hand to look at the gold watch on her own wrist. "One forty-seven," she replied.

The woman behind the counter appeared stupefied and at a momentary loss for words. Maggie didn't notice.

And the final reason I'm going to have an affair with Rush, she thought on a high-cresting wave of courage, *is because I want to. I'm a forty-year-old woman. I know what I want to do!*

"Have a nice day," the saleswoman added, handing the package to Maggie and studying her with a face screwed into tight lines of scrutiny.

"Yes, settled," Maggie answered firmly, took the package and marched from the store.

The saleswoman watched, wide-eyed and open-mouthed, as her customer disappeared out onto the tourist-busy street. The woman ended by shaking her head, a rueful little tilt that seemed to say that the fair tropical winds blew many strange ones her way.

Maggie's confident mood lasted the duration of the taxi ride back to the plush hotel; it lasted the duration of her walk down the thickly carpeted hallway to her third-floor room; it lasted as she opened the door, closed it behind her and eagerly snatched the gown from its sack. And then it vanished, like the prismatic twinkling of sunlight on the sea that shone turquoise beyond the window.

Easing to the side of the bed, she clutched the diaphanous nightgown to her breasts. "Oh, my God," she breathed softly into the silence, "what am I doing?"

Something was wrong. Something was definitely wrong, Rush thought, as he openly studied Maggie's disinterest in the food on her plate. She had picked and shoved her way around the conch salad, had played her way through soup and was now dabbling with a shrimp and pastry entrée.

He watched as her beautiful mouth formed a graciously murmured "thank you" to the waiter who removed her plate and refilled her wineglass with an amber liquid that matched almost exactly the sunny color in the three-toned gold necklace embracing her throat. Rush thought of the simple gift in his pocket, a gift that couldn't in any way compare with the beauty of what she was wearing, and for the second time in two hours experienced a sinking feeling in the pit of his stomach. The first time had been an hour before in Giles Sutherland's suite, where they'd gone for cocktails.

The famed artist, who was as renowned for his amorous tendencies as for his paintings, hadn't been at all what Rush had expected. After his New Year's introduction to Rafael Brown, he had erroneously assumed all artists to be only shades away from weird, only tints away from wildly eccentric.

Giles Sutherland had blown his theory sky-high. Not only was the man not eccentric, he had the audacity to be uncommonly handsome in his normalcy. With loden-green eyes and black hair that was dramatically silver-gray at the temples, he was more than handsome, more than distinguished, more than normal. And that *more* translated into one thing: He was Maggie's age.

Give or take a few lousy years. That realization, along with the fact that Giles Sutherland had money, that he was already established and successful in his chosen career and that he had a good twelve to fifteen years of maturity and experience that Rush couldn't match no matter how hard he tried, had caused him to feel a sense of insecurity. By comparison, was he nothing more than an immature youth? With a shallow intelligence? With unseasoned sensibilities? With a slim hope of interesting someone like Maggie?

He had comforted himself with the fact that she seemed oblivious to Giles Sutherland's charm and charisma. He had consoled himself that she had been all business, had been intent only on discussing contracts. Rush hadn't been consoled, however, over the fact that Maggie seemed unable, unwilling to fully meet his eyes. Then or now. Nor had she been able to all day. Something was wrong. It might be nothing more than the fact that it was February thirteenth, a day April had sensitively warned him about, but deep in his heart he suspected it was something else. And with his insecurities now breathing with life, that something scared him.

"You didn't eat much dinner," he said quietly.

Maggie raised her face to his. A gentle breeze fluttered the long, dark wisps of her hair and the strawlike fringe of the thatch roof covering the patio restaurant of the hotel. Not very far in the distance the night sang with the song of surf. She smiled and gave a delicate shrug of shoulders bare except for the thin straps of a blue sundress. "I guess I just wasn't very hungry."

"Are you feeling all right?" he countered.

"Yes, of course," she answered, thinking that her reply was really a lie. How could you be feeling all right when your stomach was tied in more knots than a professional sailor had ever seen? Telling herself that she had to stop acting like an adolescent out on a first date, she forced a smile to her lips. "How did your studying go?"

Broad shoulders strained against yellow knit in a repetition of her shrug. "Fine. I'm all ready for the exam Monday." He brought the wineglass to his lips and sipped slowly, then returned the glass to the table where it made tiny concentric circles on the white tablecloth. "How did your shopping go this morning?"

Maggie's wineglass hesitated ever so slightly en route to her lips. "Fine," she answered in a voice bordering on the shallow.

"What did you buy?"

The tablecloth at her fingertips instantly grew interesting. "Oh, the usual tourist stuff." The usual tourist stuff? A black gown tucked in a drawer along with her foolish notions of seduction did not fall under the heading of normal tourist purchases. Oh, God, how she wished she had left that gown in the boutique! How she wished she felt no attraction for the man sitting across from her! How she wished today was not her birthday! And if it had to be her birthday, how she wished she could be younger than forty! Thank heavens no one knew it was her birthday. Thank heavens . . .

"Happy Birthday, Maggie," Rush's voice stole gently into her reverie.

Maggie's head whipped up, her eyes colliding with his. "How . . . How do you know . . ."

"April told me."

"April?"

Rush nodded.

Maggie dropped her head forward, her hair forming

a curtain about her like rich, thick, dark brown velvet. "That settles it," she grumbled. "I'm going to kill her." Raising her head, she once more found Rush's eyes. At the same moment, a horrible thought crossed her mind, causing her own eyes to narrow slightly. "Is that all she told you? I mean, she didn't tell you how old I was, did she?"

"I believe she did say something about forty." There was a gentle smile on his lips, a spark of sensitivity in his brown eyes, a consoling hand now reaching across the table for hers.

Maggie's only response was a tortured groan and a lowering of her eyes back to the tablecloth. Her hand refused to mesh with his. He forcefully laced their fingers together anyway.

"Look at me," he ordered as softly, as firmly as spring coaxes hesitant, shy flowers into bright bloom. "Look at me, Maggie."

Slowly, bravely, she did.

"Why should it bother you that I know today is your birthday and that you're forty?"

The dark intensity in his still darker irises demanded only the truth. And strangely, she found that she wanted to speak honestly to him.

"I don't mind the birthday part. It's the forty I mind."

"Turning it or my knowing it?"

She gave a half laugh of self-consciousness. "Both." She shrugged. "Age never used to bother me. Suddenly forty sounds so very old at a time in my life when"—she hesitated, looked down at their entwined hands, then back up into Rush's eyes—"at a time in my life when I'd like to be younger."

A tiny smile of understanding curved Rush's lips.

"Would you believe I was just sitting here wanting to be older?"

"Older?" Maggie repeated in disbelief. "Why in the world would you want to be older?"

"For a reason about as stupid as yours." His fingers tightened on hers. "Ah, Maggie, why can't we be content with who we are? Why can't we just say to hell with the fact that we weren't born at the same time?"

The pressure of his hand on hers, the slow, satin texture of his voice, the way his eyes were tender and fiery and sleepily seductive unleashed tiny, tingling sensations that coursed and skipped the length of her body, settling restlessly and at last in a most feminine recess.

"To hell with age," she breathed.

"To hell with age," he repeated in a husky voice.

She smiled.

He smiled.

"Close your eyes," he said suddenly.

"What?"

"Close your eyes."

When her lashes formed crescents against her fair cheeks she felt his hand withdraw from hers, felt also the air spilling onto the moist spot where their hands had lain together. "What are you doing?" she asked, a giggle suddenly teasing her voice.

"No questions, Ms. Spencer. Just keep those beautiful eyes closed."

Her hand stirred impatiently, but when she started to remove it from the table, Rush's fingers gently clasped about her wrist. At the same moment, something cool nestled into her palm. Her eyes flew open.

A small crystal heart, no larger than a quarter and strung on a fine gold chain, stared back. Maggie's eyes went from the heart to Rush's expectant face, then back to the heart. "Oh, Rush," she whispered, taking the chain in her other hand and dangling the heart from its end, "it's beautiful."

"Do you like it?" He made no attempt to hide his eagerness.

Her eyes, round and sincere, met his. "I love it."

"I bought it at Have A Heart."

Maggie knew the little shop, located in the Faneuil Hall Marketplace, and was doubly delighted with the gift because Rush had brought it all the way from Boston to give to her.

"I thought it was appropriate, since today is your birthday and tomorrow is Valentine's Day," Rush added.

Maggie, caring not one whit whether it was appropriate or not, slipped the necklace about her neck. The crystal heart fell inches below the expensive gold choker she wore and settled into a strangely handsome alliance. Her fingers still at her throat, her eyes glowing with a tender emotion, she added, "I love it. I really do. Thank you."

"I wish it could have been more," he said sincerely. "It's not what a man like Giles Sutherland would have given you."

Quiet moments passed, moments underscoring a masculine vulnerability, a feminine sensitivity.

"No, it isn't," she agreed, "but then I wouldn't have liked anything he'd have given me a fraction as much."

A slow smile of relief curved Rush's lips. "To hell with money."

Maggie smiled, pushing the corners of her mouth upward. "To hell with money."

Then, as slowly as it appeared, Rush's smile faded.

"Now I want something from you. I want to know what's been bothering you all day."

"What do you mean?" she asked, her pulse stumbling.

"You've been distracted and as nervous as a cat about to have kittens."

"I haven't . . ."

"At first I thought it was just your turning forty, but I don't think that's it. Not all of it."

Again, Maggie laughed self-consciously. "There's nothing wrong," she lied, damning herself for her earlier unsophisticated obviousness and her present cowardice.

"Don't insult my intelligence, Maggie. If you don't want me to know, just tell me to mind my own business, but please don't lie to me."

None of his business? Suddenly she wanted to laugh. If it wasn't Rush's business, she didn't know whose it was.

"Maggie . . ."

She swallowed down the fear suddenly choking her.

". . . tell me." Time sauntered by before he added the one heart-stirring word, "Please."

Taking a deep breath, she said, "I . . . I did something very silly today." Her hands clenched tightly together on the table, as if they could hold her emotionally intact. Her eyes, unable to connect with his, studied her hands.

Rush waited a full ten seconds before sensing no further comment was coming. "What silly thing did you do?"

"I . . ." Her eyes met his, held, then fell away and back to her hands, which she now fancifully envisioned folded in prayer. "I bought a sexy black gown." It was out, the words whispered into the room. Maggie felt relief, embarrassment and an apprehension so painful it was smothering her.

Rush said nothing, though his eyes devoured every nuance of expression on her face.

She glanced up, saw him watching her and felt compelled to explain. "I, ah . . . I made up my mind that I was going"—she swallowed back the knot in her throat—"going to have an affair with you . . . if you asked me again."

She waited for his reply, but none came. He simply looked at her as if he'd been struck dumb with shock. Maggie suddenly felt sick.

"I'm sorry . . ." she mumbled, shoving back her chair, rising and moving at almost a run through the restaurant. She was only vaguely aware that Rush called her name, then cursed when she didn't answer. Her sandaled heels took her out into the hotel corridor, her eyes zeroing in on the two elevator doors that beckoned to her wounded pride. She longed for nothing but the solitude of her third-floor room.

Her heart was pounding a cruel cadence when she jammed her finger against the button. Automatically, she glanced upward to see where the two elevator cars were located. One was moving down, one up. Maggie began to pray.

The down elevator had just pinged its arrival, the doors had just started to slide open, Maggie had just taken a step forward when firm fingers curled around her upper arm and hauled her around.

Eyes, sapphire-blue and dulled with the pain of mortification, welded with eyes brown and bright and glowing with a wealth of emotion. Time stopped . . . and restarted to match the rhythm of two hearts.

"I'm asking," he whispered huskily. His hand released her upper arm and moved to the curve of her neck, where it disappeared from view beneath the fall of her hair. "No," he amended as his head began to lower, "I'm begging." His lips met hers in soft supplication . . . and were granted all they asked for.

Behind them, the elevator door whooshed open, whooshed closed and once more the elevator started upward. Neither Maggie nor Rush noticed. Their attention was absorbed by silken kisses, whispered words and the promise of the night.

The hot shower had steamed the bathroom mirror, but not enough, Maggie thought. She could still see her image. She'd been standing before the silver devil for the better part of five minutes. She was scared. Not of making love. Oh, God, she wanted that. She wanted to finally ease this ache that was gnawing her into a delicious state of insanity. She was scared instead of not pleasing Rush. He was so virile . . . so sensual . . . so experienced. He had to be experienced. No man who looked as he did—she'd seen the women at the hotel eyeing him—was inexperienced. In contrast, she'd been with only one man. And, she groaned as the steam dissipated by degrees, leaving her gown-clad image in clearer view, she was forty. Forty years old.

Forty years old and close to tears, she admitted, feeling utterly stupid. She wasn't going to cry. A woman who had seen four decades did not cry simply because she was jump-out-of-her-skin nervous!

Oh, God! She *was* going to cry, she thought frantically, watching tears pool in her eyes and observing, almost disinterestedly, one oval tear slip down her cheek. She brushed it away, but another hurriedly replaced it. She moaned. This was crazy! she thought. Absolutely crazy!

This was crazy! Rush thought, glancing at his watch for the tenth time in the same number of minutes. Striding across the bedroom he'd found empty nearly a quarter of an hour before, he rapped softly on the bathroom door. No answer. He frowned, rapped again, still receiving no answer. His hand curved around the doorknob and pushed gently.

"Maggie? Are you all ri . . ."

She whirled to face Rush, who now stood filling the open doorway. She heard his breath catch as he took in her shower-damp tendrils of hair and the becoming pink flush along her cheekbones; she saw his nostrils flex involuntarily at the smell of cleanness and misty perfume; she saw his eyes lower to take in every detail of her body so provocatively revealed by the sheer black gown. But she knew all of this registered in his senses in the fleeting span of a second before he focused on the tears flooding her blue eyes and coursing down her cheeks.

"Maggie?" The whispered word was raw with concern.

"I need a face lift," she said, as if it was the most normal of settings for such an announcement.

He frowned for a swift millisecond before comprehension dawned.

"You don't need a face lift," he replied, holding back the smile he wanted so much to give.

"I need my wrinkles smoothed out."

"What wrinkles?"

"The ones around my eyes."

"Don't you dare touch them."

"I'm too old."

"No."

"You're too young."

"No." He took a breath so deep it seemed to come from his soul. "Maggie, don't . . ."

"I want . . ." she continued as a tear dropped from her cheek onto the ivory skin of her chest and disappeared into the folds of the nightgown, "I want to be pretty for you, sexy for you."

His eyes raked restlessly over the pale flesh in the sultry shadow of the gauzy black fabric—the gentle swell of dark-budded breasts, the gentle flair of perfectly curved hips. "If you were any prettier, any sexier," he said in a voice he was having trouble controlling, "I wouldn't live to tell about it."

"I want you to want me," she whispered, her blue eyes swimming in shimmering, translucent moisture.

Three steps. He took three steps, until he was standing so close she had to angle her head to hold eye contact. Taking her hand in his, he laid it fully on the masculine bulge straining forcefully against the tennis shorts he'd hastily thrown on. Her other hand instinctively braced against his bare, hair-matted chest.

"The law calls that prima facie evidence, Maggie-Mine. I call it wanting you so badly I'm about to die."

When he pulled his hand away she brazenly left hers where he had placed it. Her fingers, never quite so eager, never quite so bold, slid the length of his arousal in an up-and-down motion that momentarily shuttered his eyes and dragged a deep groan from his throat. Then, in one beautiful motion, his lips claimed hers, warmly, passionately, reassuringly, and his arms lifted her from the floor and cradled her against his chest. Walking from the steamy bathroom in a long, even stride, he headed for the bed. In less time than it took for her to admit that she had never before experienced this rapturous feeling of anticipation, she felt the softness of the bed beneath her and the hardness of Rush's body above her. She knew with an irrefutable certainty that whatever else happened in her life, she would always remember this night, this man.

Chapter Eight

$\mathcal{B}$ush's body lay on top of Maggie's. His upper body was propped up by bare forearms resting on either side of her head, enabling him to look into her face. "Sssh . . ." he whispered.

Her face. Maggie's still swimming sapphire-colored eyes found his. Her lashes clung together in long, wet spikes, and an occasional teardrop burst the dam of her almond-shaped eyes and trickled down her temples into the shining hair fanning out from her face in dark rays.

"Sssh . . ." he repeated softly, leaning down and pressing his mouth to the corner of one eye, sipping the salty potion of her tears with minuscule kisses and finding that they filled him with a powerful, heady sensation. Everything about her caused a crazy, drunken exhilaration to spread through his body. A body whose eagerness was carefully checked by Maggie's trembling vulnerability . . . her insecurity.

A deep, shuddering breath racked her as she struggled to control her tears. Rush switched his ministrations to the other tear-drenched eye.

"Rush . . ." Her quivering voice sounded lost and held a little-girl quality that seemed to say, "Make it all right. Help me."

"What is it, Maggie-Mine?" he asked in a deep, rumbling voice.

Her eyes shifted from his and returned, while her mouth quirked in an attempt at laughter that ended in a sob. Her eyes filled again. "I'm afraid!"

"Afraid?"

She nodded, her throat moving up and down in a nervous swallow. "It's been so long . . . and what if I don't please you . . ."—she shrugged her shoulders in an embarrassed gesture, the sentence trailing away.

He chuckled deep in his throat and lowered himself to his side, pulling her over to face him, their faces close together on the pillow. His hand ran from her shoulder to her elbow and back up in a comforting caress. "Maggie, Maggie, just being on the same planet with you pleases me."

Rush's hand slid from her shoulder to her hand. He laced his fingers through hers, resting his forearm against her breasts, turning the back of her hand toward him. He pressed his lips to the delicate bones of her wrist, to the pad of her thumb, then to each finger individually. He gave each finger his undivided attention, tracing her knuckles with his tongue, then probing the soft flesh between each with a breathtaking thoroughness that caused a throbbing ache to build inside her. And all the time he kissed her hand, his eyes were entwined with hers, seeking her reaction, gauging her pleasure.

Her legs moved restlessly against his and her eyes drifted closed, unknowingly fanning the embers of his need. Rush rested the back of her hand against his jaw, and rubbed it slowly back and forth as he calculated the length of her lashes. "What are you thinking, Maggie?"

Her head moved slowly from side to side, and she partially lifted eyelids weighted with desire. "I can't think," she confessed, the words nearly a groan.

The honesty of the throaty reply surprised Rush. Most women wouldn't admit so freely the feelings a man created. But then, he should have realized artifice had no part in the life of Maggie Spencer. It was obvious that monitoring her response had never occurred to her.

"Good." Rush released her hand and slipped his arm beneath her, bringing her slender form closer to him, the softness of her breasts burning his hair-roughened chest. His hands soothed up and down the silken expanse of her back and caressed the slight sweep of waist and hip. He took her mouth in a kiss that bordered on reverence and exhaled a long breath against her forehead. "You feel so good."

"Do I?"

"If you're fishing for compliments, you're out of luck. I have better things to do right now," he teased.

"Such as?"

Rush sobered instantly. "Such as make love to you. All night, over and over, until I absorb you into my very soul . . . until there's no one left but the two of us."

"Rush . . ." Maggie started to touch his face, then stopped.

"Go ahead. Touch me. Do what you want to do."

"There's something I've wanted to do since the first time I saw you," she said.

"What?"

"This." Maggie lifted a hand and rested coral-tipped

fingers against his freshly shaven face, her index finger barely touching the corner of his mouth. It began a slow stroking, as if the texture of his face intrigued her. Then she dipped one slender fingertip into the cleft in his chin. It fit perfectly. Almost as if hers was the sculptor's hand who'd decided his strong, angular chin needed the softening of a dimple and had promptly gouged it out. "It fits," she said wonderingly.

"Yes," he agreed. "What else?"

Her hands stretched out, palms flat, and settled against the dark down covering his chest and belly. Her fingers curled and tightened, grasping loose fistfuls of hair that was surprisingly silky to her touch. Her eyes met his in surprise. "I thought it would be coarse."

"Does it feel good to you?" he asked.

A half-smile curved her mouth. "Oh, yes!"

"Good." Rush released her and stretched out on his back. His voice was firm with decision as he commanded softly, "Make love to me, Maggie. I want you to."

"But what if I do something . . . wrong . . . something you don't like?" The words gushed from her in a flurry of fear and self-consciousness.

Rush smiled tenderly. "I'll just try to tough it out."

Maggie looked at him as he lay there, an arm folded behind his head, imitating the pose he'd struck the day before at the pool. He was clad only in a pair of formfitting white tennis shorts that were as stimulating as his swimsuit had been. They delineated the long, firm length of his body just at his hipbones, obliterating the dark trail of fine, silky hair and encouraging further exploration. His tanned, hair-dusted legs were crossed at the ankle.

Tentatively, she leaned over him and placed her hand on his knee. He was so warm to her touch! Curiously, cautiously, her fingers trailed up over his hairy thigh. Rush's eyes drifted shut and his breath trickled from him in a long sigh.

This was easy, she thought, pressing her lips to the dimple in his chin and barely letting her tongue peek out from between her lips.

"Mmmmmm," he murmured in approval.

Maggie began to toy with ideas that might please him. What if she did to him what he did to her? So thinking, her lips left his chin and moved to his throat, while her fingers roamed through the hair on his chest in search of his flat, brown nipples. When she touched them they responded as hers did to his touch, becoming instantly hard. Hesitantly, she slid lower, causing her gown to ride higher up her thighs, and pressed her lips to one nipple before circling it with her tongue.

"Ahhh, Maggie!" Rush growled, shifting restlessly as one hand found her bare thigh.

Emboldened by his response, she raked her nails lightly down his muscle-corded ribs. "Do you like this?" she breathed.

"Do you?" he countered without opening his eyes.

"Oh, yes!" As if to prove her point, Maggie's fingers trailed through the path of hair that grew down Rush's stomach. He sucked in his breath, and her hand slid between the hard flesh of his abdomen and the fabric of his shorts. She realized with a dizzying clarity that he wore nothing beneath.

"Ah, dammit, Maggie!" he groaned, arching his hips into her touch.

A smile of pure witchery teased Maggie's mouth as she touched it lightly to his and spoke in a teasing, regretful tone against his lips. "Oh, you don't like this?"

She felt Rush's mouth curve upward against hers in a brief smile. "I'm not sure, but I think I just might be able to tolerate it. That is, if you don't stop—you know—give me time to get used to it."

Maggie giggled delightedly, never before having experienced the emotions coursing through her. She had never been the instigator of any lovemaking between her and Jarrell. Never been the explorer instead of the explored. She'd never known you could actually talk while making love, or that laughing and teasing were an accepted part of such an intimate act.

Her head lowered, and her mouth moved tantalizingly over his chest.

"Maggie . . . Maggie . . ."

Down, down over his belly her lips roamed, her tongue tracing whorls in the silky hair tickling her nose before delving into the deep indention of his navel.

"Mag . . . gie . . ."

She was enveloped with lethargy, her movements slow and deliberate, her mind barely able to think beyond the sound of Rush's voice as he encouraged her to unzip the tennis shorts . . . to touch him . . . like that . . . oh, yes . . . just like that. His words, like her thoughts, sounded thick, sluggish. The intensity of feeling ravaging her body left her weak and aching with a throbbing emptiness at the very core of her being that only Rush's total possession could fulfill.

"Rush, please," she begged softly, lifting, then lowering herself onto his body. She hadn't realized how stimulating it would be for her to do the touching, the kissing, the caressing. She hadn't known that once she had tasted intimacy, she would be so eager to partake of the entire repast.

Rush shook his head, rolling her over beneath him

with one deft movement while one hand worked to rid himself of the hindering shorts.

"No. Not yet." His voice was saturated with desire, low and husky. "I've waited almost thirty years for you, and dammit I'm going to do this right."

He raised up briefly, lifting the hem of the black gown to her waist, then lowering his hard, hot body between her legs to rest in the cradle of her femininity.

Maggie gasped and arched her back at the pure, sweet pleasure that pierced her. Dear God! If just the touch of his body against her felt this good, she would die, literally die, when he entered her.

His lips whispered across her shoulders, and his fingers slid the straps of the gown lower, lower, until it caught and hung on the pouting tips of her breasts. Rush's lips followed the gown's descent and when it stopped, so did they. He nuzzled the sheer, black fabric aside, then cupped his tongue around one aching nipple, drawing it into his mouth and bathing it with a gentle suckling. The flexing of his mouth caused her to thrust her bare hips upward against his blatant maleness, blindly seeking surcease of the sweet burning blazing inside her.

"Oh, Rush, please!" The plea, caught on a sob and torn from her heart, was rooted in the pain-pleasure threatening to tear her apart.

Rush looked down at her. Her eyes were closed and her head turned restlessly from side to side while her teeth punished her bottom lip.

"Look at me, Maggie," he rasped huskily, with the sudden realization that he, too, could wait no longer.

Her eyes, glazed with passion, met his. Rush lifted

her hips, positioned himself, and with a single, slow stroke, eased into the wet willingness of her body. The breath Rush must have been holding escaped in a soft hiss as he struggled to comprehend that the moment he'd waited for so long was finally at hand.

Maggie sucked in a quick breath and blinked rapidly, fighting back the tears threatening to start again. So many things tumbled through her mind . . . a fleeting guilt, a sort of sorrow, a sense of rising freedom and joy and, beyond that, on a more elemental level, how good it felt . . . how incredibly, wonderfully good . . .

For long moments they lay still, Rush buried in the warmth of her, his lips pressed against her temple while they both gathered themselves. Finally, slowly, it began, the barest movement of his hips. More of an awakening of motion, a stirring, than actual movement.

Then the emotion he saw in her eyes changed the stirring to a gentle thrust against her. Maggie, devouring his beautiful, masculine face and trying to memorize his facial features by the touch of her fingers, met the thrust with a parry of her own. Gradually . . . oh, so gradually . . . their movements increased in strength and frequency until they were both bathed in a fine film of perspiration.

Even when Maggie thought she had reached the outer limits of physical pleasure—simply could not take any more—her body still moved against Rush's, countermanding thought, countermanding the mind's and body's limitations. Their movements, punctuated by quickened breathing and sprinkled with murmured words of love, became faster, deeper, harder, as they raced toward fulfillment. Then, with her name on his lips, love in his eyes and peace in his heart, Rush drove into her with one last soul-shattering thrust that hurtled them to the edge of eternity.

And beyond.

Dawn brushed away the night, leaving the morning sky streaked with tattered wisps of pink and lavender clouds as the sun stretched its golden rays upward in search of a new day. Nassau awoke slowly, with the sounds of cars in the distance, the slide of a patio door across the way, the hushed murmur of the hotel maids as they arrived for another day of changing sheets and dusting.

Maggie stood on the balcony facing the sea, watching a solitary runner jog along the water's edge and hugging herself against some imaginary coldness. Something had roused her from her peaceful slumber beside Rush, filling her instantly with a sense of sorrow. A sense of finality.

They would go home today. Back to Boston, where she would once again pick up the threads of the life she'd woven for herself since the divorce. Where would Rush fit into that life? How would she fit into his? Would he even want her to? She couldn't pretend the weekend hadn't happened. Not when the very thought of his mouth against her willing flesh filled her with erotic yearnings and an eagerness for physical fulfillment she hadn't experienced in years.

Walking back to the opened French doors, Maggie peered into the semidarkened room. Rush was still sleeping. Her soft footfalls carried her to the bed, where he lay on his stomach, one arm relaxed at his side, the other resting on the pillow, almost cradling his face. The single sheet had slipped low, emphasizing the breadth of his back, the curve of his spine and the rounded swell of his buttocks, which were only partially covered.

She wanted to touch him. Wanted to crawl back into bed with him and recapture the night. Maggie watched the rise and fall of his even breathing, recalling the exquisite pleasure of his touch, the tender wooing of his mouth, the unsurpassed pleasure of his possession. With swift, deliberate movements, she lifted the black gown over her head and slipped into bed.

He stirred a little as her slight weight shifted the mattress. On her knees, Maggie feathered slow, moist kisses down his spine, her lips making a thorough inventory of each vertebra. She wasn't certain when she realized he was awake. She only knew that by the time she reached his lower back there was an almost tangible tension in the room. Her lips meandered lazily over the swell of his hip.

Rush's voice was thick with sleepy desire as he murmured softly, "I'll give you an hour to stop that."

Maggie's throaty laughter filled the room with its rich, velvety sound. Rush turned, twisting the sheet tightly across his lower body, straining the bounds of the cotton fabric. Her eyes dropped to the obvious evidence of his arousal, and her hand soon followed the path of her eyes. Her fingers stroked the hard maleness of him through the sheet, further abrading his rapidly dwindling restraint.

Rush's arms went around her as he growled his pleasure into her ear and tangled his hands through the dark cloud of her hair. Bringing her mouth to his in a slow, provocative kiss, his tongue slipped past her lips, leisurely exploring the warm moistness of her mouth. Maggie moaned and leaned into him, surrendering herself, at least for the moment, to whatever it was he offered.

His mouth curved warmly, lazily, sexily. "What a fantastic way to wake up on Valentine's Day."

A seductive smile arced Maggie's mouth, and her heavy-lidded eyes were filled with promises as her fingers moved the sheet aside and her mouth lowered hungrily to his.

With a low cry of passion, Rush rolled, pinning her to the mattress with one heavy leg, pressing the hard, hot length of him against her hip. His mouth captured her breast, his tongue coaxing the tumescent tip to pebble hardness, his hand making a thorough reconnaissance of her stomach and lower, his marauding fingers urging complete surrender. Hands stroked. Mouths fused. Two hearts beat as one. And when, only moments later, flesh joined to willing flesh, minds and souls fused into a single emotion.

Love.

Rush reveled in the physical mirroring of what his heart harbored.

Afraid, Maggie called it by another name.

Later . . . later . . . long after sunshine gilded the surface of the ocean, Rush raised himself up on one elbow and smiled down at her with an overflowing heart. She no longer looked like prim and proper Margaret Spencer. This woman, with her mouth swollen from their ravenous kisses, whose blue eyes were still hazy with desire and clouded by fatigue, whose boneless body, cradled within his embrace, radiated the scent of flowers and love—this Maggie—his Maggie— was all fiery passion, just as he'd known she would be.

Maggie's eyelids drooped, the violet circles beneath the sapphire eyes a testimony to the sleep-starved night. Rush brushed each blue-veined lid with his lips.

God, he loved her. And it was so hard not to say the words. He knew, though, that it was too soon, that it would take time for her to accustom herself to what they felt for one another before he brought up the subject of love and commitment. Her scars were too deep, her fears too great. In a moment governed by protective anger, Rush hoped he never met Jarrell Spencer.

"What happened, Maggie-Mine?"

The words, spoken as they were after a storm of lovemaking, should have held no meaning to Maggie. But somehow, after the night, with its melding of minds and bodies, she knew exactly what Rush's seemingly random comment alluded to.

She drew a deep, fortifying breath. "H . . . he . . . found someone else." Her voice held the emotional tone of one whose heart was no longer involved, but whose pride was. "Her name is Rita. She worked for Jarrell at the agency. She's beautiful, sexy and young. So very *young*. Only nine years older than Lacey."

With a sudden, frightening clarity, Rush understood her preoccupation with the age difference between them. He pulled her closer to him, his body curved around the rigidity of hers as if to shield her from any more hurt. He pressed his lips to her temple.

"Lacey is your daughter." The words were as much statement as question.

She nodded, her eyes still closed, her hands lifeless at her sides.

"Are there any other children?"

"No."

"And your divorce, and the reason for it, is why you're so worried about us."

Her blue eyes met his. "Yes."

"Maggie, age doesn't matter." His voice was low, husky and vibrant with sincerity. A sincerity that was echoed in his eyes.

"How can you say that!" she cried softly. "You're not quite thirty years old. I'm ten years older than you! Ten years!" She laughed, the sound weary and edged in bitterness. "And it's a known fact that men want younger women, not older ones."

"So how do you explain what happened between us last night and this morning?" he asked quietly.

"I don't know."

"Why did you make love with me?"

Maggie hesitated. "I needed you. Physically."

"I'm flattered," Rush said, his voice a subtle blend of sarcasm and pain. He wanted more from her. He wanted to hear that last night was special, that, like him, she'd never quite felt such a depth of emotion from a sexual encounter. He couldn't dismiss what was between them as she was trying so hard to do. But then, he knew and understood why she was trying so hard to forget. It was because of the insecurities left by her failed marriage.

He wanted her. Not just for an occasional weekend, but for always. In his bed. By his side. Just across the room. A smile away. He wanted her enough to use his love for her and the physical relationship they'd just begun to help replace her fears and insecurities. Love could change things, couldn't it? And if love couldn't, willpower could. There was nothing in his life that he hadn't received in the end if he'd stuck with a plan to get it.

"Last night did happen, whether you're ready for it

or not," he said, his voice soft, but firm. "And it wasn't something I went into lightly. I don't think you did either."

He pressed his lips to her forehead.

"We're playing by your rules, Maggie. So where do we go from here?"

Chapter Nine

From there, they went back to Boston.

As the silver, giant-winged 747 sliced through the night sky to cover the last miles of the flight, Maggie stared silently and thoughtfully out of the small, squat window to her right. Beside her, one leg loosely squared over the other, sat Rush, the open law book on his lap actively absorbing his interest, except for an occasional sweep of his eyes in her direction. Beneath the book, hidden from the inquisitive eyes of other passengers, two hands entwined in secret enchantment.

They had tried so hard not to touch since boarding the plane, as if they were seeking to give the relationship some perspective through distance, but no sooner were they airborne and settled in than Rush's hand had found hers. And hers had willingly been found. The armrest separating them had been shoved impatiently out of the way, and their bodies had melted into inevitable contact. But for all of the touching, all of the exchanged glances, quick and lingering, there remained an emotional aloofness, a determined restraint.

Where *did* they go from here?

Maggie didn't know now any more than she had earlier, when he'd asked the question as he'd held her love-sated and damp body in the silken bondage of his arms. She had no idea what she was feeling for him—or maybe she did, a secret corner of her heart responded, and just considered it best not to say it in words, or put the thought into concrete terms. She could allow herself to admit, however, that she had never felt the complete unity that she had felt when making love with Rush. It was a feeling, scary and wonderful, of losing yourself in someone else. It was as if her heart, her body, her mind, her soul had always—*always*—been preparing for him as a lover. She had felt sensations with him, subtleties of sexual satisfaction, nuances of kiss, caress and communion, that she'd never felt before.

So what was the problem?

Rush's thumb languidly, absently traveled the length of her thumb, then slowly trailed upward again. Maggie's attention shifted toward him. He was lost somewhere in the world of law, not even aware that he was making shadow sketches on her skin. It was a totally natural gesture, a completely comfortable gesture. A gesture that felt right.

And that was the problem, Maggie thought. It shouldn't feel this right with this man. This *young* man. Because the world—strangers, family, friends and her daughter—wouldn't see him as right. They'd see him only as young. Like the woman seated across the aisle, who'd tactlessly stared at her and Rush a dozen times since leaving Nassau.

A ping sounded, dragging Maggie's gaze from the curious woman to the fasten-seat-belt message above the cabin door. At the same time a stewardess's practiced, well-modulated voice came over the address system announcing their impending arrival at Logan Airport.

"We're home," Rush spoke softly.

"We're home," Maggie said in the same feather-light tone.

There was both sadness and happiness in the statement, both finality and hope. The same emotions were captured in blue and brown eyes. Slowly, with the hesitant reluctance of those forced against their will, their hands disengaged, and for a moment Maggie felt as if she'd been set adrift in a lonely world. Rush, too, seemed to be cruelly without anchor. Maggie reached for her purse; Rush closed his law book. Both readied themselves for arrival; neither seemed able to ready themselves for a good-bye.

"Your seat," Rush pointed out.

"What?"

"You have to return your seat to an upright position for landing."

"Oh," she acknowledged, depressing the button on the arm of her chair. Nothing happened. The seat remained in a resting position. She tried again. Still nothing.

"Here," Rush said as he leaned over her and, pushing in the button, jogged the seat. It whipped upright. And when it did, their faces were but mere inches apart. He didn't move; she didn't move; the world didn't move. His breath grew ragged and thin, while hers seemed suspended completely. Their eyes hazed and darkened, and both swallowed back sizable chunks of emotion. An expectancy weighted the moment.

"Thank you," she whispered. Her words focused his

attention on her lips, lips that only hours before had known him in every way a lover's can—had known him, teasingly tortured him, unselfishly pleasured him and had begged him to do the same to her.

"You're welcome," he whispered back as his mouth, of its own volition, eased toward hers. Suddenly, as if just remembering where they were, he stopped, drew in a harsh, forceful breath and pulled away from her.

She thanked him, she damned him, she said to him as teasingly as possible, "Why are men always so much more mechanical? With seat buttons, nuts and bolts, and screws and things?"

A smile stole to his lips, making them full and devilishly inviting. "You're talking to a man who once had a serious altercation with a manual can opener." The smile ebbed, then vanished, along with the one that had sprung to her lips. "Maggie . . ."

"Don't . . ." she broke in, her whole countenance pleading with him not to complicate matters any more than they already were.

The plane's sudden and jarring contact with the runway determined the outcome in Maggie's favor. With a deep sigh, Rush leaned back and waited for the plane to taxi its way to a stop.

Which it did in minutes.

Neither Maggie nor Rush spoke as they debarked from the plane or as they traveled the tubular jetway connecting it with the terminal. No words—only glances—were exchanged as they walked the long corridor to the baggage claim department. As they waited for their luggage, he helped her into her coat, then slipped his arms into his own. Minutes later, luggage in hand, they stepped out into the crisp Boston night. Frigid air, so different from what they'd left behind in Nassau, curled chilling tentacles about them, forcing puffs of white from their lungs and lending swiftness to their feet. Above them, millions of stars shimmered in white-hot radiance.

Rush looked about for a cab.

"Let's take two cabs," Maggie suggested, breaking their self-imposed silence and brushing back a froth of hair blown into her face by a cold gust of wind.

"I'll see you home," he negated, hailing a taxi that seemed to suddenly appear from nowhere.

"No," she said firmly.

He looked hesitant, as if he wanted to argue with her suggestion. Then, before he could speak, the cab pulled to the curb; the driver got out, mumbled a few words only a longtime Bostonian had any chance of interpreting, then grabbed up the luggage pointed out to him. As he stored it in the car's trunk, Rush opened the door to the backseat. Maggie had just started to ease in when the pressure of his hand on her upper arm stopped her. For a span of time that seemed to last forever, they stared at each other.

"I won't let this end," Rush said. "I'm determined to have you in my life. And, lady, you don't know anything about determination until you see it Barrington-style."

Monday morning came early.

By eight-thirty Maggie had risen to a breakfast of buttered toast and coffee, had dressed in a black and beige wool suit, and was busy at her desk in the gallery. Going over the Sutherland contract, she congratulated herself on the success of the weekend.

The weekend. Rush. Was he in class at this very moment? Was he taking his exam? Or was that later in the day? Funny, she hadn't asked the time of the exam; she wished now that she had, so that she could have gone through it with him if only in a long-distance manner. She wished . . .

When the phone rang her heart jumped into fast gear in a betrayal of every decision she'd made since waking. She'd told herself over and over that she hoped he didn't call her—that it would be better for both of them—but now, with the shrilling ring bouncing off the venerable walls, she found herself praying that it was his voice at the other end of the line.

It wasn't. It was April's. The two women laughed and talked the better part of fifteen minutes, Maggie jokingly promising to get even with April for telling Rush about her birthday. April remained adamantly unrepentant.

The rest of the day passed busily, but uneventfully. At least until four thirty-three in the afternoon. Then a delivery man bounded into the gallery and left a bouquet of perfectly petaled daisies in the hands of a startled Maggie. Staring down at the white, satinlike spikes radiating from amber-eyed, velvet centers, she asked a thousand silent questions, questions that a single note supplied with a thousand answers.

I want to see you. Call when my courting gestures have won you over. The card was signed simply, predictably: RUSH.

Maggie's first reaction was woefully inappropriate— she wanted to crush the flowers to her heart. She settled for putting them in water. That evening she carried the bouquet home under the curious glances of fellow commuters, and put it in a Lalique crystal vase on the bedside table. In a Lalique crystal vase near the phone on the bedside table. She wanted to pick up the phone and call him, and almost did, but in the end she told herself wanting something did not make it right. She needed time to sort through the maze of her mind.

She could not help, however, but hope that Rush would call her. He didn't, and it was with a disappointment that she readily acknowledged as illogical that she drifted off to a daisy-dreaming sleep.

Tuesday afternoon saw the arrival of a nosegay of sweet-smelling purple violets. Snuggled in among the heart-shaped leaves was a note with two words: *I'm waiting.* This time no signature revealed the identity of the sender, but then, none was necessary.

New England asters, pink and plump, sashayed in on Wednesday, accompanied by the now-smiling delivery man. He disappeared with the usual "Have a nice day," which Maggie acknowledged absently. Her attention was on the words scrawled across the white vellum card. *Still waiting.* That evening, with the flowers sending their subtle fragrance throughout the living room, she almost called Rush. Almost.

Thursday, in the middle of selling a three-thousand-dollar picture, lemon-yellow dahlias arrived with the note: *Ah, hell, Maggie, I'm being as charming as I can.* She felt the foundations of her resolve gently crumbling under the weight of Rush's persuasion.

Friday noon Maggie spent lecturing at the Institute of Contemporary Art on Boylston Street. As a guest speaker in the institute's "Art Sandwiched-In" program, she spoke before a group of art lovers who had paid a two-dollar fee to eat a brown-bag lunch during a discussion of the current exhibition. Afterward, she stayed for coffee and dessert, and it was almost two-thirty before she returned to the gallery. When she did she found Jerri Fitzgerald admiring the latest floral acquisition: a single, crimson-red rose.

"This just came," Jerri said as she finished placing the stem into a silver bud vase and arranging some greenery and cloud-white baby's breath with it. "I took the liberty of putting it in water for you."

"Thanks, Jerri, I appreciate it."

"There's the card," Jerri said gesturing with a casual nod of her head.

Maggie picked it up from the desk, inched it from its small envelope and read: *I'm going to send flowers until you call. No guilt intended (well, maybe a little), but I really can't afford this. I'm already reduced to peanut butter and tuna.* Maggie's lips twitched in response, and she would have given a month's salary to share the laughter she was feeling with the slightly crazy guy who'd been sending flowers all week. God, she missed him!

"There, how does that look?" Jerri asked, stepping back to admire her arranging skills.

"Beautiful. Thanks."

Jerri Fitzgerald's gray eyes held firmly with the sapphire blue of Maggie's . . . held until Maggie felt she owed the woman some explanation about the rose. In fact, her employee had been politely, if unnaturally, quiet about the weekly parade of flowers.

"The flowers . . ." Maggie unconsciously eased into her chair. "Rush Barrington sent them."

Maggie watched as the name went from unknown to known. "The man who bought the oriental etching?"

"Yes," Maggie answered. Here it comes, she thought. The first witnessed act of censure. Oh, it would be a subtle censure. It would begin with a look of surprise Jerri couldn't quite hide despite her supreme effort. Then would come the quick acceptance—the quick, false acceptance—that said "How nice," when what it really meant was "My, God, he isn't dry behind the ears yet!"

A flicker of surprise did flit across the woman's face, and Maggie cringed.

"I liked him," Jerri returned with a sincerity that could never be faked. "He has warm brown eyes." She smiled faintly, reminiscently. "Just like my husband." She turned, started to walk away, then turned back. "There's something real special about warm brown eyes, isn't there?"

Maggie could only nod, an action of agreement and thanks.

It was of warm brown eyes that Maggie thought minutes later as she dialed the number listed for M. R. Barrington. She told herself she was calling to put a stop to the spending Rush couldn't afford, but she knew she was lying to herself. She was calling because of the way warm brown eyes looked when laughing, when teasing, when making love.

She checked her watch. Three-oh-seven. She had no idea what time he got out of class. The phone rang and rang and with each ring disappointment coiled more tightly in Maggie's heart. Damn! she thought. He wasn't there! She promised herself she'd try later. She did. At three-fifteen, three-thirty, three forty-five and finally at four o'clock. She still got no answer.

She made herself wait until she got home to call again, but it was the first thing she did when she entered the condo. She dialed the number and took a deep, impatient breath.

Rush answered on the first ring. "Hello?"

She had waited all afternoon to hear his voice, and now that she had, her own fled as surely as a thief in the night, leaving silence the only communicator.

"Maggie," he breathed at last, his words laced with certainty and relief.

How had he known it was she? Easing to the edge of

the sofa, she told herself it didn't matter as long as he'd known.

"Hi," she breathed.

"Hi."

The cord of the phone coiled around a beige-tinted nail. Coiled. And coiled again. "I got your flowers. Thank you."

She could imagine his lips arcing into a smile. "You're welcome."

Another silence stretched between them.

"I've missed you," she said at last. It was serious, it was simple, it was more than she'd intended to say.

Rush answered with a drag of air into his lungs, followed by a moment's quiet. "I want to see you," he said with the same undisguised candor.

The cord tightened around Maggie's finger until it should have choked her flesh with pain. She was aware of nothing but the rapid beating of her heart.

"I'm working tonight and tomorrow, but what about Sunday afternoon?"

She nodded her head, then foolishly realized he couldn't see. "Sunday's fine."

"What about a movie?"

"Okay."

"Two o'clock?"

"Two o'clock."

"How about one o'clock?"

"One, then."

"Ten-thirty?"

They were both laughing.

"One o'clock," she said as firmly as a woman quivering like jelly could.

Another brief silence invaded the line before Rush added, "Then I'll see you at one Sunday."

"Yes . . . Sunday."

"Bye."

"Bye."

Each waited for the other to hang up, which Maggie finally did with a reluctance that weighted her hand. Standing, she hung her coat in the hall closet and moved mechanically toward the bedroom. Raking her hair back from her eyes, she wondered about the prudence of what she'd just done. She wondered why she hadn't remembered that his voice was so rich and full and so capable of sending ribbons of excitement scurrying through her. She wondered just how many lonely hours were left before one o'clock Sunday.

Rush laid the receiver back onto the cradle and glanced down at his hand. It was trembling. God in heaven, *it was trembling*. He sank into the softness of the unmade bed and allowed himself a full-chested sigh. He wanted to open the window and shout to every stranger below that Margaret Spencer, the woman he loved, had missed him, had called him. He wanted . . . What he really wanted, he thought on a mental groan, was to know how many damn hours he had to live through before one o'clock Sunday.

Chapter Ten

The doorbell pealed a full twenty minutes early.

The pleats of a turquoise and black wool skirt had just settled about Maggie's knees and she was fumbling, with fingers that shook noticeably, at the hook and eye at the skirt's waistband. At the strident buzz, her head jerked upward and her heart fell into a frenzied rhythm.

Oh, God, he's early! Oh, God, he's *here!* she thought as she padded on stocking feet toward the door. Once there, she groped a final time with the stubborn skirt fastener, then, finger-threading her hand through bouncy-clean hair, she pulled open the door.

She pulled open the door and feasted on the man before her . . . just as he seemed to be feasting on the sight of her. His eyes roved from the top of her dark hair to the unshod feet standing on the plush rug, while her eyes touched on his mussed hair, the heavy, fur-lined jacket sheltering shoulders straining the cable knit of a steel-gray pullover and the tight—the unmistakably, unforgettably tight—denim jeans encasing his long legs.

After a span of time just shy of awkward, she managed to say, "You're early."

A smile tilted the corners of his perfectly shaped mouth—dear heaven, it was perfect, wasn't it? she thought. "I could wait out here until straight-up-and-down one," he suggested with nothing even akin to seriousness.

Her mouth did what it did so naturally around him: it smiled. "That won't be necessary." She stepped backward and he followed her into the room, automatically removing his jacket as he did so and tossing it on a nearby chair. He then rammed both hands into the back pockets of his jeans.

His eyes were on her again, hungrily on her—a week's worth of hunger—and hers were equally devoted to him. Had it been only seven days since she'd seen him? she thought. Had it been only seven days since he'd held her? Kissed her? Made love to her?

"How . . . how did your exam go?" she asked, trying to change the direction of her single-tracked mind. She nervously, but unconsciously mimicked him by jamming her own hands into the side-slit pockets of her skirt.

"Which one?" he asked, dragging his eyes from the pure curve of breast filling out her black sweater. "I've had three this week."

"Monday's," she replied, forcing her eyes from the firm, taut fit of his pants and forcing her toes to uncurl in the carpet. "The one you took Monday."

"I aced it," he said so matter-of-factly that there wasn't the least bit of smugness in the announcement. It was as though he had gone into it allowing no less.

She smiled and moistened her cotton-dry lips. "I'm glad."

"Actually, it's a wonder I passed it at all." His eyes were once more sensually canvassing her face, as if he was having a hard time getting his fill of something long-denied him. "Considering all the other things I had on my mind."

"What . . . other things?" she asked in a soft voice, her heart thrumming at the time-honored man-woman game they were playing.

He gave his head one quick jerk. "Come here and I'll show you what other things." His eyes burned brightly into hers, compelling her, urging her, daring her.

But she needed no compelling beyond the lonely hours she'd already spent, no urging beyond the fact that he now stood before her, no daring beyond the sensations sparking her body. Closing the distance to him, she arched her neck to stare fully into his face. Without her shoes on, she had to angle her neck considerably.

"What other things?" she whispered again, in her own provocative challenge.

"Things like missing you, wanting you, waiting for you to call. Things like"—one hand eased from his pocket and captured her cheek—"touching you." His hand caressed her silky skin as his thumb made tiny movements near the curve of her parted lips. His eyes dropped there, then sauntered back to hers. "Things like memories of you and me and Nassau. Things like"—his head tilted and lowered—"kissing you."

His mouth closed over hers in a perfect union, flesh confronting flesh, warmth colliding with warmth, need clashing with need. He groaned a sound of pleasure-pain, pulled his other hand from his back pocket even as hers left their hideaways and drew her against him. His lips opened completely over hers, claiming them in sweet urgency, an urgency that swept her up in its velvet talons. Hands roamed, wandered over fabric and skin, plied through hair and reacquainted themselves with curves and angles and body points that mysteriously distinguish male from female. Both were greedy, both eager, both insatiable.

Both were supremely satisfied; both were supremely unsatisfied.

"Do you know how long a week can be?" he murmured as they drew apart in search of a sustaining breath.

"Yes," she admitted hoarsely. "Oh, yes." Her hands framed his face and pulled his mouth back to hers. She had dreamed too long and too hard of his kisses to settle for a single offering. As their lips joined again, Rush's tongue penetrated the sanctity of her mouth—penetrated, met her tongue and gently ravished in a love-dance that sent the emotions of both whirling and swirling.

"Oh, Maggie . . ." he whispered, pulling her close and resting his lips beneath her ear. "Oh, Maggie . . ." He held her tightly, fiercely, as if loosening his grip meant the slipping away of his very life-force.

Moments short, moments endless eddied by as two hearts beat wildly.

"Do you really want to go to the movie?" he breathed, his wide hand palming the crown of her head.

"No," she answered quickly, firmly. She pulled back and her eyes met his with total honesty. "No. I want to stay here and make love."

The moan he gave was eloquent approval, total agreement.

Minutes later the skirt that had rebelled against

fastening lay in a heap on the bedroom floor, alongside a black sweater, a gray sweater and ebony-colored undergarments with frilly filaments of lace. A pair of jeans lay sprawled at the foot of the bed, only inches away from a pair of hose turned wrong side out because of a hasty removal. A pair of tan briefs reposed in an attitude proclaiming love's silent victory.

In the bed, on sheets flowered in blue, breath mingled with breath, kiss with kiss, body with body. Maggie's knees flexed, allowing Rush to thrust boldly, deeply, but always tenderly, into the core of her femininity so vacant, so empty without his complementary maleness. Her hands rested on his dimpled, sweat-slicked buttocks, urging him in his rhythmic undulation. Her own hands were wet, wet with his perspiration, her passion.

"Being deep inside you is my only reality," he whispered, the words slurring from his mouth to hers as he kissed her over and over and over again.

"Having you deep inside is mine," she breathed back, draining his lips of each word, each kiss.

His mouth—nibbling, softly biting, tasting—trailed her neck, her shoulder, fastening at last on a dark nipple hard and hurting and begging for his touch.

She moaned, writhed, arched against the healing of his lips. "Oh, Rush, why does everything you do to me seem so right?"

"Because it is, Maggie-Mine. It is."

In blissful seconds right became perfection as dual cries bounded off quiet bedroom walls. In time bodies stilled, hearts slowed, lungs filled more easily with air. Passions were sated. For the present.

As Maggie lay lethargically snuggled in the enclosure of Rush's arms, her mind drifted in unison with his finger roving lazily up and down, down and up her body from shoulder to hip. It had been inevitable, she thought. Inevitable. Her week of clinging to sanity, to prudence, had been all in vain, for she now knew it was inevitable that she and Rush be lovers. It was what she wanted. It was what he wanted. And the years between their ages be damned. Though the future would demand a price—it always did—for now, for this moment, for tomorrow, for however long it lasted, she would allow herself this sweet indulgence. She would allow herself to bask in the sublime rightness of Rush Barrington.

They began to date. Scrimping and saving minutes and hours from two busy schedules, they shared their treasured time with each other. Each night of the following week they had dinner at Maggie's. They laughed about trivial, even foolish things; they talked of the same trivia, sometimes adding the element of seriousness, the seriousness of law dreams, the honesty of emotions following a divorce, the earnest admission of the pleasure they found in each other's company.

Since Rush had the weekend off at the escort agency —a rarity, but an occasional necessity for health and sanity—they spent that time together, too. Friday night found them at a movie, in the back row doing what could only be called necking.

Saturday night they heard Rachmaninoff brilliantly played by the Boston Symphony Orchestra, though the hand each held seemed far more interesting and stirring, far more arousing to lovers' starved senses. Sunday they spent with books: Rush, textbooks; Maggie, romance novels that paled by comparison with the honest-to-goodness romance unfolding in her life.

Throughout that week and the one that followed, the two made love. Everywhere. Anywhere. In the feather-softness of the bed, in the warm drizzle of the shower, before the crackling, red-orange embers of a winter fire. They even made love without touching. Sometimes when her eyes would merge with Rush's— across the room, the car, the table—something so powerful, so elementally sensual would pass between them Maggie could have easily sworn she had been physically caressed. The essence of Rush mated with the essence of Maggie. At these times she felt awed. At all times she felt alive . . . tearfully happy . . . unbelievably content.

And then on a Friday afternoon in the first week of March she felt unbearably miserable.

Humming a song, she dialed Rush's phone number, eased herself into her chair, and, wedging receiver between ear and shoulder, straightened a pile of order forms on her desk. At the back of the gallery, she could see Jerri hanging three new pictures—all with Rafael Brown's nearly illegible signature—on the wall. The hum ended mid note when a deep, masculine voice answered miles away.

"Hello?"

"I just had a great idea," she began with no preamble.

Rush laughed softly and with a seductiveness Maggie always inspired. "Hello to you, too."

"Hush, counselor, you're interfering with a great idea." Her own voice had grown a tad husky at his phone presence, and the pencil that suddenly appeared in her hand absently began to scribble the initials *RB* across a note pad.

"Sorry," he said, shoving aside paper and pen and book and settling back on the bed. "What is this great idea of yours?"

"There's this murder mystery on TV . . ."

"I didn't know you liked murder mysteries," he interrupted.

"I love murder mysteries."

"I thought you liked romance," he teased.

"I love romance, but man—pardon me, woman—cannot live by love alone."

"Wanna bet?" The sultriness of his tone did more than suggest she'd lose if she did.

"Rush . . . my great idea," she insisted as her heart pounded in a responding rhythm.

"Sorry."

"There's this murder mystery on TV at eight o'clock. What if I go by the deli and get cold cuts and you stop by the bakery and get those jelly doughnuts . . ."

"Tonight?" he again cut through her words. His voice suddenly sounded strained.

"Tonight," she concurred innocently. The silence that followed caused her hand to halt in the second loop of a *B*. "What's wrong with tonight?"

"Don't you remember, I'm working tonight? I have that escort assignment at eight."

She had forgotten. The shared weekend before had driven away unpleasant thoughts of ones spent apart. The pencil eased from her hand to rest diagonally across the small tablet. "I forgot," she said simply.

"I'm sorry," he said. When she made no response he added, "Maggie, I said I'm sorry."

She shrugged shoulders in a gesture that no one saw. "It's all right."

"It's not all right, but it has to be."

"I know."

"You know I'd rather be with you."

She said nothing. Instead she wondered why it should hurt so much that she wasn't going to see him for one evening. It was only one evening, she reminded herself. She frowned, knowing full well why it hurt so badly. It wasn't altogether that she wasn't going to see him, but that another woman was. She suddenly felt the crisp sting of possessiveness.

"Maggie? Tell me you know I'd rather be with you."

"Would you?" she asked, battling jealousy and dismally losing. Maybe the woman would be young and beautiful and . . .

"It's only a job," he said, reading her mind as thoroughly as he'd moments before been reading his law book. "It's what I'm paid to do. Those women mean nothing to me." He smiled slightly. "But I'm glad you're jealous."

"I'm not jealous," she lied.

"You're not? I would be of you."

"Well," she relented, "maybe I'm just a little jealous."

Time spun about them in silent, silken threads.

"Maggie," he whispered at last, "I lo . . ." The word trailed off, and she heard him sigh deeply, wearily before adding, "I'll call you when I get in tonight. Okay?"

She had a feeling that he hadn't said what he'd wanted to say, but she answered, "Okay. I'll wait up for you."

After she hung up she sat staring at the phone. Her chest suddenly seemed far too small for her lungs, as if they couldn't expand to get the air they needed. She remembered thinking that yesterday's happiness would exact a price and couldn't help but wonder if she'd already begun to pay the bill.

"One, two . . . three, four," Maggie puffed as she bent at the waist to touch right hand to left foot, straightened and bent again to touch left hand to right foot. The woman beside her, who was red-faced and long tired of exercising, struggled to keep up.

"Are you sure this is good for you?" April Newbern asked. She stopped in midbend to tug the elastic of her leotards back over the curve of her buttocks. She was wearing hot pink and a skeptical look.

"It's good for you," Maggie answered, never slackening her pace. Well-honed muscles moved beneath white tights, while black and white polka-dot leotards stretched in a measured rhythm. Black leg-warmers cuddled at her ankles, and a white terry band kept hair and perspiration from her brow. She was relentless in the task before her.

April, sensing her friend's determination, sighed, shook her head in resignation and resumed the grueling activity that promised her fitness . . . if she didn't die first.

"One, two . . . three, four," Maggie chanted over and over into her quiet living room.

The TV sat silent following the gory murder mystery, and the crusts of two corned beef sandwiches lay hardening on plates abandoned on the coffee table. When April had called minutes after the upsetting conversation with Rush, Maggie had been thrilled—after all, misery loves company—to hear the same monotone of unhappiness in her friend's voice. It seemed both their men were tied up, Rush on the agency assignment, Sam Larson on out-of-town business. It was only natural that the two suffering women should spend the Friday night commiserating.

"You're slowing down," Maggie accused in a tone peculiar to drill sergeants.

"I'm dying," April wheezed.

Another one minute, five seconds passed before April collapsed onto the floor, holding her side with both hands and gasping for breath. "I . . . I quit. There is . . . no way . . . I'll do another . . ." She never defined what she wouldn't do another of. Instead she lay moaning and groaning and clutching at various aching body parts.

"Quitter," Maggie taunted.

"Yeah, well, I'll live to go to your funeral."

Finally, after taking several solid breaths of air into her lungs, April rolled to her side and propped herself on an elbow. Her free hand scooped up a fistful of diet-be-damned peanuts and plopped them into her mouth. She watched her friend.

"How many of those things are you going to do?" she asked after a while. Her voice had grown noticeably more serious.

"As many as it takes," Maggie answered, her breath now reedy with overexertion.

"As many as it takes to what? Forget Rush is with another woman?"

Maggie threw her friend a barbed glance. "Yes," she answered truthfully.

"For criminy's sake, Mags," April said, pushing to a sitting position while she pushed kinky blond hair from her eyes, "it's business. It's not as if he's doing it for fun. It's purely for the money."

"Don't you dare assail me with logic," Maggie countered, hurling another look in April's direction. "How would you like it if Sam were with a woman right now . . . on business, of course?"

The blonde bundle of energy thought a moment. "I wouldn't like it a damned bit, but then"—she stretched for another handful of peanuts, watching Maggie carefully as she did so—"I'm in love with Sam Larson."

"Yeah, well, I'm in love with Ru . . ." The words, uttered in such natural innocence, brought Maggie to a stop somewhere in midstretch, at a place where nose met knee. Her mouth open, her eyes wide, she straightened and glanced at her friend. Her friend was looking studiously at her.

Slowly, April smiled, the kind of smile that spells amused, the kind of smile that spells caught-you. "You really didn't know, did you?" The smile turned to soft laughter. "Oh, Mags, you're priceless. You're the only one who doesn't know you're in love with the guy . . . except maybe the guy himself." She gave her friend a contemplative look. "Yeah, I'm certain he doesn't know you're in love with him. He has the same dumb look you have."

Grabbing a towel, with which she dabbed at the tearlike beads of perspiration dotting her forehead, Maggie eased to the floor. "Oh, April . . ." she whispered, her blue eyes bright with bewilderment. "I never meant this to happen."

"Why not? What's so bad about being in love? It's not as if it's unrequited. Rush is in love with you."

Maggie's eyes widened even further, and her heart actually skydived at the possibility. "He is?"

April shook her head in disbelief. "You are blind, aren't you? No, he's not in love with you," she teased. "He just breathes at half capacity when you're a-round because of atmospheric conditions." She patted Maggie's hand as one would that of a slow-witted dolt. "Of course he's in love with you."

Rush in love with her! Maggie passed the towel over her forehead and finally draped it about her neck. He'd never said he was. But then, from the total way he made love to her, she could almost believe it true. Oh, God, did she want it to be true? The answer came quickly. An unequivocal yes. What woman didn't want the man she loved to return that tender feeling? And she did love him. As impractical as that was, she did love him. She now clearly saw that . . . as clearly as she saw the new problems that it brought.

Sighing, she asked April and the keeper of the wisdom of the universe, "Why is everything always so difficult?"

"What's difficult? The situation seems simple to me. You're in love. The man loves you."

Maggie's shoulders slumped as if under some unseen weight. "We're not exactly your average couple."

"What's average?"

Two pairs of eyes met. "You know what I mean."

"I think you're making a lot more out of this age thing than it deserves. I think . . ."

April's words were cut short by the sound of a key fumbling at the door. Both women glanced toward the rattling sound, then at each other.

"Are you expecting anyone?" April whispered.

"No," Maggie whispered back.

There was a moment of panic before the door opened and Rush stepped in. His eyes immediately moved to the two women sitting on the floor.

"Hi," he said, closing the door and pocketing the key in navy wool slacks.

"Barrington, you just took a couple of years off my life," April teased as she reached for her tennis shoes and slid her feet into them. "How did the assignment go?" she asked, suddenly becoming the good business-woman she was.

"Fine. The client just wanted to make an appearance at a reception." His eyes shifted to Maggie. "Hi," he said especially to her.

The brief moment of uncertainty as to who was at the door had left Maggie's heart pounding. That pounding became a deafening throb at the sound and sight of the man now moving across the room toward her. Suddenly her mouth went dry, her head spun, her palms grew moist. She was in love with Rush!

"You said you were going to call," Maggie heard herself say.

"When I 'reach out to touch someone,'" he said, his lips dipping to hers, "I like to reach out and touch someone." He pulled to mere inches away, found her eyes with his, then kissed her once more. "That sure as hell beats the telephone." When he straightened, he removed his suit jacket, tossed it on the sofa and unfastened his tie and two shirt buttons. "What did I do? Interrupt a hen party?"

"Not at all," April answered, coming to her feet. "We had an orgy. The guys just left."

Maggie came to her feet as well, and her waist was immediately encircled by Rush's arm. He hauled her close . . . which was exactly where she wanted to be. "She better be kidding," he said, his eyes finding hers.

"She's kidding," Maggie answered with a smile as she slipped her arm about his waist.

"Well," April said, starting for the door, "I can see what they say is true. Three is a crowd."

"Don't go," Rush and Maggie said together.

"There's an embarrassing lack of conviction in your voices," April teased, then added, "I've got to go. Or, as we say in Texas, I gotta mosey. Maybe I'll get lucky and Sam will call."

"When is he coming back?" Maggie asked, following her friend to the door after reluctantly tearing herself away from Rush. He had just as reluctantly released her.

"Tomorrow." They were both standing with the door open and April half out it. Both smiled.

"Thanks for the company," Maggie said.

"Thank you." The smile inched away. "Simple, Mags. Don't complicate what's simple." And then she was gone, leaving Maggie with the man she loved . . . and a thousand doubts.

She turned and, leaning against the closed door, stared across the room. Rush crouched before the fire, banking the dying embers in a way that was homey and comfortably familiar. His shoulder muscles rippled with the activity he was performing, and he swayed slightly on the balls of his feet, causing thigh muscles to shift beneath pants fabric in a way that could be distracting to a woman. It was to Maggie.

Standing, Rush put the poker back in its rack and turned. It was then he saw her watching him. For timeless moments each absorbed the sight of the other. Wordlessly, she pushed from the door and started toward him. Wordlessly, he watched her approach. Closer. Closer. Ever closer, until she stood directly before him. Then, in a lover's silence, she slipped into his waiting arms, and his lips took possession of her willing mouth.

The kiss was gentle, tenderly given, tenderly taken, yet for all of its silken subtlety, it was arousing. Ribbons of warm desire spiraled as lips opened and meshed, as tongues touched and taunted, as arms held and curled closely.

"I missed you," he whispered, his breath a vapory mist against her mouth.

"I missed you," she whispered back. She tilted her head to allow his sweetly marauding lips to trail along her throat, then eased her head backward in a slow, sensuous, exposing movement as those same lips found the vulnerable hollow of her throat. Her eyes closed, finger roving lazily up and down, down and up her body she expelled a slow, ragged breath. Nuzzling aside the towel still draped at her neck, he kissed shoulder, collarbone, collarbone, shoulder.

"You taste salty," he said, his words husky and blurred.

"I need a shower," she said, fighting to give voice to her thoughts.

"Un-uh. I forbid it. You taste sexy . . . and like a woman."

"How does a woman taste?"

"Like you," he said, again taking her mouth with his. His hands roamed over her body, the thrusting swell of her breasts, the trim firm derriere tucked into leotards. When he pulled away from her he was smiling. "What in the hell are you wearing?"

Her lips twitched. "My exercise outfit. You don't like it?"

"Oh, yeah, I like it." This he said as his palms once more skimmed her thinly concealed breasts and to his and her pleasure, the nipples beaded in a sensual response. "I like it a whole bunch."

Lacing her hands about his neck, she asked flirtatiously, "Yeah?"

"Oh, yeah."

.He smiled, she smiled, smiles that slowly died away. Both swallowed low in their throats.

"Spend the night," she pleaded softly. "Wake beside me in the morning."

They had shared many hours of loving, but because of tight schedules they had not shared an entire night as lovers since Nassau, never watched the sun glimmer over their bodies in the molten glow of a Boston dawn. In that moment, standing emotionally naked before him, waking with him at her side suddenly seemed the most important thing in the world.

"Please," she begged.

His kiss was his answer.

Naked. They stood before the bed, in the lamp's gilded glow, naked. Her leotard had been traded for a wine-colored shirt, tights had been exchanged for navy wool pants, leg-warmers bartered for shoes, and masculine briefs bargained for their lacy, feminine counterpart. Love looks and tender touches had been tossed in for free.

His eyes on hers, her hand in his, he eased a knee to the bed and tugged her down with him. The bed's softness captured them even as his lips moved to capture hers.

"No," she begged softly, stopping the advancing kiss with fingers placed gently across his lips. "Let me make love to you." *Let me show you how much I love you.*

He studied her, watched the dark, intangible something sweeping across sapphire-blue irises, then slowly released his hold on her. He lay back, snuggling into the pillow, and raised one arm to curve about his head, while the other reposed at his side. One knee flexed outward in an invitation that mercilessly stole Maggie's breath.

"Love me," he whispered.

Her eyes caressed him with the warmth of the emotion swelling her heart, caressed, touched, brushed every cell of his body, from the dark hair tousled about his head to his toes lying tanned and masculine against her flowered sheet. God, he was beautiful . . . perfect . . . and so sensual he made her ache with a delicious pain. With a hesitant reverence, her fingertips reached out to rub against the softness of his full lower lip, then slid lower to plunge seductively into the cleft of his chin. The same hand transferred its attention to the arm flung casually toward the bed's headboard. She traced his forearm, moved the length of his biceps, then trailed her finger through the hair under his arm, trailed lower and lower until the hair became wiry curls sprigging his chest in a dark, thick matting. Then lower still, until the hair changed coarseness, just as his breathing changed to an irregular pant that seemed forced from his throat. But he made no move, flinched not a muscle, made no attempt to dictate the moment. Even when she slipped between his parted legs, even when she slid up his body in the wake of summer-warm kisses, even when her lips found the sweet sanctuary of his.

"Oh, Rush . . ." she moaned, her own control slipping to the brink of madness. "Oh, Rush . . . love me."

In one swift, purposeful movement, he rolled her to her back, joined them as one and, with a maddening motion, drove them higher and higher, faster and faster, toward love's golden reward. Both gasped, then groaned at the zenith of their passion. Maggie also cried. Cried because their loving had been so flawlessly perfect.

"It was different," Rush said quietly a long time later.

The woman in his arms stirred and raised her chin until her eyes, now dry from repeated kisses, found his.

"Our loving was different," he said in answer to the silent query he saw etched on her face. "You gave me a part of yourself you've never given me before. I know I didn't imagine it." His eyes questioned her in the same wordless way she had just questioned him.

Her finger inched upward and strolled across his lips; those lips planted a tiny kiss on the sweet invader. "No, you didn't imagine it," she admitted, but could go no further because of the sudden lump in her throat.

Slowly levering his weight to an elbow, he stared down at her with eyes both caring and compelling. "What, Maggie? What made the difference?"

She wanted to tell him. She didn't want to tell him. She wanted to hear the same confession from his soul, yet she didn't, for it would hurl the relationship into a new, different and more difficult sphere.

"Maggie?"

"I . . . I made a startling discovery tonight." She gave a fleeting, self-conscious smile. "At least it was startling to me."

He waited, but when she said nothing, he brushed a strand of hair back from her forehead and said, "And what was this startling discovery?"

She felt precariously poised in the middle of a rickety, swaying rope bridge with danger on each side—the danger of denial, the danger of admission.

"I . . . I'm in love with you."

Time slowed to the pace of lovers' heartbeats and the only sound alive in the room was the drugging ticktock of the bedside clock. Maggie, her breath held, watched as a million emotions flashed across his face, none of which she could read except the initial and eye-widening surprise. He said nothing; he did nothing. His own breathing seemed labored and lost. And then he lowered his head, leaving Maggie to stare at his dark crown of hair.

A million shafts of pain pierced her heart. He didn't love her. And her admission had embarrassed and saddened him. She reached out to touch his head—for her solace or his, she didn't know—but pulled her hand back without doing so.

"It's all right," she consoled. "I don't expect you to love me."

He raised his head, and eyes as dewy as springtime grass met hers. "Do you have any idea how long I've waited to hear you say that?" His voice was so husky she had to strain to hear it. "Sometimes I thought I'd never hear it."

Her own eyes were growing moist at the same rate that her heart was soaring with hope.

"Rush?"

"I love you, Maggie. I think I must have loved you from the first moment I saw you." He smiled faintly. "From the first moment you wanted to kick me out of here for being too young."

Her lips tried a feeble smile. "I don't think I really wanted to kick you out."

"That's not how I remember it."

Smiles widened and ebbed, giving lips the chance to merge in a new and wondrous possession.

"Marry me," he breathed against her parted mouth.

The sweet command splintered her heart with pain. How could she make him understand? How could she tell him that, ironically, loving him negated marriage because she couldn't tie him to a future he might one day regret? How could she tell him that she had to leave him free to walk away from her?

"No," she breathed back.

He pulled from her, his eyes probing hers for an explanation.

"I'll have an affair with you until the end of forever, but"—she swallowed—"I won't marry you."

"Why?" The one word spoke eloquently of his confusion.

"Because," she answered, her palm finding the side of his cheek, "I love you too much."

Chapter Eleven

$\mathscr{M}$arch was almost over when Maggie agreed to leave the gallery in Jerri's capable hands and spend the afternoon with Rush. He'd teasingly promised to show her his world and wanted her to meet some of his Trivial Pursuit buddies. Reluctantly agreeing, Maggie took the Red Line of the T to the Brattle/Harvard stop in Cambridge, where Rush had promised to meet her.

What would his friends think of their May–December romance? While it was true that her acquaintances hadn't been shocked at their relationship, Maggie wasn't certain they counted. Very little shocked April, who proudly considered herself the perpetrator of the entire scheme. And Jerri . . . well, Jerri was so nice, she would never give a clue if her sensibilities were offended. Besides, Jerri was a sucker for warm brown eyes, too.

But then, it really didn't matter how the world reacted, Maggie thought. What mattered was her daughter. A daughter she'd always been close to. A daughter whose love she didn't want to jeopardize.

She sighed, wondering just what Lacey would think of Rush. Would she be resentful that her mother was seeing someone? Would she think Maggie was foolish for falling for someone ten years younger than she was? Or would she, like Jerri, fall for the warmth of Rush's brown eyes? Or like April, fall for his obvious physical beauty? Maggie felt like gnashing her teeth and pulling out her hair. Life had been much simpler before the Newbern Agency had sent Rush Barrington into her life. But then, it had also been much more dull.

Thinking of him reminded her of just how much she really did want to see him. She was worried about him.

Weekends he now spent at her apartment—when he wasn't working at the law offices or escorting for April. If Maggie thought he looked tired before the trip to Nassau, it was nothing to what he looked like now. Only when he woke up in her bed and in her arms after a night of loving did there seem to be a measure of peace and relaxation on his face. When she'd mentioned his fatigue to him it only served to launch another of what she referred to as his attacks on her defenses as he tried to get her to agree to marry him.

The arguments, if they could be called that, always ran along the line of the one two weeks ago, when she had declined Rush's invitation to share his life in marriage.

"What do you mean, you love me too much?" he'd demanded. "How can you say you'll have an affair with me forever, but you won't marry me? It just doesn't make sense."

Maggie, who had never seen any sign of temper from Rush, and who was trying hard to keep from flinging herself at him and telling him she would be his wife, swallowed and said gently, "Rush, what you think you feel for me might die in two months . . . or six months. Can't we just enjoy what we have until that time, then go our separate ways with no regrets?"

Rush swore soundly and planted his hands on his lean hips, his head shaking in a bewildered, negative motion. "What I 'think' I feel for you? Good God, Maggie! I'm almost thirty years old and a pretty good judge of my own feelings. I don't *think* I love you. Dammit, I *know* I do! And it isn't going to go away in six months or six years. And regrets? What I regret the most right now is that Jarrell Spencer did such a job on you."

As he stood glaring down at her, flinging the reminder of just how insecure she had felt because of Jarrell's rejection until he, Rush, came into her life, Maggie's eyes flooded with moisture.

The sight of her struggling with incipient tears melted his anger and left him with a hollow feeling instead. It was a feeling he was on intimate terms with these days. He wondered why he'd longed for and waited for love so desperately all his life. The songwriters were right. Love hurt.

His hands left his hips and cupped her shoulders, drawing her against his chest.

"I love you. You're far too special to tuck away in a back corner like some casual affair. What I feel for you isn't the least bit casual. You're the woman I've looked for all my life. The woman I want to go to bed with every night, and wake beside every morning. You're the woman I want to have my children. For all intents and purposes, Maggie-Mine, you are my wife . . . my wife . . . my wife . . ."

Someone jostled Maggie, bringing her back to the present and the fact that people were disembarking from the subway in the usual Boston hurry. She straightened the shoulder strap of her purse and hoped Rush was waiting for her. As she stood, the image of a miniature Rush Barrington scampered through her mind and softened her lips into a smile. There had been conviction in his voice when he'd said he loved her and wanted her to have his child. Good Lord! She certainly wasn't getting all sentimental and thinking of the possibility of having another baby! Was she? Her anxiety turned to annoyance. Damn Rush Barrington for planting such thoughts! And he'd darn well better be waiting for her, or she'd catch the T right back home!

She needn't have worried. Rush was waiting for her, his mouth warm and hungry, his arms hard and possessive as he held her close, his dark eyes drinking his fill of her. Her wind-ripened cheeks glowed; the cold breeze played tug-of-war with feathery wisps of her hair, snatching at her joyous laughter and bringing a glimmer of moisture to her jewel-bright eyes. Rush's breath caught in his throat at the surge of emotion that the sight of her always brought. He smiled down at her.

"Ready?"

Maggie's eyes glittered up at him, her fears and annoyance disappearing with the same speed of the subway passengers who were rapidly scattering toward their various destinations. "Yes! Where are we going?"

"We're meeting Mike and Larry at the Blue Parrot."

"Wonderful!" Maggie said. "I've never been there."

"You're gonna love it!" Rush promised, taking her

hand in his and starting off at a brisk pace toward the waiting Monte Carlo.

And she did.

Maggie and Rush entered the welcome warmth of the Blue Parrot after a walk across the Harvard campus. The airy restaurant and coffee house, located on Mount Auburn Street, was one of more than a dozen such establishments that catered to the Harvard and Radcliffe students.

Maggie caught sight of a group of preppies laughing over a pitcher of sangria. A beautiful Oriental girl pored over a thick book, absently tucking back a swathe of obsidian-colored hair gleaming with the reflected colors of the overhead Tiffany-style lamp. Two turbaned Indian men sat watching the people come and go from their vantage point near one of the two large windows. The people, all pursuing different interests, lent a certain relaxed, no-pressure ambience to the room.

Maggie, following Rush to an unoccupied table near the windows, had expected to see a boisterous crowd of young people. She was pleasantly surprised to find such an eclectic gathering of humanity under one roof.

"You look happy," Rush said, seating himself opposite her.

Her eyes smiled into his, loving everything about him, everything that made him who and what he was. Just loving him.

"I like your world."

"I'm glad."

"And I'm glad I came."

"So am I, though I can think of things I'd rather be doing, things that definitely do not include Mike and Larry."

Maggie propped her elbows on the tabletop and cupped her cheeks in the slender palms of her hands, her wine-colored fingertips framing the lustrous blue of her eyes. She was just succumbing to the sensation of drowning in his warm gaze when someone rapped sharply on the window beside them.

Startled, her head turned and she saw a vivacious cheerleader-type with her nose pressed against the glass, smiling widely at Rush. She wore a bulky, cable-knit sweater of an aqua tint that contrasted nicely with the cascade of bouncy copper-colored curls brushing her shoulders. The sweater was paired with gray wool slacks tucked into gray suede boots. The entire ensemble was topped by a heavy quilted coat that hung casually open, revealing the fact that the girl was stacked, as they had phrased it when Maggie was in school. She was incredibly beautiful, Maggie thought. She was also young.

Rush smiled and waved. "Carrie Upshaw," he offered. "She works for the law firm on the weekends, too."

"Oh?"

Rush looked at the woman sitting across from him, hearing the new coolness in her tone. His eyes frosted over the merest bit as he warned in a low tone, "Lady, if you don't want to have your backside warmed in a public place, I wouldn't even *think* what you're about to say."

Maggie's chin lifted a fraction.

"Yes," Rush confirmed. "She's lovely. Yes, she's younger than you. Yes, she's made a play for me . . . on several occasions. No, I have never taken her out, nor do I want to. My taste runs to older, more sophisticated women, not gauche young things barely out of their teens. Good Lord! Carrie still smells like baby powder."

Maggie realized what she was doing, realized the futility of it. She was actually looking for wedges to drive between herself and Rush. She'd fought the attraction from the very beginning. Fought and lost. She'd fought and lost having an affair with him. She'd fought and lost loving him. Now she was fighting his pleas for them to marry. And all, she told herself, for the same reason.

She was afraid. Afraid of the age difference, afraid of failure.

Failure.

Even after two years the word *divorce* left a bad taste in her mouth. She was scared to death to even contemplate marriage again . . . with anyone. She was scared to death it wouldn't work again. And the age gap between her and Rush just seemed to be a strike against them.

Now he said he wanted children. It seemed like every time she thought she was adjusting to the rules, Rush threw her a curve. And her batting average wasn't the greatest in the world. Could she give him a healthy baby? And if she couldn't . . . or wouldn't . . .

Strike two.

Three strikes, you're out.

"Maggie . . ."

She jumped, startled at the sound of Rush's voice. Her troubled eyes found his. He stretched his arm across the table and lay his hand palm upward in a gesture that seemed to say, "Trust me. It's going to be all right."

Maggie untwisted the fingers of her clasped hands and slowly raised one, allowing it to rest in the large hand extended toward her. Rush's fingers closed firmly around hers. His dark eyes, the color of the coffee the waitress was just setting before them, held her own blue gaze, and her heart.

"I love you."

She knew he meant it; suddenly she vowed to stop trying to tear what they had apart. She'd love him back, and they would just wait and see. Rush wouldn't push. Whatever happened would just happen.

"I didn't think they'd ever leave!" Rush declared some six hours later, and a bare thirty minutes after he'd closed the door to Maggie's condo behind Mike and Larry. He raised his gaze from the massive law book in his lap, closed the book with a slap and set it on the glass-topped table in front of the sofa.

Maggie, who sat curled up in the opposite corner of the couch reading a historical romance, looked up in surprise at the outburst that came hard on the heels of a lengthy silence. She'd known something was the matter from the strained atmosphere between her and Rush ever since his friends had gone. And from the outrageous flirting both Mike and Larry had indulged in, she also had a sneaking suspicion what it was. She rested her elbow on the fat arm of the floral-patterned sofa and pressed the knuckles of her hand tightly against her lips to stifle a threatening smile.

"Well, hell, I just thought I'd introduce you to them, we'd have some coffee, say good-bye and everyone would go their merry way. But no! You're having such a good time, you invite them over to your place for soup, sandwiches and a movie!"

Maggie struggled to control a giggle. "Why, counselor! If I didn't know better, I'd think you were jealous."

"I'm not jealous, dammit!" he shouted.

"Well, mad then."

"I'm not mad!"

"Then why are you yelling?"

"I'm not . . ." he began loudly, the tone of his voice lowering several decibels and the sentence trailing off, ". . . yelling." A sheepish grin curved his mouth. "I was yelling."

"It sounded like it to me."

Rush began an agitated pacing of the living room. "Well, Mike kept touching you all evening. And Larry!" Rush paused and placed his hands on his lean hips, snorting in disbelief. "He fawned over you like some lovesick teenager."

"'Fawned'?" Maggie asked with raised eyebrows. "'Fawned'? Have you been reading my romance books? That word is straight out of the nineteenth century."

A wide smile slashed his features. He was beginning to feel extremely foolish. "I'm acting crazy, aren't I?"

Maggie raised the book and said, "As Belinda would say, 'You're making a rogue's royal ass out of yourself.'"

"Belinda?"

"The heroine."

"Ahhh," Rush nodded, sitting down beside her. "Is it good?"

"Jessica Jerome is always good." Maggie placed her hand over her heart. "Her love scenes are ab-so-lute-ly divine."

"'Ab-so-lute-ly divine'?" Rush repeated, a wicked gleam in his eyes as he reached for the book.

"Rush!"

Unheeding of her protestations, he snatched the paperback from her and flipped through several pages. "Oh-ho!" he chortled. "What's this?"

He cleared his throat and began to read. "'Ryder's strong, tanned hands pinned Belinda's wrists to the feather mattress. He straddled her, his firm buttocks'" —he frowned slightly—"'resting . . . on the most . . . feminine . . . part of her?'" Rush's eyes, alight with mirth, met Maggie's as his tone transposed the sentence from a statement to a question. "The most feminine part of her?" he repeated.

Maggie grinned and nodded. "Romance has its own language. Readers want the act of love to be beautiful."

"It is beautiful," Rush said, adding huskily, "especially with you."

Their eyes locked—sapphire blue with darkest chocolate. The mood in the room changed from lightly teasing to electrically sensual in a matter of a few words. Rush put the paperback book on top of his law book, pulled Maggie on top of him and stretched out on the sofa, his body blanketed by her slight weight. His fingers began to pull on one end of the green silk bow at her neck.

"What are you doing?" she asked breathlessly.

Rush smiled lazily, caught both ends of the now untied bow and tugged, bringing her face close to his.

"We're going to create a love scene that will put Jessica Jerome to shame," he told her throatily. "You start."

Maggie saw the teasing gleam in his eyes, which was negated somewhat by the thread of seriousness in his voice. She began to speak, matching her actions to the words. "Maggie's fingers traced the arrogant sweep of one dark brow, then she trailed her fingertips down over the whisker-stubbled line of Rush's jaw. Her mouth hovered above his . . ."

Rush grinned a naughty grin, then broke in, continuing their game. "Unable to wait, Rush threaded his fingers through the silky texture of Maggie's hair and pulled her toward his waiting lips."

Silence permeated the room as the storytellers kissed. The fire crackled and hissed in the grate. Two pairs of hands fumbled with buttons. Maggie's fingers pushed aside the cotton fabric of his shirt, her nails skimming lightly over the crisply textured hair covering his chest. Rush moaned.

Breathing stopped as his tongue made a sensuous, thorough investigation of the warm cavern of Maggie's mouth. When the kiss broke off she gasped for air and rested her forehead against his chin, her hair a soft caress against his face.

Warm fingers dipped into the lace-and-satin bodice of the camisole she wore in lieu of a bra. Maggie half lifted herself, giving him freer access to the aching heaviness of her breasts. She sighed. Rush's voice was husky with emotion as he said softly, "Rush eased aside the fabric covering her breasts. They were perfect . . . beautiful. As soft as velvet to his touch." His eyes met Maggie's. "Rush looked into her vivid blue eyes and said, 'I love you, Maggie. Marry me. Be my wife. Have my babies.'"

"Rush . . ." Her voice held a tone almost of warning.

"This is the way I'd write my love scene," he said seriously. "How does the heroine answer?"

Maggie leaned forward, letting her breasts overflow the cup of his hands and pressing her lips to his, once, twice, three times. Her breath was a soft cloud against his cheek. "She says she loves him, too. So very much. Perhaps too much."

"You can't love too much."

"No?"

Rush's mouth planted tiny kisses against the side of her throat. "No. And her answer? Will Maggie marry Rush?"

Maggie collapsed against him, and his arms closed tightly around her. The hair of his chest felt deliciously erotic pressed to her bare breasts. She spoke into the hollow at the base of his throat, acutely aware that they both knew the game had progressed from fantasy to reality. Still, she played her role. "Part of her wants to. Most of her wants to. But part of her is afraid."

"Of what?"

"Afraid that when she's a graying fifty, Rush will be a handsome forty. That younger women will start to look better to him than she does."

Rush shifted so that they lay on their sides, Maggie sandwiched between his body and the back of the floral-print sofa. "That will never happen."

She rested her thumb in the cleft of his chin and traced the sensuous curve of his mouth, her eyes clinging to the love in his. "How can Rush be so sure?"

Suddenly Rush forgot his role, or simply tired of playing. "Because you're everything that I've always dreamed of having in a woman." His hand rubbed up and down her silk-covered arm. "Say you'll marry me."

Maggie's eyes met his. "You're moving too fast! First you talk of marriage. Then you talk of babies."

Rush smiled. "I wasn't, but let's. Have my baby, Maggie." He placed one hand flat against her abdomen. "I want to see you heavy with my child. And I want the pleasure of making that baby with you."

Maggie's hand rested on his. "Rush, I'm forty. There are sometimes problems with pregnancy at that age. I don't know if I can give you a healthy baby."

"Okay, if you're worried about something happening, we'll adopt a child."

Maggie sighed. "Rush, I don't know if I *want* a baby. I have a business now. I like my work. I'm good at it. I'm not sure I want to complicate my life by raising another child."

His eyes clouded.

One wine-tipped nail rasped against his beard. "See," Maggie said with a sad smile, "even with love there are problems."

"Uh-huh," he agreed as his lips lowered to silence any further protests, "but that same love can supply a lot of answers."

As his body moved atop hers, neither thought of problems or answers. They thought only of feeling.

An hour later after making love slowly, sweetly and most satisfactorily, Maggie and Rush shared a leisurely shower. They were standing together in the middle of the bathroom floor, halfheartedly drying each other off and constantly being distracted from their efforts by wayward hands and promising kisses, when they announced simultaneously, "I'm starving!"

"Jinx! You owe me a Coke!" Rush chanted laughingly, dabbing at some moist droplets on Maggie's shoulder before reaching for his jeans and sweat shirt.

Maggie, who was just tying the belt of a fleecy, navy robe, directed a wrinkled-nose face toward him. "Yeah? Well, only if you pour it."

Dropping a light kiss on her soft, happily curved lips he teased, "Yes, ma'am."

She instantly towel-popped his bare derriere.

Ten minutes later they carried plates piled high with crackers, peanut butter, cheese and Mettwurst into the living room and stretched out before the fire, laughing, talking, drinking rosé and falling more deeply in love.

A cracker with a bit of Brie was on its way to Rush's

mouth when the doorbell rang. Maggie's hand paused in midair. She frowned and glanced at the mantel clock. "Who can that be?"

She started to rise, but Rush caught her wrist and guided the cracker to his mouth before releasing her. She smiled, rose and leaned over to ruffle his hair in an affectionate caress before making her way to the door. Peering through the peephole she saw only the back of a woman's head. With a shrug, Maggie shot back the dead bolt and turned the knob, opening the door the barest crack, a hesitant smile tilting the corners of her mouth.

The woman at the door turned with a joyful grin.

Maggie's smile died a sudden death.

"Hi, Mom!"

Chapter Twelve

*L*acey!"

The single, breathless word was snatched from Maggie with all the force of disbelief. Even as she spoke, her heart catapulted to her throat and her hand traveled upward to where that heart now beat a fluttery pulse in the indented hollow of her neck.

"I forgot my key," Lacey Spencer announced, her blue eyes bubbling over with youthful enthusiasm and showing not the least contrition for her usual forgetfulness where keys were concerned. Shouldering a canvas bag and reaching for a piece of luggage, Lacey booted open the door that curiously remained only a thin slit of welcome.

"I thought I'd surprise you," the vivacious blonde said, depositing her things just inside the door. "I hitched a ride with Mary Ellen. You remember Mary Ellen Foley, don't you? We went to high school together. She always had that disgusting four-point-oh average. Anyway," Lacey continued in a chatty way as she slipped from her coat, "she and I have dates tomorrow night with these two rad guys from Harvard. We met them in the Poconos and we . . ."

The words halted as Lacey's eyes caught sight of the man standing before the sofa. For excruciatingly long seconds the room was as quiet as a centuries-forgotten tomb.

Clutching her coat to her, Lacey stared at the man . . . and at her mother . . . then back to the strange man.

Maggie, unconsciously smoothing her hand down the side of her fleecy, damning robe, looked at her daughter . . . then at Rush . . . then back at her daughter, who Maggie thought had turned a shocking shade of pale.

Rush, threading his fingers through hair still damp from their shower, did the only thing he could to make the situation a little better: He grappled for the loafers hiding at the sofa's edge and slipped his bare feet into them.

Maggie momentarily closed her eyes to the scene her daughter was taking in—a mother in nightclothes, a man in too-casual dress—and prayed that it was not as evident as a morning sun what had just happened in the room. Were her cheeks still flushed from lovemaking? Was there a telltale fragrance of man and woman and love still lingering in the air? Was there a condemning indentation in the sofa that spoke clearly of Rush's weight pressed seductively against her? At this latter thought, her eyes flew open and, as ridiculous as it was, she couldn't help but make a survey of the floral sofa that stood so innocently in the face of her guilt. She moaned silently, thanking whatever powers guided the heavens that Lacey hadn't arrived thirty minutes earlier . . . when she and Rush had been lost to all except the exquisite feelings possessing their bodies.

The man who had shared in those exquisite feelings finally shattered the growing silence.

"Hi," Rush said, stepping around the coffee table and extending his hand. "I'm Rush Barrington."

Lacey took the hand he offered—automatically, it was obvious—and almost dropped the coat she was holding in the process.

"Here, let me have that," Rush said, taking the woolen garment and laying it across the arm of the chair.

He straightened just as Lacey was stuffing her fingertips into the front pockets of black corduroy jeans that fitted so tightly over her curvaceous hips that Maggie thought it surely defied some physics principle that the seams didn't burst wide open.

"Oh! I'm Lacey Spencer," Lacey replied belatedly and nervously as long, attractively flyaway blond hair splayed about her shoulders.

Rush's hands slipped into the back pockets of his worn jeans. Maggie grimaced at the way the fabric tautened over his male form and thought that the same physics principle had once more been defied.

"It's nice to meet you, Lacey," Rush said, for all the world as if this was a typical meeting. "Your mother's spoken of you often."

"Yeah?" Lacey asked, throwing Maggie a surreptitious glance.

"Yeah," Rush answered with a smile that, even under the circumstances, did quivery things to Maggie's emotions. It obviously warmed Lacey as well, for she smiled slightly.

The room grew quiet once more, with the stark silence of people who don't quite know what to say next.

"So," Rush plowed in again, "you're at Skidmore, aren't you?"

"Yeah," Lacey answered, adding, "I'm a sophomore."

"What's your major?"

Lacey shrugged, shifted her weight from one foot to another and gave a sheepish look. "It kind of keeps changing."

Rush laughed, a sound that somehow mingled comfortably with the tangible tension. "It takes a while to settle in. Most everyone changes a time or two."

She shrugged again and, digging deeper in her pockets, gave a self-conscious laugh. "Tell that to my mother."

Rush raised his eyes to Maggie. "Everyone changes a time or two."

Maggie smiled slightly. "Every week?" There was a round of weak laughter before Maggie added, "Rush is at Harvard."

Lacey's eyes once more met the dark, intense eyes of the man before her. "Oh, yeah? That's neat. What's your major?"

"Law," both Maggie and Rush responded. Rush quickly glanced in Maggie's direction. There was a hint of an apology in both pairs of eyes, an apology that went beyond each having overrode the other's answer and went into the area of I'm-sorry-you're-caught-in-the-middle-of-this-embarrassing-scene.

"I know some guys at Harvard," Lacey was saying and Rush's eyes reluctantly drifted back to the younger woman. "Matt Russell and Chad Konrath."

Rush shook his head. "I don't know them. Unless they're in the law school . . ."

"No," Lacey interrupted, "they're undergrads. I met them at Christmas," she added in the way people tack on irrelevancies when seized with a case of nerves.

"Poconos, right?" Rush asked, accurately determining that one of the young men was her date for the following evening.

"Yeah," Lacey admitted, then set her top teeth to gently gnawing her bottom lip.

They succumbed to another round of silence, a silence that lasted a full quarter of a minute before three people all spoke at once: "I", "We", "Lacey."

Each looked at the other two; each gave a little strained laugh.

"I was just going to say," Rush pursued, "that I've got to be going." He glanced meaningfully at Maggie, telling her with the dark hue of his eyes that he understood that his overnight stay had just been canceled . . . and that he understood why.

She silently thanked him.

"If you two will excuse me . . ." Rush said as he moved past Lacey, then Maggie, and into the bedroom.

He was gone a couple of minutes that seemed a couple of lifetimes to the two who still stood in the living room exchanging comments so empty of meaning that they didn't even fall under the heading of inane. When Rush returned, both women seemed visibly relieved . . . until Maggie realized Rush was carrying some of his personal belongings. She could have died at the obviousness of their original plans.

"Nice to have met you, Lacey," Rush said. "Hope to see you again."

"Nice to have met you," she returned.

An awkwardness once more descended on the room, and a trio of unspoken questions buzzed about: "Should I kiss her good night?"; "Oh, God, is he going to kiss me before my daughter?"; "Is this strange man going to kiss my mother?"

Everyone but Rush was satisfied with the ultimate decision. He, however, had no intention of remaining totally unsatisfied.

"You want to walk me to the door?" he said to Maggie. She nodded and fell into step beside him. Once he was standing in the hallway, he turned.

"Rush," Maggie whispered, "I'm so sor . . ."

His fingers lightly touched her lips. "Sssh . . . It isn't your fault." The easy lines around his mouth tightened almost imperceptibly. "I'm leaving this time, Maggie. But never again. We belong together. The world and you are just going to have to face that." He raked a strand of hair back from her forehead with a touch gentler than any she'd ever known. His fingers lingered, brushed the curve of her cheek, then fell away as if sorry to leave her satin skin. Both sighed sounds of frustration. Then, with a sweetly delivered "good night," he was gone.

Maggie found Lacey sitting on the sofa, absently nibbling at a cracker and swirling a glass of rosé that somehow made Maggie feel guilty all over again. It was Rush's glass—unfinished and accusing.

"Are you hungry?" she asked, seizing on the topic as someone drowning seizes on anything of substance. "How about an omelet?" she offered, her steps already moving toward the sanctuary of the kitchen. "I could . . ."

"I'm not hungry," Lacey cut in.

"An omelet would be no trouble . . ."

"I'm not hungry, Mother." Their eyes locked and held.

Stress, powerful and struggling to relieve itself, charged the room. Maggie slipped trembling hands into the pockets of her robe and wished she was anywhere else on God's sweet earth but where she was. She fleetingly wondered if Jarrell had felt this awkward—this guilty—the first time Lacey had met Rita. She felt a sense of compassion for him if he had.

"I didn't mean to interrupt anything," Lacey said, looking up at her mother with eyes that seemed neither those of a child nor a woman.

"You didn't interrupt anything," Maggie returned quickly. "Rush . . . Rush was just leaving." It was a lie, and Maggie knew that Lacey saw right through it, but thankfully Lacey allowed her that escape. The two women stared at one another, stared and measured and gauged.

Long moments crawled by.

"Lacey, I . . ."

"I'm tired, Mother. I think I'll go to bed."

In the end Maggie didn't push; in the end she realized Lacey was shelving the issue for another time, and that it was probably best for both of them, probably best that they had some time to think.

"I'm glad you're home, honey," Maggie whispered, her eyes locking with her daughter's.

"I'm glad to be home."

Suddenly they were in each other's arms. Maggie held Lacey closely, possessively. Lacey returned the embrace with a force that bordered on fierceness. Then, wordlessly, she pulled away and picked up the suitcase.

Maggie watched her daughter leave the room, then

spent restless minutes cleaning up the snack she and Rush had so quickly abandoned with Lacey's unexpected arrival. Turning off the lights, she ultimately headed for the bedroom. But hours later she was still awake. Awake because her bed felt so empty without Rush and her heart so full with her daughter's confusion.

"You're sleeping with him, aren't you?"

The pitcher clanked against the side of the glass, and the orange juice, caught in midcascade, spilled on the countertop. Her heart racing suddenly and wildly, Maggie grabbed up a rag and started to wipe up the juice just as Lacey, too, snatched up a dishcloth. The orange juice streamed down the side of the oak wood cabinet. Both strove to make the task take as long as possible.

The question, however, hovered in the room, and Maggie could still feel its bluntness, a brazenness that was foreign to her soft-spoken daughter. The fact that it was so atypical only made it all the more harsh.

"I'm sorry," Lacey said moments later, laying the stained cloth aside and forcing her eyes to her mother's. "Let me rephrase the question." She took the glass of juice Maggie offered and headed for the table that was brilliantly bathed in morning sunshine.

"I think that might be a good idea," Maggie agreed.

Lacey pulled out a chair and sat down, leveling vivid blue eyes on the woman across the room. "Is Rush your boyfriend?"

Boyfriend? It was a curiously juvenile-sounding word to Maggie, but she understood that it was Lacey's way of asking if she was dating Rush, if the two had made some kind of commitment.

"Yes," Maggie said, praying she wasn't alienating her daughter with the admission.

"I see," Lacey said.

Maggie, pulling out a chair across from her daughter, hoped she did.

Both sipped at their juice without either really tasting it.

"Lacey," Maggie began, hesitated, then screwed up her courage, "We . . . Rush and I . . . we didn't mean to upset you . . . I mean, about last night." Oh, darn, Maggie thought, where were the right words when you needed them? But were there any right words to tell a daughter about your affair?

Lacey Spencer gave a smile that Maggie wasn't at all expecting. "I was, you know. Upset."

"I know," Maggie assured her. "So was I." And so was Rush, Maggie thought.

The two women quietly studied each other before Lacey rose and moved to stare out of the window, which overlooked the whiteness of yesterday's snowfall. When she turned back she jammed her hands into the front pockets of her cropped corduroy pants.

Maggie recognized the pale blue pants as those she'd given Lacey for Christmas; the top, a pastel argyle sweater Jarrell and Rita had given her the year before. At the time Maggie remembered feeling resentment that her daughter had something Rita had obviously picked out. Right now it seemed a silly thing to have felt. She silently wondered just how much her love for Rush was responsible for that change in feeling, then decided it was probably totally responsible.

"Can we talk?" Lacey suddenly cut through her mother's thoughts. "I mean, woman to woman, not mother to daughter?"

Maggie nodded her head, scattering rich, brown hair about shoulders that were drooping slightly from emotional strain. "Of course."

"About last night," Lacey began, her eyes finding the toes of her shoes, the edge of the ecru tablecloth, then moving more boldly to the eyes so intently watching her. "You know what my first feeling was?"

"No. What?" Maggie asked.

"Betrayal."

Tiny creases formed in Maggie's forehead. "Betrayal? I don't . . ."

"Dad has Rita," Lacey sliced through her mother's words, "and I guess since the divorce, I'd come to think of you and me as a team. Sort of like you and me against the world. Certainly me and you against Dad and Rita. When I saw you and . . . Rush, my first thought was, where does this leave you, Lacey? Now you have no one. Just you against the world."

Maggie's heart constricted. "Honey . . ."

"Let me finish. Please. You see, when Daddy first left that's exactly how I viewed it. *Daddy* left us. I see now that was very selfish. I was seeing it only from my point of view. The same way I saw it only from my point of view when I walked in on you last night. As I lay awake . . ."

Maggie couldn't keep the wry smile from her lips. "You didn't sleep either?"

"Very little," Lacey said, returning the smile with one that Maggie thought was so beautiful that it didn't even have the right to be real. "As I lay awake," Lacey said, picking up the threads of her thoughts, "I realized for the first time that when Lacey Spencer's dad left, Maggie Spencer's husband walked out on her. And for a younger woman. And at a time in Maggie's life when she was no longer blissfully young. Oh, not that you're old, Mom," she hastened to add, momentarily forgetting it was a woman-to-woman talk.

Maggie fought the smile trying to form on her lips, fought it with the tears forming in her eyes. She wasn't sure she'd ever loved Lacey as much as she did right at that moment!

"As I lay there, I wondered what I would feel if a man I loved had done that to me. You know what I decided?"

Maggie shook her head, unable to find words, unable to trust herself to voice any if she had.

"I thought I'd feel terribly hurt. But more than that, I thought I wouldn't be sure I was a woman anymore. You know what I mean, Mom?"

Oh, God, yes, I know! Maggie thought, but managed to say a soft, "Yes. I know exactly."

Lacey's eyes pierced her mother's, blue on blue, woman to woman. "Did Daddy make you stop feeling like a woman?"

"Yes," Maggie answered simply.

"Does . . . does Rush make you feel like one again?"

"Yes."

"Do you love him?"

"Yes."

"Does he love you?"

"Yes."

Moments long and forever marched by.

"I'm glad," the younger woman said finally.

"He's . . . Rush is . . . He's younger, Lacey. Ten years younger." Maggie waited for her daughter's comment with a heart that was as close to death as it had ever been.

Suddenly a smile teased the features of Lacey's lovely face. "I won't tell anyone if you won't."

And then it happened. How Maggie didn't know or care, but suddenly, sweetly, the two were in one another's arms, and laughter and tears were flowing in equal proportions.

"Oh, Mom, I love you . . . more than chocolate-ripple ice cream."

Framing her daughter's cheeks with two trembling hands, Maggie said, "No one, *no one* can ever fill the place you hold in my heart. You know that, don't you?"

Lacey nodded. "Yes. We'll always be a team."

The tears would have started again if the phone hadn't chosen that propitious moment to ring.

"Thank heaven," Lacey sniffled, "this was getting maudlin."

Maggie laughed and brushed at a tear as her daughter grabbed for the phone.

"Hello?" Quiet moments reigned. "Oh, hi. Not much. No, we decided against breakfast. Watching our figures and all." There was a sudden smile in her daughter's voice.

Assuming the call to be from one of Lacey's friends, Maggie turned, picked up the juice glasses and carried them to the sink.

"Sure, I like to skate," Lacey was saying over the running of the kitchen faucet. "Sure. Fine with me. Let me put on the boss and see what she thinks."

With that, Lacey shoved the phone at her mother.

Maggie's brow wrinkled as she dried off her wet hands.

"Lover boy," Lacey teased in a whisper. "Yours. Not mine."

Maggie took the phone and watched her smiling daughter flit from the kitchen.

"Hello?" she said into the receiver.

"You two want to go skating?" Rush's sexy voice came tripping over the wire.

Maggie smiled. Maggie teared. Maggie whispered, "I love you."

It wasn't the answer he'd expected, but it was one he happily settled for.

Maggie pulled her ice skates from the back of the closet and wondered just how long it had been since she'd last used them. She decided it had been years. A shiver of excitement ran down her spine. Part of it had to do with the anticipation of a fun-filled, carefree Saturday morning. Most of it had to do, however, with seeing Rush again.

Rush.

His very name trebled the rhythm of her heart and caused her head to spin with a thousand romantic fantasies. He could be so gentle, so tender, so seductively sensual. She smiled. He could be so persistent! He wanted her to marry him, and he had plied her with every tempting reason he could think of to get her to accept his proposal.

And she had countered with every reason she could think of. Reasons that right this moment, with the warm glow of Lacey's approval and the still warmer memory of Rush's voice in her ear, seemed pale and without merit.

Dabbing a rose pink gloss onto her lips, Maggie grabbed the brush and raked it through hair that seemed unruly and wayward following a night of tossing. Throwing down the brush, she headed for the nightstand and a pair of ivory combs she thought were in there. Her fingers fumbled over a ring of keys, a pair of tweezers she'd already replaced because she'd thought them lost and a purse calendar for the year before. She spotted the combs at the same time her eyes came to rest on the black velvet case.

Jarrell's cuff links! The combs forgotten, she eased open the case and stared at the jade jewelry that had haunted her for so long. She waited to feel something. Waited, but was denied any emotion except the practical one of thinking that she really ought to give them to Lacey to give to her father. She smiled, a smile that finally gave way to an appealing laugh.

Tossing the case onto the bed, she picked up the combs and threaded them through her sable-brown hair. Whirling—turning was just too anemic an action —she snagged the ties of her skates, hiked them over a shoulder and started from her bedroom.

It was a beautiful morning! she thought. A morning when anything seemed possible. Even marrying Rush Barrington.

The shriek, mingled with laughter, escaped Maggie's lips as her legs, tottering on thin blades of steel, traitorously bowed inward. Her arms flailed at the empty, unsupporting air. She was going down . . . down . . . down . . .

Suddenly an arm snaked around her waist and hauled her flush against a ruggedly masculine body. Maggie's eyes flew upward and connected with the electric brown eyes of Rush. Both smiled; both exhaled a feathery frost into the March Saturday morning.

"I . . . I almost fell," Maggie got out around a heavy gust of breath. Her fingers, protected against the chill by white woolen gloves, clung tightly to Rush's shoulders, while her eyes, peeking from beneath a matching white woolen cap, devoured him as romantically as any just-rescued damsel does her knight in armor. Especially a knight she loves.

"I couldn't let that happen," he said huskily. "I wouldn't want anything to damage that sweet tush."

Rush's words would have caused Maggie's cheeks to blush if the crisp air hadn't already done so. His hands sliding, gliding down the denim of her jeans, to a spot just shy of that part of her anatomy they were discussing, did give her a ruddy complexion that the weather could take no credit for. Her breathing grew shallow.

"You think I have a sweet tush?" she asked coyly, thinking that she had never so outrageously flirted in her life . . . and thinking that she had wasted a good part of that life by not doing so.

"Lady," he said with a grin that revealed two even rows of white teeth, "I not only think it. I know it for a fact."

One of her hands eased from his shoulder and traveled to his waist, then slipped to his jacketed back and just a millimeter onto the curve of his hip. "And here I was thinking all this time that *you* were the one with the sweet tush."

He gave a slow, slumberous smile. "You think I have a sweet tush?"

"Mister," she said with a smile as bright as love could make it, "I not only think it. I know it for a fact."

Rush's breathing changed to a fluttery, airy pattern. And his sunshine smile dipped behind a cloud of seriousness. "Keep this up, Maggie, and I swear I'll kiss you right here."

Maggie feigned a look of shocked disbelief. "Right here?" she asked, glancing about her at the two dozen or so skilled and unskilled skaters having the time of their lives on the ice of the small outdoor rink. "Right here?" she repeated. "In front of all these strange people?" As she spoke, two skaters whizzed by in metrical tandem, followed closely by a third and a fourth.

"I'd have no trouble with it at all," Rush returned, his eyes traveling from Maggie to the figure sitting on a bench. Lacey had just limped off the ice to retie a skate lace that insisted on being stubborn. "Except," he added meaningfully, "that your daughter is watching."

Maggie turned in the circumference of his arms and glanced over at Lacey. She waved, a salute the younger woman returned. When her eyes met Rush's again, she asked, "Is Lacey all that's stopping you?"

His eyes narrowed to a point somewhere between question and seduction. "I would have thought after last night . . ."

"We'll talk about last night later," Maggie interrupted. "Right now, why don't you kiss me?"

Brown eyes widened and warmed and then touched every feature of the face before him—blue eyes already half-shuttered in anticipation, cheeks red and rosy from the day and his nearness, lips full and delectably inviting. His breath shuddered slightly as he lowered his head and his mouth took hers in an adoring kiss. His lips opened, and he freely took all she gave.

And she gave all that propriety allowed. When she felt one finger ease into the hip pocket of her jeans, an anchor to the emotions claiming them both, she moaned softly and parted her lips to the gentle plunder of his tongue. A quick, but sweet plunder molded to circumstance and place.

"Oh, Maggie," he rasped, "for five cents I'd do something that would get us arrested right here!"

A teasing light flashed in her eyes, and her lips, still wet from his mouth, twitched at the corners. "If you know a good lawyer, I have a nickel in my pocket."

Rush's face broke into the same smile. "I don't know a lawyer good enough for what I have in mind."

"Then I guess we'd better skate, huh?"

"It's a damned poor second, but let's do it."

And they did skate. For three whole seconds, before Maggie's left skate became entangled with Rush's right. Steel blade bumped steel blade. Foot ensnared foot. Ankle mated with ankle. Bodies crashed and thrashed in a desperate effort to save self and the other.

"Rush!" Maggie screeched seconds before her derriere connected with cold, cold ice. And then Rush was sprawled atop her, knocking her flat on her back and even further into the unyielding frigidness beneath her. Arms, legs and gusts of breath mingled.

"Are you all right?" Rush wheezed, looking down into her face with concern. Her cap had been knocked from her head, and brown hair, coffee-colored and wildly tumbled, spread over the marble-white ice.

She nodded, adding breathlessly, "Funny, I don't remember your weighing this much last time we made love."

"Funny, I don't remember your being so clumsy."

Both mouths began to quiver into smiles and, as he rolled from her and onto his back beside her, the smiles turned to laughter. They laughed in the chill March air that would soon sing with the promise of spring. They laughed in appreciation of the ridiculous spectacle they must be making. They laughed in grateful acknowledgment of the love they shared.

Blinking back tears of laughter and glaring sunshine from her eyes, Maggie was the first to notice Lacey standing over them. With hands on her hips and a smile on her lips, the young woman glanced from one to the other of the supine figures.

"Good heaven, you two are total clods on ice," Lacey condemned teasingly. "And I don't mind telling you I'm thoroughly embarrassed."

This set all three of them to laughing.

"Your mother's clumsy," Rush said, moving to a sitting position before rising carefully to his feet. He smiled as he added for Maggie's benefit, "On ice."

"I know," Lacey said, not noticing the secret glances or the half smiles that were quickly exchanged.

"Thanks, you two," Maggie retaliated as she took the hand Rush offered and was yanked to a standing position. Even then, her rebellious legs wobbled. "Well, this proves one thing," she said, trying to dust the wet from the back of her jeans, "skating is not like riding a bicycle."

"Want to try it again?" Rush asked, brushing back the fallen hair from his eyes.

Maggie shook her head defiantly. "Not on your life. I'm going over to that nice, safe bench for a much needed rest." When Rush glided to one side of her and Lacey the other, Maggie added, "You two go skate. I'll watch."

Rush threw a glance in Lacey's direction. "Want to?"

"Sure," Lacey answered, "but I have to warn you that clumsiness on ice runs in the family."

"Well, as you can see," Rush tossed back, "I wasn't exactly part of the last Olympic skating team."

Seconds later Maggie eased her assaulted derriere onto the wooden bench. Even as she collapsed into a relaxed pose, she became aware of trillions of little pains in trillions of little places over her body. The fall was already exacting its toll. Trying to shift to a more comfortable position—should she try to ease the ache in her shoulder, her foot or her tush that at that moment seemed anything but sweet?—she watched as

Rush and Lacey circled the rink. Effortlessly circled the rink, she admitted with a note of envy. For all of Lacey's denial, she skated beautifully . . . and Rush didn't seem in the least affected by the fall. Face it, Maggie, ol' girl, being forty is not like being twenty . . . or even thirty.

For a brief second she felt another ache, this one in her heart. For the first time that enchanting Saturday morning something had blighted her perfect mood.

"You're good," Rush said to the woman who skated at his side.

Lacey shrugged. "Not really. I'm just doing my best to impress you."

Rush's eyebrow arched. "Impress me? Is that what you're trying to do?"

"Sure," Lacey answered, swiping at a blond strand of hair that streamed across her nose. "Just the way you're trying to impress me."

"Point well taken," Rush admitted with a grin. "Well, you think we should tell each other how we're doing?"

Lacey threw him a glance as they took the curve of the far side of the circle. "Yeah. Why not? You first. How am I stacking up as a daughter?"

Rush considered a moment, even slackening their pace to do so. "I like you," he announced honestly. "You seem open, warm, friendly. You seem intelligent. You don't come apart in a crisis." Rush knew she knew the crisis to which he referred. "You're also pretty," he added, "but not what I'd expected Maggie's daughter to look like." He started to say that the black-and-white photograph by Maggie's bed didn't do Lacey justice, but realized just in time that Maggie's bedside might be a good topic to avoid just now.

"The blond hair, right?" Lacey asked, turning to skate backward as they talked.

"Yeah, I guess that's it," Rush admitted.

"I have Mom's eyes and Dad's hair, and I guess basically I look more like Dad. I wish I looked more like Mom. She's pretty."

"Yeah," Rush agreed without the slightest hesitation. "But then, so are you. Just different looks."

"Thanks," Lacey said. "So I pass muster, huh?"

"You pass," he said. "With flying colors." She had fallen back to his side, skating in a forward pattern with him. He threw a quick look in her direction. "Well, want to give me your verdict?"

Lacey Spencer studied him openly, with an intensity that might have been insulting under other circumstances. Rush thought her blond-brown lashes blinked in the same rhythm as a judge's gavel pounding a judicial imperative. Finally she spoke. "I haven't entirely made my mind up yet. I need to ask you a question."

"Fire away," Rush insisted, hoping to God he wasn't being led to the slaughter.

"What are your intentions?" Lacey asked simply.

The brow that had hiked once, hiked again. "What are my intentions as in 'What are my intentions'?"

"Right. What are your intentions concerning my mother?"

The question was straightforward, shot from the hip, and Rush intended to be no less direct.

"Simple. I'm going to marry her." Their skating had slowed again, this time to a crawl other skaters were having to dodge. Rush's eyes had once more found Lacey's, and a faint challenge seemed to be written in both pairs. "Is that going to be a problem for you?"

Lacey, never wavering in her gaze, answered, "I

don't think so. It's going to take me a while to adjust to the idea, but I don't think there'll be a problem."

"You're not concerned about the difference in our ages?"

"Not at all," Lacey answered candidly. "Statistics show it makes a lot of sense."

As this last comment was made, the couple glided past Maggie. Lacey waved and Maggie returned the gesture with a smile. Another woman had joined her on the bench.

Stuffing her hands into the pockets of her jacket, Lacey added, "When you kissed Mom a little while ago . . ." She trailed off and Rush felt his heart slam into a pound.

". . . it was the first time I've ever seen a guy besides Dad kiss her," she continued.

"And?"

Their eyes brushed, hers skittering away first.

"It felt strange."

There was a silence filled with the laughter of other skaters and the faraway rumble of vehicles going about weekend chores. Nearby, at the rink's icy edge, a red-cheeked child cried at having to call his Saturday outing over.

"I'm sure it did," Rush responded sensitively. Coming to a halt, he watched her carefully. What he saw was a young woman striving hard to leave youth behind and embrace the hard world of adulthood. He saw a child-woman who'd had her home split and now wasn't quite certain where she belonged in the scheme of things. "We're not rivals," Rush reminded gently. "I think we could even be friends."

Lacey apparently needed no time to consider the possibility. "I think we could, too," she said, giving him a soft smile. "I like you." The smile faded as quickly as it had come, replaced by a look of nearly defiant earnestness. "But there're two things I have to say."

Rush's hands moved to bracket his hips. "Let's hear them."

"Don't hurt my mother." The words came out grimly, with a hint of a threat, a threat Rush found incongruous with Lacey's delicate looks. "My dad hurt her enough for a lifetime."

"I give you my solemn promise, Lacey, that I'll never willingly, knowingly hurt your mother."

"You'll never leave her?"

He shook his head. "No." She seemed to absorb his answer, seemed to be relieved by it. "Now, what's this second thing?"

The smile was back, this time multiplied in its intensity. "I have no intention of calling you 'Daddy.'"

Rush was so surprised that it took the laughter several seconds to bubble up from his deep chest. When it did it spilled forth in warm waves that urged Lacey to join in. Hand in hand, they circled the rink, laughing, talking, at last skating.

She was beautiful, Maggie thought as she watched Lacey skate by, her hair swirling about her like a banner of sunny golden silk. And Rush, his hair dark as some bewitching wintry night, was so handsome it strangled the breath from her chest. In that moment Maggie felt such a strong sense of possessiveness, for them both, and such an overwhelming feeling of pride, that she experienced a prickling twinge of fear. How could she have managed to get so lucky? She instantly cast the fear aside as a feeling totally inappropriate for such a lovely, sunny day.

". . . lovely."

Maggie jerked her head toward the sound, realizing

the woman sitting beside her had spoken, but not having the least idea what she'd said. The two women had sat exchanging occasional smiles ever since the middle-aged woman had arrived minutes before with a carload of children. Maggie had suspected them of being grandchildren and friends of grandchildren.

"They're a lovely couple," the woman repeated, nodding toward a laughing Lacey and Rush, who were just passing in front of the benched observers and favoring Maggie with another wild wave.

Maggie's eyes moved from the couple back to her companion. "Yes," she answered, that prickling of fear once more slithering to the forefront. "Yes, they are."

"Is she your daughter?" the woman asked with a smile.

"Yes," Maggie replied, knowing in her heart what the next question was going to be, and willing to give anything if she could stop it from being voiced. But she couldn't.

"Is he your son-in-law?"

Son-in-law! Maggie swallowed painfully. It was worse than she'd suspected; she'd thought the woman would wonder if Rush was Lacey's boyfriend.

"No," she said, struggling to give the word sound. "No, he's my . . ."

My what? she thought. *My boyfriend?* She could see the woman's surprise. What about *my lover?* She could see the woman's surprise melt into censure. *The man who's asked me to marry him?* Maggie could see the woman's censure turning into pity for Rush's obvious foolishness. *The man whose proposal I've just been considering?* Maggie could see the pity turn to accusing shame for what she'd been contemplating doing.

"No," Maggie said in a tone dulled with fresh pain, "he's not my son-in-law."

Time ticked by in slow, torturous beats, beats she finally realized were the rhythm of her own heart. She watched as Lacey and Rush skated toward her, bright smiles giving their faces a mocking youthfulness. They had never looked so young; she'd never felt so old. Nor so damned stupid!

"Hi," Rush said, skating up to her and leaning down to brush a kiss on her lips.

Skillfully, she avoided the intimate contact, rose and gave a smile so fake it made rhinestones look like precious gems.

"Ready to go home?" she asked, not bothering to wait for an answer. Instead, she trudged off toward the Monte Carlo . . . leaving behind her a bewildered Rush, who hadn't the foggiest idea what the hell had just happened.

Chapter Thirteen

$\mathcal{S}$he's a great kid. I like her," Rush told Maggie only moments after Lacey and her date, Chad, the "really rad hunk" she'd met in the Poconos, left the condo.

"Thank you."

Maggie picked up Rush's fallen scarf from the floor and draped it back over the brass hook of the antique hall tree near the door. Then she walked back to the sofa and began to plump the already fat pillows that languished against the floral print like brightly fallen petals.

Rush, just barely arrived, stood warming himself at the fireplace. His long legs were planted a few feet apart and looked even longer in the knife-creased black pants of his tuxedo. His hands were clasped behind his back in a pose that would look casual to any observer. Maggie, however, wasn't fooled. She hadn't spent the last two-plus months involved with Rush Barrington at varying levels of intimacy without learning something of his moods.

He was on to her. No doubt about it. He knew something was wrong. Why else would he come over before leaving on his evening's assignment for April? He'd said he wanted to tell Lacey good-bye, but Maggie felt there was more. She had a strange, something-is-about-to-happen feeling. She could feel a reckoning in the wind.

Maggie sighed, a shudder rippling through her still aching body. How had such a beautiful, sunshiny day turned so emotionally cloudy? She'd been ready to throw common sense and caution to the wind and say yes to Rush's next proposal. As long as her family and close friends approved, what did it matter what the world thought? But all that had been changed in the span of a heartbeat by a few ill-timed words that knocked the props out from under her recent resolution and sent her newfound self-confidence tumbling just as she'd tumbled onto the ice earlier that morning. The woman's question about Rush being her son-in-law had undone all the progress she'd made. Maggie's emotions were back to square one. She felt . . .

"Maggie," Rush's voice broke into her thoughts.

Her head jerked guiltily toward him, their eyes colliding with a gentle jolt. Oh, God, he looked so wonderful. Was so wonderful. "Yes?"

"Come here."

She straightened and moved slowly forward, her eyes clinging to his, her footsteps whispering quietly across the rug separating them. She stopped before him, and his hands, warm on her shoulders, slid around her back and drew her close. Maggie's arms went around his middle, and she breathed in the musky scent of his cologne and the clean, starched scent of his pleated shirt.

"What's the matter?"

Maggie burrowed closer to him, an ache, rooted in some abstract fear, growing in her heart. "Nothing."

"Sure?"

"Yes."

Rush sighed. "So what did Lacey have to say about last night?" he asked, releasing her and leading her toward the sofa. "I've had very little time alone with you since she arrived."

Maggie sank down beside him and nestled in the shelter of his body, her slight weight resting against him while his lips foraged in the softness of her hair.

"We neither one had the courage to talk about it last night," she confessed. "After all, finding your mother in her nightgown and robe with a man is pretty condemning evidence."

"Strictly circumstantial," Rush murmured.

"Maybe," Maggie agreed. "But this morning, during breakfast, Lacey and I had a good talk about things. Jarrell, mostly, and what his leaving meant to her then, and what she sees and feels about it now that she has a couple more years and a little more maturity on her."

"And?"

"She realizes I lost a big part of my life. That my loss was as great, if not greater, than hers. And she realizes I'm still young enough to enjoy a relationship with a man."

"Good for Lacey!" Rush smiled against her hair.

Maggie tipped her head back to look up at him. "What about you? You two spent a lot of time together today. What did she say to you?"

He smiled, the action crinkling the corners of his

eyes. "She was a little standoffish at first, but basically she wanted to know what my intentions were."

"What!" Maggie sat up straight and turned to face him. "Oh, surely, she didn't . . ."

"I assure you, she did," Rush chuckled. "I believe those were her exact words. 'What are your intentions concerning my mother?' And of course I told her what you know. That I want marriage. A family. A home."

Maggie's eyelids fell to hide the pain his words evoked.

Rush's voice was low, husky, suddenly serious. "I love you, Maggie. You love me. Your daughter approves. So do your friends. Does anything else really matter?"

Maggie opened her eyes to look at him. He looked older somehow, the grueling pace of the past few weeks exacting payment for the sleepless nights and the constant strain of juggling his work with school. Fatigue lurked in the dark depths of his eyes and etched lines in the lean masculinity of his face.

She reached out and touched his smoothly shaven cheek with the fingertips of one hand. "I do love you. And I had decided that if you asked again I was going to say yes."

Rush's head dropped and his shoulders slumped in a gesture of relief. Then he drew a deep breath and raised his head, his eyes glittering with a peculiar moistness as they clung to hers. "I'm asking," he said softly.

Maggie inhaled deeply, her breath catching in her throat as she fought back the feeling of déjà vu sweeping over her. It seemed like an instant replay of the scene in Nassau when she had decided to say yes to his persuasive demands that she sleep with him. Only it wasn't quite the same. This time the answer was different. This time the answer was no.

Her head moved slowly to the left . . .

The joyous glow in Rush's eyes dimmed.

. . . and slowly to the right.

The flame in his eyes flickered once and died, snuffed out by old hurts, insecurities and a woman's careless words.

"No?" His voice was hardly more than a whisper. "You aren't going to marry me?"

"Oh, Rush, I can't!" Maggie cried, leaping to her feet and whirling toward the fire so she wouldn't have to look at the ravages left behind in the wake of her answer. The joyous light had been swept away by a typhoon of disbelief and pain that left only hopelessness and the tattered remnants of the love she'd thrown back in his face.

She didn't hear him leave his place on the sofa, but felt his hands close over her shoulders in a grip whose pain rivaled that in her heart. He hauled her around to face him.

She had never seen Rush really angry. His eyes blazed with the intensity of his feelings, his nostrils flared as he struggled to draw in the harsh breaths that wheezed in and out of his lungs. His mouth—the beautiful mouth that was able to bring her to the heights of rapture—was drawn into a thin, uncompromising line. Maggie, blaming herself and damning the circumstances that had brought them to this, cringed away from the fury contorting his handsome features and hoped she'd never have to see him this way again.

"Why?" The single, heart-wrenching word was torn from his very soul and squeezed through gritted teeth.

Maggie felt tears burning beneath her eyelids and

blinked rapidly in an effort to hold them back. "You know why," she said, losing the battle as two tears escaped the fragile defense of her lashes and spilled down her pale cheeks.

Rush released her and turned away, swearing softly and explicitly. The low, succinct epithet held more power than if he'd yelled it.

Maggie flinched at the harshness oozing from him.

"Why?" he repeated.

"Because I'm so much older than you!"

Maggie was beginning to feel like a record stuck in one agonizingly monotonous groove as she attempted to explain once more the fears that were so inconsequential to him, yet so heartrendingly real to her.

"If it were only a year or two, it wouldn't make that much difference," she said in a placating tone. "But it's ten years, not two. And that was brought home to me very clearly today by a woman who asked if you were my son-in-law."

"The woman sitting next to you at the rink." It was a statement. He'd . somehow intuitively known the woman had been responsible for Maggie's change of mood.

"Yes."

"Are you going to let some stranger you'll never see again ruin our lives? I don't give a damn how many years separate us, or what people think!" he snarled.

Maggie wiped at the tears bathing her cheeks with ever increasing speed. "Not now you don't. But what if I decided I didn't want to have a baby . . . didn't want to adopt one."

"Maggie, don't do this," he begged.

Ignoring the earnest plea, she continued, "How would you feel about me a few years from now? Will you love me so much then if I deny you the child you want so badly?"

Rush placed his hands on his hips and stared up at the ceiling. He was suddenly tired of fighting her and her fears. Tired of fighting the whole damned world. Futility filled him. "I've been patient, Maggie. I've tried to bide my time and give you some space to work things out for yourself. But my patience is about gone. And I've bided about all the time I can spare." He lowered his head, his gaze locking with hers. "I'm not getting any younger either. I need to get on with my life. Either with you or without you."

Maggie drew in a harsh breath at the subtle inference of his words and the finality in his voice.

"I want you. But I want you for my wife, not as a casual affair. Not for an hour here, two hours there. Not just for the weekends. I want all of you. All or nothing."

Maggie held out her hands, pleading. "Rush . . . please. Can't we go on as we have been? It's been good . . . it's been . . ."

"All or nothing," he reiterated.

Maggie stood staring at the man she loved, at the man whose body had brought her to new plateaus of feeling, both physically and emotionally. At the man who stood regarding her with a strange succession of feelings in his dark eyes. Hurt. Fear. Defiance. Love. Maybe even hate.

A shaft of pain pierced her heart, pierced so deeply and hurt so badly that one hand came up to cover her breast in a gesture of solace. A deep, ragged sob shuddered through her.

Rush saw a hand come up to rest on the curve of one perfect breast. A breast he'd touched, caressed, kissed. She was shaking so badly she could hardly stand.

"I can't," she whispered, tears shimmering in her eyes. "I love you too much."

Rush's eyes closed against the pain as his heart crumbled inside his chest, leaving a cavity that might never be filled again. There was a dull roaring in his ears that must have been the aftershock of his world as it came tumbling down around his shoulders. Deaf, mute, he turned and retrieved his coat from the hall tree. The door was open, and he was halfway out when Maggie's voice halted him.

"Rush!" she cried softly. "Can't you see that I'm doing this for you?"

He turned and looked at her, his eyes unnaturally bright. "Don't do me any more favors, Maggie."

Maggie's eyes hungrily devoured the black-and-white photos that comprised an entire newspaper page of men's spring clothing, all worn by models from a local agency. After seven days of staring at the now tattered, dogeared page, she still couldn't have said what was in style for the well-dressed man. Her eyes invariably and unerringly zeroed in on one model's face, the face of the man who haunted both her waking and sleeping hours. Rush. Maggie dragged her gaze away from the week-old newspaper with a soft sigh that spoke eloquently of her feelings.

It was Thursday. Three weeks and—her dull blue gaze dropped to the ten o'clock spelled out by the gold watch encircling her slender wrist—ten hours into the fifth day since Rush had left her apartment and her life. Even now when she closed her eyes she could see him standing there, could hear the words, "Don't do me any more favors, Maggie." Could recall how the door crashed shut behind him with a force that shook the walls and shattered her brittle, breaking heart into myriad, minuscule fragments. Fragments so small that in three weeks and four and a half days she hadn't even gathered them all together, much less tried to repair them.

She remembered standing for long moments staring at the door, certain from her feeling of emptiness that she was dying . . . or already dead.

And then, like her heart, her composure shattered.

She cried.

For hour upon hour she cried—hard, ugly sobs tearing at her throat and shaking her already trembling body. She'd cried until it was time for Lacey to come home, then she'd burrowed into her bed, curled into a fetal position, and tried to shut her mind to the memories . . . a task she soon realized was impossible.

After a sleepless night that tormented her with the horrendous scene of the evening before and then tantalized her until just before dawn with what had been and what might have been, she'd crawled out of bed to make coffee.

When Lacey bounced into the kitchen at about ten the bright smile on her face had vanished with comical rapidity when she saw the state Maggie was in. She had stared at the dark circles, the red-rimmed eyes and her mother's haggard features. Her fair brows had drawn into a frown of concern. "Are you all right?"

Maggie gave Lacey a wan smile and cradled the warmth of the coffee mug in both hands. In a voice that was barely audible from her hours of weeping, she whispered the lie, "I think I'm coming down with the flu."

Lacey leaned across the table and placed the back of her hand against Maggie's forehead. "I don't think you have a fever."

Maggie caught her daughter's hand and pressed it

against her cheek, touched by the maternal gesture. "Maybe it's just a cold. I'll be fine."

"Are you sure? I can stay today and go back to school tomorrow," Lacy offered, worrying her bottom lip in a manner that was both endearing and familiar.

Maggie gave her daughter a halfhearted smile. "I'll be okay. There's no need for you to stay here and miss school."

"How about me calling Rush to come stay with you?"

"No!" Maggie cried. Then her voice softened. "No. Not now." Her laughter sounded embarrassed. "I wouldn't want him to see me like this. Besides, I think he had some studying to do today. I'll give him a call later on this afternoon."

"Okay . . ." Lacey acquiesced, though she still didn't sound convinced. She had sighed, looked at her watch and announced that she'd better get her things together. It was barely an hour until Mary Ellen would arrive. Maggie had smiled in return and told her to go on and not to worry—and prayed for the hour to pass quickly so she could sink into the misery trying to tow her under. Lacey had gone with a promise to call soon and check on her.

And Maggie had allowed herself to be dragged down by her heartache.

She was still under. Even after all these weeks. Almost a month. Easter was upon them, and Mother Nature's warm breath caressed the naked trees that blushed with red-hued buds. Crocuses and daffodils sprouted in sunny places, or against buildings where the ground had been helped to an earlier thaw from the heat inside. A brave few poked their heads above the snow that still lay in shadowy patches. The sun shone weakly, trying to push away the gray clouds. The nights were still cold and crisp and there was a halfhearted snowfall in early April, sent, no doubt, to remind the Boston residents that winter still retained the upper hand in the never ceasing struggle for final control of the season.

Maggie's emotions were still cold; her heart was still broken. And she doubted that it would ever feel the rebirth of spring again. Staying at home was hell. She saw Rush lounging on the floral sofa, resplendent in his black tux; she saw him sitting at the kitchen table studying, his hands running through his hair in agitation; she saw him standing before the fireplace to warm himself. The memories were everywhere. Rush Barrington filled every pore of her being.

The bedroom was the worst. She'd found one of his socks beneath the bed and remembered the haste in which he'd stripped them off. She could picture him sprawled in seductive splendor, the sheet barely covering him. She could close her eyes and actually feel the touch of his lips on hers. She'd even tried sleeping on the sofa, *tried* being the operative word. The memories were as vivid there as they were in the bedroom. She couldn't even escape him at the gallery. It, like her home, was filled with haunting pictures.

Maggie had tried throwing herself deeper into her work, but even that panacea hadn't helped. Oh, she was tired. So tired, in fact, that she could barely put one foot in front of the other at the end of the day. But she still didn't sleep; still didn't eat. The headaches seemed to come with increasing regularity, and her nerves were stretched to the snapping point. She despaired of ever being better. She despaired.

The shrill ringing of the telephone shattered her

endless introspection. Maggie picked up the receiver and nestled the phone to her ear. "Simon Gallery. Ms. Spencer speaking."

"Mom? This is Lacey. How are you?"

Maggie couldn't help the smile that curved her mouth. Lacey always answered in the same way. She always opened with "Mom," then identified herself.

"I'm fine, honey," Maggie said, conjuring up a mental image of her only offspring.

"You don't sound fine. You sound tired," Lacey commented with disgusting honesty.

"Well, I've been working pretty hard lately. Trying to catch up before I make that trip to Florida next month."

"Oh, the pastel lady, right?"

"Right."

The conversation lagged. Then both Maggie and Lacey spoke at the same time.

"How's . . ."

"Have . . ."

They both laughed. "Age before beauty," Lacey quipped cheekily.

"Thanks," Maggie said dryly. "I was going to ask how the chemistry class was coming."

"Oh, about a *B* I think. It sure isn't getting any easier. The only way I can hold on is to keep telling myself that I only have about a month to go."

"It's hard to believe it's already the middle of April."

"I know," Lacey agreed. "Oh, by the way, I gave Daddy the cuff links for his birthday last week. He loved them."

"Good," Maggie said, meaning it.

Another silence stretched over the phone lines. Finally Lacey asked hesitantly, "Have you heard from Rush?"

"No."

Both women were silent again. Maggie had confessed to her daughter that she and Rush had had their first fight, omitting only that it was also their last. Lacey had naturally assumed that no matter what the problem, they would work things out.

"It's serious, isn't it, Mom?"

"Yes."

"Do you think you can fix it?"

Maggie's eyes welled with tears. "I don't think so."

Lacey's voice held a note of anger as she demanded, "Did Rush break off with you?"

"No, Lacey. I did."

"But why?"

"Because I thought he needed someone younger for a wife . . . to have his children."

"Children?" Lacey said, as if the thought of her mother having another child had never occurred to her. "Children? Gee, Mom. Brothers and sisters. I never thought about it. It might have been nice."

Maggie couldn't be sure, but there seemed a wistful quality to her daughter's tone. She gave a short laugh that ended on a sob. Her voice was thick with unshed tears as she lied, "Look, honey, I've got to go. Jerri's out and I see a couple of women coming through the door."

"Okay," Lacey said agreeably. There was another brief pause. "I love you, Mom."

Maggie dabbed a stray tear from the corner of her eye. "I love you, too, honey. Take care."

"I will. And Mom!" Lacey added quickly.

"Yes."

"Think about it, will you? I mean, you love Rush, and a blind person could see that he's crazy about you. I think with that going for you, you could work out any other problems that came along. Besides, I think you make a really rad couple."

Maggie smiled through the mist of tears. "I'll think about it."

"Promise?"

"Promise."

"Okay. Bye, Mom."

Maggie heard the soft click at Lacey's end before she could tell her daughter good-bye. She replaced the receiver and buried her face in her hands, her tears trickling through her fingers.

"Get your clothes on. We're going to lunch," April announced in a no-nonsense tone as she stood planted in the doorway of the condo. Her hands rested firmly on her hips as she stared at Maggie, who was still dressed in her nightgown and robe at eleven o'clock the following Saturday.

Maggie forced a smile to her lips and pushed back a strand of tousled hair. "Come on in, April. The coffee just finished dripping through."

"Just finished . . ." April began, then shook her head, entered the apartment and hung her jacket on the hall tree. She followed Maggie into the kitchen, tugging the cranberry sweater she wore down over her slender, jean-encased hips. She perched on one of the small table's matching chairs and propped her rounded chin in her palm. Her free hand raked back a tendril of frizzled hair. April's heart ached at the ravages of misery etched on Maggie's face as she watched her friend pour two mugs of coffee.

Maggie turned and caught April's scrutinizing look. "Still cream and sugar?"

"Of course," April said, grimacing at the thought of taking her coffee black.

Maggie fetched the coffee condiments and seated herself across the table from April, wrapping her hands around the mug and taking a preliminary sip.

"You look like hell," April said amiably, stirring two healthy teaspoons of sugar into her coffee and adding a generous dollop of half-and-half from the cardboard container.

"Thanks," Maggie said dryly. "Look, April, I just got out of bed. I haven't put on any makeup, haven't even combed my hair. What do you expect on Saturday morning?"

"Something that looks at least a notch above a corpse," April said shortly. She reached out and touched Maggie's hand, two parallel lines drawn between her brows that were half hidden by her blond bangs. Her voice held love and concern as she whispered, "Oh, Mags, what are you doing to yourself?"

"I'm just trying to survive," Maggie admitted, fighting the tears gathering in her eyes. "Just trying to get from one day to the next."

"How much weight have you lost?"

Maggie shrugged.

"You couldn't afford any of it," April told her bluntly. "Do you eat at all?"

Maggie looked at her friend and said hesitantly, "When I think about it."

"Which doesn't appear to be too often," April observed. "How about sleep? You said you just got up."

Maggie's eyes slid guiltily away from April's. "I think I finally dozed off some time after four this morning."

"God, Maggie! Look at yourself! Lacey will be home soon. You can't go on this way! You can't be like this when she gets here!"

"It'll be better by then."

"Will it?"

Maggie shook her head. "No. I doubt it." She traced the rim of her mug with one fingertip. "I don't know what to do. How do I make the hurt go away?"

"You go to Rush and tell him you've changed your mind," April said, her voice firm with conviction.

"That simple, huh?" Maggie's eyes met April's over the rim of the red mug as she raised it to her lips.

"I've said all along it was that simple."

"April, I told Rush I wouldn't marry him. Not once, but several times. Do you think he's forgotten that?"

"No. I know he hasn't, because, if possible, he looks worse than you."

Maggie's cup thudded to the tabletop. "You've seen him?"

"He works for me. That's how you met him, remember?" April said with a hint of her usual teasing self. "I'll shoot straight with you, Maggie. I'm worried about you both, but especially Rush. He isn't eating or sleeping either. I have to really twist his arm to get him to take an assignment nowadays. And I've gotten the impression that the studying has been shot to hell, too. Which means the grades can't be too good."

"Oh, God!" Maggie threaded her fingers through the sides of her hair and scraped them back, tugging the hair tightly away from her face, an action that accentuated the new fragility of her features due to her weight loss. "He's got to get that degree!"

April shrugged. "I think he's finally found something that means more to him than his sheepskin. And I think that if he can't have it, nothing else matters."

Maggie's eyes were anguished. "Me?"

April nodded. Her smile was sad as she said softly, "Give it some serious thought, huh, Mags? I don't care a diddly-damn about how much age difference there is between you and Rush. What the two of you feel doesn't come along very often."

"But it isn't fair of me to take his youth and give him nothing in return."

"What's that supposed to mean?" April asked with raised eyebrows. "If you love him back, you're giving, too. And whether you believe it or not, you have a helluva lot to give to any man."

Maggie concentrated, tracing a pattern on the table-top with her fingernail. The polish was chipped, she thought randomly before she raised her gaze to April's. "He wants children."

"So? So does Sam."

"But you're younger . . ."

"Are you afraid to get pregnant because of your age?"

Maggie nodded. "I guess so. What would people think, me marrying him and having a baby at my age?"

"Everyone I know will be pea-green with envy, sugar," April told Maggie with a throaty laugh.

"Be serious," Maggie said, a ghost of a smile hovering around her lips.

April's eyes widened playfully. "I am! Look, Maggie, what the world thinks doesn't matter. You don't have to live with the world. You have to live with Rush and Lacey."

"Lacey likes him," Maggie offered.

"Then you don't have any problem. If you're worried about the other, go see your doctor. But according to the paper, more and more women are waiting until their late thirties and older to have their families."

"Really?" There was a thread of hope in Maggie's voice and a glimmer of excitement in her eyes that April didn't fail to pick up on.

"Really. Now, how 'bout getting your act together. I'm taking you to the Parker House for lunch."

Rush pulled off his glasses, slammed the law book shut and rose from the dinette table. He placed his palms at his back and arched against the strain of sitting hunched over too long. It hadn't done any good. For two hours he'd read words that didn't mean anything. With a sigh, he went to the refrigerator and reached for a can of light beer.

His long legs carried him to the living room, where he sank into a corner of the corduroy sofa and picked up the Monday newspaper. He thumbed through it, more for something to do than with any actual interest in its contents. A small article caught his attention: WOMEN SUFFER MORE AFTER BREAK-UP. Rush read the article, gave a disgusted snort and threw the paper aside. No one could be any worse off than he was right now. Hell, he'd have to get better to die.

He downed a large mouthful of beer and set the can on the coffee table at precisely the same moment as the phone rang. He stretched to the opposite end of the table and picked up the receiver. "Hello?"

"Hi, sugar! What's up?"

Rush covered the mouthpiece briefly, hiding a tired and disappointed sigh. "Not much, April. How about you?"

She gave her husky laugh. "Well, I'm a whole heap better now that Sam's back from Texas. The stubborn fool refuses to sell out and move up here, so he spends a lot of time flying back and forth." She made a sound of frustration. "It's miserable."

"Why don't you pack up and go back to Texas like you're always threatening to do?" Rush asked, lifting his feet to the coffee table and crossing them at the ankles.

"Look, Barrington, stay out of my love life, huh?"

Rush chuckled. "Sure. So why did you call? Surely you know I can't work during the week."

"Yeah, I know. Or the weekends either," she said, then added, "I saw Maggie Saturday."

"So?" Rush's voice was carefully noncommittal.

"So, she's lost so much weight she looks as if a good puff of wind would blow her away."

Rush raked his hand through his already tousled hair. "Look, April, she told me to take a hike. What do you want me to do? The long and the short of it is that the lady just won't marry me."

"Do you love her?"

"What kind of asinine question is that?"

"Does that mean yes?" April asked sweetly.

"April . . ." he growled.

"I called because I thought you might want to know that she has an appointment with a doctor this afternoon."

Rush could barely think for the sudden questions roiling inside his head. Why was Maggie going to the doctor? Was she sick? Oh, God! Was his Maggie sick?!

"Rush! Are you still there?" April asked.

"Yes," he said, shaking his head to scatter his troubled thoughts, "I'm here."

"Well, I just thought you might want to call and check on her or something. I talked to Lacey earlier and she's really getting worried about her mom."

"I'll think about it, April," he said.

"Okay. Look, I've gotta go. Sam's due any time and I've got to make every minute count."

"I told you how to fix it."

"Stay out of my love life, Barrington," April repeated.

"I will if you will," Rush said.

They laughed, and on that note, hung up. Rush crossed his arms, pondering what April had told him. And across the river in Boston, April Newbern lowered her legs from her cluttered desk, sprang to her feet and gave a rebel yell that would have made Sam proud. A wide grin was plastered on her mobile mouth. That ought to do it, she thought, with a self-satisfied giggle. She'd done her best with Maggie on Saturday to set the wheels in motion for a reconciliation. And if Maggie chickened out, she'd planted just enough worry in Rush's mind that he'd be bound to check things out sooner or later. And April's bet was that it would be sooner.

It was eight o'clock, some ten hours since April had called. Rush, now so sick with worry that he, too, needed a doctor, was pacing the apartment floor. He'd been calling Maggie's place and the gallery ever since noon—at least once every hour, always with the same results. Jerri didn't know where she was or when she'd be back. There was no answer at the condo. Rush was about ready to call out the Mounties, or at least Boston's equivalent. He stopped his restless roaming and looked at his watch. It was three minutes later than it had been the last time he'd checked. He planted his fists on his hips and stared unseeingly at the wall. Where in hell could she be?

Making a sudden decision, he ran into the bedroom, grabbed his coat from the foot of the bed and raced back toward the door. He'd go to her place and wait in the Monte Carlo until she got home. Then he'd sit her down and they'd thrash this thing out if it took all night.

And this time he'd win. He wouldn't take no for an answer. He would make her believe the strength of their love could overcome any problems they might have. He had to.

Rush was in the act of plunging his arms into his coat sleeves and was halfway across the room when the doorbell rang. He frowned. Not now. He didn't need any company now. He flung open the door with an excuse already forming on his lips. "I'm sorry, I . . . "

His voice trailed away as his disbelieving eyes took in the sight of Maggie framed in his doorway. For long moments they just soaked up the sight of each other, reveling in the fact that they stood only feet apart for the first time in a month. Gone were the memories of their hurtful words, the agony of being apart, the endlessness of the nights. Right this second there was only joy.

Rush thought that April was right. Maggie did look thinner, even in the bulky coat that she had belted around herself. She was still elegant, though. Still classy. Still beautiful. And he still loved her.

Maggie thought that April was right. He didn't look as if he'd been eating well. He looked exhausted. Exhausted, lean and . . . gorgeous . . . so gorgeous. And she loved him so much. Then she noticed that his coat was half on.

The wonderful, heady moment passed, and she began to wonder what on earth she was doing here. What could she say to him to make him listen, to make him understand, to make him forgive her and take her back?

"I . . . see you're going out," she said. "I won't stay long."

Rush stepped aside so she could enter the living room. "Come on in. I was just going . . . I was just going out for a while," he said, not wanting to tell her he'd been on his way to see her. He took off his coat and threw it onto the back of the serviceable brown sofa.

Maggie stood before his recliner, a folder of some sort clutched to her breast.

"Let me take your coat," he offered, stepping up behind her.

She jumped and half turned. "Oh. Okay."

Rush watched as she unbuttoned and untied the classic, camel-colored coat. He helped her out of it and tossed it on top of his, watching her carefully, looking for some sign of why she was there . . . and how she felt.

Rush rounded the chair. "Sit down," he offered.

Maggie perched on the edge of the recliner seat, her back straight, her feet planted close together on the beige carpet. Her tongue felt glued to the roof of her mouth. She'd agonized over this all day, practiced what she would say and how she would say it. Now her mind had turned to mush. She couldn't dredge up a single coherent thought, much less an argument that would bring Rush back to her.

Rush dropped onto the sofa separating her from him by the width of a few feet. A coffee table, with an abandoned beer can and scattered legal magazines, also stood between them. She raised her eyes hesitantly to his and saw questions in their umber depths. Both were afraid to speak, afraid to even offer an opening gambit.

Finally, after what seemed to be an inordinately long time, Maggie cleared her throat. "I brought some new evidence." *Fool! That isn't what you were going to say!*

A frown drew Rush's heavy brows together. "Evidence?"

Maggie nodded. "For the case."

What's going on here? "What case?"

"Barrington versus Spencer." *Are you crazy, Maggie Spencer? Your whole life is at stake, and you're treating this like some sort of comedy routine.*

The question in Rush's eyes was slowly replaced by the dawning of comprehension. He nodded. *What are you getting at, Maggie-Mine?* "I remember."

"Well, about a month ago the case came to trial." Her voice trembled as she remembered the events she was alluding to. Her eyes were bleak. "I believe I'm right when I say that both Barrington and Spencer lost."

"Yes," Rush agreed.

"It was poor strategy on Spencer's part," Maggie rushed on. "She didn't know what to expect from the merger Barrington wanted since her last one was such a dismal failure. She was inexperienced and afraid. She wasn't certain she could comply with all of Barrington's demands."

"I guess they were demands," Rush said with a nod, "but more than that, they were wishes." *Thank you for this game, Maggie, that helps us say the things we might not be able to say otherwise.*

"I know. Spencer would like to"—she swallowed—"reopen the case if Barrington is agreeable." *Oh, God! How silly can you get?*

Rush sat very quietly for a moment. His elbows rested on his spread knees, hands laced tightly together. "A case is only reopened if there *is* new evidence," he said at last.

His words told Maggie he wouldn't settle for what they had before. He hadn't changed his mind. It was still all or nothing.

"I know." She took some papers from the folder and handed them to Rush.

He scanned the copied page of the ragged scrawl that he soon realized was a rambling medical dissertation. Something about the current state of health of one Margaret Spencer. Too thin at 108 pounds, but she had a good blood count. He flipped to the next page, which was the lab report on some sort of hormone level test. His frown returned. He looked up at the woman seated across from him. "What is this, Maggie?"

She licked suddenly dry lips. "It's a copy of the doctor's report. I went today to see if . . ."

"April told me you were going to the doctor. Is everything okay?" he broke in. "You're not sick, are you?"

A happy smile burst through Maggie's somber attitude. "No. I'm not sick. In fact, I'm very healthy. That's what I came to tell you. My doctor sees no reason I can't have a healthy baby . . . I mean, there are no guarantees, but I *am* healthy . . . I could probably have your baby . . . that is, of course, if you . . . if . . ."

Rush's eyes closed. He felt the load he'd carried for a month begin to lift. *Play the game a little longer, Barrington. Don't rush her. She needs to do this.*

He opened his eyes and saw that her trembling hands were extracting another paper from the file. Her smile had faded, and there was a sort of grim determination molding her features. He held his own relieved smile at bay. *Ah, Maggie, Maggie, it's going to be so good . . .*

"And this is . . . an application for a . . ." She peeked up at Rush from beneath her lashes and saw the laughter lurking in his eyes. She saw the way he pressed his lips tightly together to keep from smiling. Saw that he still loved her. *It's going to be all right.* She felt relief, joy and a sudden overwhelming surge of love for the man across the table from her. Her throat tightened with the despised tears that had been a constant threat lately. She moistened her lips and continued doggedly, "It's an application for a marriage . . . license . . ." Her voice faded away, her face and her composure crumpling.

In less than a second Rush was across the table separating them and had Maggie in his arms, where she belonged. Where she had always belonged. Her face was pressed against his chest, her arms held him close. He whispered his love to her and rained kisses on the top of her head in a gentle reassurance of his feelings. Finally, Maggie pushed herself from the comfort of his embrace. She might have cried longer, but her common sense was returning rapidly, and there was one final thing she needed to say before she gave in to the promise burgeoning in her heart.

Lifting her tear-streaked face to his, Maggie smiled up at Rush and whispered, "I love you, Michael Rusheon Barrington."

"And I love you, Maggie Spencer." He leaned forward and shut the manila folder. "And I believe with those confessions that this case is closed," he teased.

"Not quite."

Maggie's eyes glowed with happiness and peace and a quiet self-assurance as she said, "How soon can you get a blood test?"

"Ma'am?" Rush asked, a look of shock scurrying across his face.

"A blood test, counselor," she repeated with a grin. "And surely among all your high-and-mighty acquaintances, there's one who has the authority to waive the three-day waiting period."

"Why, ma'am, are you asking me to marry you?"

Maggie's tremulous smile broadened. Her words were hardly more than a whisper. "I'm asking."

Rush swept her up into his arms, his long legs carrying them unerringly toward the bedroom. His mouth hovered just above hers. Their eyes met in love and commitment. The teasing dimmed, then disappeared. Rush's voice held the barest quiver as he said fervently, "Maggie-Mine, I thought you never would."